THE PRINCE OF DEMONS
AETHER UNIVERSITY
BOOK ONE

HANA HAHM

Copyright © 2023 by Hana Hahm

All rights reserved.

No part of this book may be reproduced in any form or by any electronic or mechanical means, including information storage and retrieval systems, without written permission from the author, except for the use of brief quotations in a book review.

This book is a work of fiction. Names, characters, places, and incidents are either products of the author's imagination or used fictitiously. Any resemblance to any living persons, alive or dead, is entirely coincidental.

To everyone on #BookTok—
Thank you for reminding me that I deserve true love, too.

CAMPUS MAP

Welcome to Aether University!

Reminder to all incoming students: fighting demons is not a valid excuse for littering! Make sure to dispose of any blood, gore, and weaponry in portals conveniently located on the edge of campus!

PROLOGUE

Luna was a mistake.
    Her mother knew it from the moment she cradled her tiny, darling baby girl, with eyes as black as an abyss.

Her father knew it as soon as his one-night stand came running back into his life, sobbing and panicking.

All their friends knew it when the shotgun wedding invites went out.

But her mother was determined for Luna not to know it. From the second she came out of the womb, covered in skin so fragmented it mirrored her mother's broken heart, she knew that her daughter was her fault, and her fault alone.

Never mind that the baby was so lovely, all her pets were entranced, despite Luna dissolving their collars. Or that she was so vibrant, she smiled at her mother more than any other child ever would, while sapping the electricity from the house. She was unplanned. Uncontrollable. Unruly. So, her mother had to overcompensate.

Luna's mother bought toys, sang songs, and planned walks in the park with her newborn, showing her off to the world. Showing the world she was wanted. That it wasn't the alcohol-fueled consequences of teenage naivety. She devised a list of excuses, of go-to-explanations whenever something died, or decayed, or disintegrated in her daughter's presence.

She couldn't tell her—couldn't risk her precious child's self-worth—by letting her know.

Her father, a very happy-go-lucky man, was happy to let his wife take over their strange baby. Her grandparents, able to do basic math, knew by her delivery four months after the wedding that she was not the first granddaughter they wanted. But in true Korean fashion, they always praised their daughter when questioned publicly.

Yet her mother knew, and she knew from the moment she felt the shadows swirling in her belly, that this baby was never supposed to exist.

So, when the time came for her Dol ceremony–Luna's first birthday party and presentation to society—her mother knew it had to be spectacular.

Quietly, she was hopeful. Her husband said his entire family would be there. She had confronted her own family publicly, ensuring they'd attend. Everyone would be present, and everyone would celebrate the baby, because nobody would dare to call her a mistake with so many others around. Such was equivalent to declaring war between two groups who already hated each other, but united in their desire to one-up the other side.

By one year old, nobody had ever bothered to visit. Why would they? Each blamed the other for Luna's existence.

Please, her mother hoped.

Please love her.

Luna's grandmother would be there, and she'd never shown an ounce of love to her own ward. But this time would be different. Luna's mother was determined for it to be so.

The Dol ceremony was deeply rooted in tradition, an occasion predetermined by the fates, designed to impress even the coldest of families.

Parents from around the neighborhood dressed their kids in their finest to observe. Grandparents, aunts, uncles, and cousins came to watch her in vibrantly colored hanboks. The traditional gowns swayed with the guests, splashing the room in bright bursts of color.

Above family, hidden in the chandelier where nobody could see, spirits also paid their dues and visited.

Traditional decorations of fans and paper lanterns adorned the room, hand-selected by the parents. Luna was placed down in the center of the room, an uncertain future ahead of her. It was a prosperous, auspicious celebration, a relic from ancient times.

The child's community brought food. The family brought well wishes. Parents brought the sacred items.

As the room filled with anticipation, Luna's eager parents propped her up on a mattress, raised slightly for everyone to see the spectacle. One by one, items were brought out to the smiling, oblivious baby.

The first was a rainbow rice cake, to prevent the baby from ever going hungry. A fine choice in ancient times, but unlikely to impress in the modern era.

A calligraphy brush came second, to symbolize intelligence and creativity. Her mother would have liked that one —everybody wanted to say their baby was brilliant.

Next, a shiny coin, to foretell great wealth and success. Luna's father hoped for that one—having a good retirement plan would be nice.

Last, a long thread was presented, to imply an even longer life. It was skipped aside, tossed over as the least interesting of the options.

The family urged Luna to choose an item. Her relatives and neighbors looked on, peering over the crowd.

Her mother waved aggressively at the brush. Her father tipped the coin, hoping the glare would catch Luna's eye.

What would the baby choose for her Dol ceremony?

Who would the child become?

Could she redeem herself?

Could she redeem *her mother*?

The crowd waited with bated breath. And they waited. And they waited some more.

Giggling, Luna snatched the long thread, waving it up in the air like a prized trophy. Huzzah went up in the crowd. Her parents captured each other in an embrace. At least she chose something, they thought. At least she didn't destroy the house in the process.

Onlookers smiled and let out a series of, "I knew it! I knew she would choose that one!"

So lost were they in their distraction, that they didn't notice what pulled at the end of the thread. All at once, applause turned to gasps. Parents yanked their children back. Surprise became horror.

Above, spirits cheered.

"How did that get there?" her father whispered.

"Impossible," her tight-lipped grandmother uttered.

"Cursed!"

Behind her, one of the relatives fainted.

In front of Luna, her mother wished she could faint, or build a time capsule to go back and prevent this nightmare from ever unfolding.

Because at the end of the glowing, luminescent thread, an onyx tiara awaited.

Silly mother. The Fates made no mistakes.

CHAPTER
ONE

THE ORACLE MUSINGS

*W**elcome to The University of Aether, freshman! You may be wondering—who's this? And you'll never know. Because I, like the future, am chaotic and hidden from most. But there is nothing I love more than a little story, some future gossip, and a riveting prediction of the future—which is why I send out all my notorious wisdom to my fans. Since you've decided to follow me, I'll let you in on secret number one—a pair of starborn lovers will meet today!*

IF THIS GOBLIN didn't shut up, I was going to throw him out the window.

"What happened to that boy you were staring at this morning? The one with magnificent hair?"

The lamp above me sputtered at the sound of my goblin's voice. It was rich and ancient, and if I weren't so devoted to him, I'd tremble from it.

I frowned. "What happened to 'just one date, and I'll leave you alone for the rest of the week'? No pressure, no drama?"

I dotted concealer over the rosy splotches on my face. The same rosy splotches I suspected prohibited me from getting dates. Gaksi wouldn't know the struggle. Demons didn't have beauty standards that called for glass skin and a transparent, pleasant personality.

A raspy chuckle swayed my overhead lamp back and forth. The light went out. My American girl doll jumped, followed by the haunting image of a 20th-century figurine laughing. Mocking me.

"That bad, huh?" the doll rasped. *"Maybe you should let me do the lover hunting. It's not like I can do any worse than you."*

I chucked a pen at him.

The doll's eyes closed before the pen knocked it off my bookshelf, and the candle beside my desk flared to life. Blue light danced above the wick, prancing in excited little jumps.

"Who are you taking to the first college party? Don't tell me you're going alone!"

His cheerful, eerie male voice haunted me from the other end of the desk. I turned my head away, ignoring him, and continued typing on my computer. This calendar wouldn't plan itself.

"You can't fall behind on your studies," Mother had warned me. *"With a face like that, you'll need every advantage you have."*

I grimaced at the memory and blocked off time for more doctor's appointments. Despite my mother being the one to hound me over my skin, I actually got my eczema from my dad's side. Not that my mother had any room to judge, given what *she* had passed down to me.

Gaksi's lackadaisical banter pulled me from my thoughts.

"*You ever think you spend too much time in school and not enough time having fun?*"

I debated whether I could throw the candle out the window faster than Gaksi could escape. If I whipped my hand out, could I at least surprise him? Or would I burn in the process? Gaksi had never hurt me before—although he had created some mischief in my past—so maybe it would be worth a shot.

I flung the candle out the open window.

"*Rude!*" My computer light flared. "*I know I raised you better than that!*"

I shut the laptop and slid it inside my backpack. "I don't have time for this right now, Gaksi."

Leave it to Gaksi to distract me on the first day of school. Maybe I should have left him at home and gotten a cat instead. Cats had less attitude.

"*Have you forgotten everything I've done for you?*" Gaksi tutted. "*Like the time you needed your volcano to explode for the science fair, and, like a dutiful goblin, I created a mess that won you first place? Or the time a boy bullied you, so I made his clothes turn inside out at school for the rest of the week? Or when you got so lost in NYC that I called your mother for you?*"

"Hush," I muttered to my backpack. As much as I hated to admit it, I didn't know what I would do without Gaksi. "I don't want anyone to think I stuffed a kid in there."

I blocked out thoughts of Gaksi and focused on my breathing instead. I inhaled, and black shadows dotted my fingertips. Exhaled. They dissolved. In. Out. Repeated three times. I used more energy with each inhale, and with each exhale, I made sure it disappeared. All gone. All controlled. No chance of any wily shadow of mine escaping unexpectedly and taking out innocent objects.

Gaksi grumbled, moving stuff noisily around my backpack. After my exaggerated huff, he silenced himself.

When I'd exhausted myself from expelling cursed magic, I checked my phone for one last burst of strength, this time of a non-magical variety.

Mother: *Have a productive day today.*

Mother: *Make an impression. No daughter of mine will end up unhoused.*

I smoothed out my clothes. They were ironed and pressed, even hemmed to the right length. A light sundress, pastel sandals, and a pink headband. Mother would be proud.

Mother: *And make sure you hide your rashes. They're almost as ugly as your shadows.*

I cringed, nearly dropping my phone.

Luna: *Do I need to be pretty to fight demons?*

There was a long wait before she replied.

Mother: *I did not raise you to be weak. Fighting is what we do best.*

My eyes narrowed. Was that a compliment? I didn't know she had it in her. Although she included herself, of course.

My hand lingered on the dorm door before I left. Stilled. Waiting for me to open it. Face the outdoors.

"The first day of school is lethal," Dad had warned me. *"The anxiety and fear draw the occult closer, encouraging more bloodshed wherever freshmen tread."*

"You're more fierce than any demon," Gaksi said in my head, present-time.

"Quit reading my mind!"

I shook my backpack for good measure.

"*Quit fearing those that are like you.*"

My shadows hummed in response.

Enrolling in a demon-fighting school didn't bode well for someone who resembled one.

"If the professor doesn't show up in fifteen minutes, we can leave, right?" A smiling redhead with glowing umber skin turned to face me.

I felt so solitary walking into the lecture hall today—everyone else seemed to be walking with their roommates, and I didn't have one. (Gaksi didn't count). I requested special accommodations for my 'service animal,' but maybe that had been a mistake. Would people think I was strange? Arriving without company?

Most of the other students hesitantly waved at dorm friends and whispered amongst themselves. The teaching assistants relieved anxious students, answering their "What can I do to get ahead?" questions with, "It's the first day, relax."

Be nice, be pleasant, be polite, I coached myself. *Make a good impression.*

Problem was, I needed another person to be nice to. Was it my skin? Did I look like a freak here? I'd plopped down on the first seat available, but nobody had come to join me.

Until this freckled girl sat next to me and started talking.

I tuned back in to our conversation.

"Maybe? I'm Luna." I gave my best smile. Would my attempts at approachability work? I hoped so.

"Cordelia," the redhead replied. With dimples and freckles that moved when she smiled, she had the most childlike, innocent quality.

"Is it okay if I sit here? The lecture hall is filled today," she said, gesturing to the class. Students packed themselves like sardines in every row, crowding themselves amongst water bottles, backpacks, and tablets. Some students even lingered at the balcony railing, peering below for empty seats.

"Of course," I responded. *Good work*, I thought to myself. At least I'd made one friend today.

"Dr. Ansi is only five minutes late, though," I said. "I'm sure she'll be here eventually, so we can't leave yet."

"Yeah, right," a smooth male voice said, sliding into the seat beside me. My head had to tilt up to smile at him. With tanned skin, blonde hair, and warm brown eyes, he resembled a bohemian surfer who had strayed too far from the beach. He was the boy with magnificent hair I'd seen out my window this morning, the one I was way too shy to approach.

"Are you guys fish?" he drawled.

"Fish?" Cordelia asked. Her face paled.

"Yeah. Fish out of water. Freshmen." The gentle tenor of his voice smoothed over the insult like we were all part of an inside joke.

"Are you not?" I asked. "This is History of Aether University 101. It's one of the first courses freshmen take."

"I'm a teaching assistant, or T.A.," he said. "I'm avoiding the overachievers and socializing here instead." He winked, making me smile.

"I'm Luna," I said. "This is Cordelia."

He nodded at us. "Lukas." He gestured to the two tall guys fielding off questions upfront. "The big broad guy is

Adam, and the shorter one is Xavier. They're Alpha and Beta of Wolf House, respectively."

Alpha and Beta of Wolf House? Powerful upperclassmen, most likely.

"If they're that important, what are they doing here?" Cordelia asked.

"Can I let you in on a secret?" Lukas whispered, leaning in toward us. Cordelia and I mimicked him. I didn't know why, but I trusted him intrinsically. He had such a calming presence.

"Lots of upperclassmen like to become T.A.s to scope out new talent for their houses," he murmured conspiratorially.

"So, are you another Wolf house recruiter?" I asked in a hushed voice.

"Even better," he practically sang. His voice was like butter. "Siren House. Where all the beautiful and charismatic people go."

"Siren House?" Cordelia sputtered. As soon as she reacted, I snapped out of whatever Siren haze Lukas trapped us in. "Is that why I like you so much? Because you're manipulating us into doing it?"

Lukas leaned back and chuckled. "I only turned on the charm a little, ginger. The rest was just you having good taste."

Cordelia shivered. "Sirens are so manipulative," she stated. "I've never seen such a pretty group of—"

HYDRA ALERT! HYDRA ALERT!

Cell phones and tablets buzzed as the university alert system rang. The sounds of zippers and shifting backpacks filled the air as a message popped up on every university-owned screen:

Run, hide, fight! A wolf stabbing has been reported on

campus, behind Einstein Tower, and across Constellation Lake! The suspect is heading toward Curie Hall!

Whoever slays the first demon of the year earns 1000 points!

"We're in Curie Hall!" Cordelia gasped.

"I'll handle this," the Alpha wolf, Adam, proclaimed, voice echoing across the cavernous lecture hall. His red frame fled the room, trailed by his brown-haired Beta, Xavier.

"No, you won't," the annoyed siren, Lukas, mumbled. "Sorry, ladies. The Housed will handle this." He shook out his hair before careening after them.

"Are we in danger?"

"What's happening?"

"What should we do?"

Frenzied panic filled the air. Several students darted away, opposite where the boys went. A couple of them stuffed themselves under seats.

"Sirens are so egotistical. They think none of the other houses can handle anything," Cordelia said. She ignored the surrounding havoc.

"Every time a House tries to do something, there's always at least one siren trying to outdo them," she told me. "Because the sirens make such sizable donations to the university—you know, by seducing rich people on the outside—they think they're better than everyone else, and that they can fix everything themselves."

"Shouldn't we be, like, doing something?" I interrupted.

"It's probably just a rogue demon. They cross the veil from the Beyond all the time. We just have to stay out of their way until one of the Housed handles it and claims the points."

"How do you know all this?" I pulled my backpack onto my lap before fleeing students trampled it.

"Me and the sirens go way back." She grabbed her water bottle from her desk and shoved it back into her backpack.

"How?" I ducked as another student jumped over me in his haste to exit.

Green specks swirled in her eye like she was under some spell. She pressed her lips together, like she was thinking, but then changed the subject.

"This is crazy!"

"Maybe someone unaffiliated should check this out," I shouted over the chaos. "Do unhoused freshmen get points?"

"Yeah!" she yelled back. "It gets calculated into grades with your class rank!"

I grinned. "Let's go then! We can split the points if we defeat it together."

"You want to go fight a demon?" Shock crossed her pretty face. "You have no House and no magic. What are you going to do to defeat it?"

"*Ah, there's where she's wrong,*" Gaksi whispered in my mind. "*You have plenty of fun up your sleeve.*"

"*Silence!*" I told him internally.

"I have some regular weapons," I suggested. Mom had sent me off with an obscene amount of pointy toys to stab villains with.

"*Maybe while you're there, you can seduce one of those boys that has just run off,*" Gaksi suggested.

"*Count your days,*" I threatened.

"*I have infinite days; I'll have you know.*" His internal amusement warmed my thoughts, smoothing out my annoyance.

"I'll be right back," I decided, chucking on my backpack

and turning to Cordelia. "Do you have anything to protect yourself with here?"

Her eyes widened. "In class?" She glanced at the commotion. "I'm sure it'll be fine. The demon was spotted outside."

I grabbed her hand and placed a silver dagger inside. "It's enchanted, so it'll strike everything but the user." She blinked, but I was already running out the door before she could thank me.

Outside, my feet shuffled off the sidewalk. Hot air breezed by. The red brick road linking buildings was spotless, and the worn brick campus buildings stood tall as ever. Birds chirped in the background. There was no blood-curdling screaming. No terror and confusion.

Was it just a false alarm? A test run, maybe?

I slid another dagger into my hand, just in case.

It was too quiet—

A body slammed into my side, knocking me over and sending my dagger scuttling across the pavement.

I whipped around, only to see a human boy running off with my pretty, floral-covered weapon.

Thief!

Curly brown hair bounced as he sprinted away from me.

I wasn't the only one who thought I could make a name for myself early.

A line of sunken-in paw prints off the trail caught my eye. I crept closer, realizing those were Adam's and Xavier's tracks.

I crept along with their paw prints. At a school like this, I was already disadvantaged by my defective skin. I *needed* to land my first kill. If I couldn't look as strong as the rest of my competition, I'd become so much more vicious that they'd be forced to respect me.

I drifted further from campus until the Whispering Woods loomed ahead. I crept forward, pushing back every nagging thought, ignoring each mysterious wisp of air. Tendrils of maroon shadow swirled thicker toward the thicket of trees near the entrance.

Eroded black gates arched above.

"*Spooky,*" Gaksi mentioned.

BEWARE OF THE WHISPERING WOODS, the rickety sign across the top of the arch read. The black writing was chipped and cracked, destroyed by time.

I resolved my nerve, flipped my dagger once, and powered forward.

Despite being daytime, the verdant forest canopy made the woods dark. Flame-colored leaves grew out of branches, covering the forest ceiling with a ruby hue. Fog clouded the air, making it difficult to see more than a few steps ahead. The trunks of surrounding trees were stained scarlet, not brown, making the forest glow crimson on all sides. If it weren't for the paw prints, I would think I was entering the belly of some beast, or into an ongoing blaze.

Another sign waved in the wind, hanging from the arched branch of a tree above. In blood-red, dripped lettering, it read: VEIL LIES AHEAD.

A few paces ahead: DEMONS CROSS HERE.

I hesitated for a moment. Was that... human blood?

"*Go,*" Gaksi said, sensing my hesitation. "*You already mess with demons. I'm your favorite goblin, aren't I?*"

I inhaled deeply and strode forth. There was no other way. I *must* make a name for myself here. Shadows pulsed along my skin, fueled by my determination. My pace slowed to a crawl when I heard the faint echoes of voices.

I slid my camera into my hand. Mother told me that the most points came from slaying a demon, second most from banishing one back home, and a meager amount came from any new information about one—like a picture.

Even without using magic, I could get a good look.

I warned Gaksi to hush—which he did—then dove deep into a rosebush. Its branches moved slowly out of the way, parting the thorns away from me. Did that mean it was friendly? I'd never seen a bush... move before. I hoped it was in greeting. Please don't swallow me like a Venus fly trap. Hidden in this mystery shrub, I had just enough eye space to see the figures in front of me.

The most beautiful voice I'd ever heard spoke.

"Looking for something?"

CHAPTER TWO

THE ORACLE MUSINGS

I wonder how universities sent out notifications before Hydra alerts? Imagine you're just minding your business in class, passing notes like a vintage caveman, when a carrier pigeon drops in to tell you that there's a hydra, or some other interesting demon, on campus. Can't relate. Anyway, expect a major commotion today—a series of events will conspire, leading to tragedy for one dear reader and a hopeless infatuation for the other. Stay safe!

P.S. Some of you have tried to outdo me via communication with the Whispering Woods. Let it be known here: the whispers you hear from those woods are rarely ever real.

"This place... is an abomination," the same sensual voice said. "None of you should be here."

"Did you do this?" Adam's voice roared. I could only see the periphery around his massive frame. He let out a deafening howl, making me shiver as the surrounding trees shook.

His wolf was as large and bright as an inferno, and as bulky as a bear. His claws dug into the earth, frame hunched back like he was poised to pounce. Beside him, Xavier's tawny-brown frame lurched forward, jaw chuffing with threat.

As soon as Adam's howl ended, he reared back. Quivering and shaking, he looked like he was fighting invisible constriction. Xavier paused mid-step, eyes blown open.

I spotted Lukas' windswept blonde hair hidden in the shadows to the left. He made eye contact with me and shook his head slowly. Message received. *Leave.*

The man owning the voice stood ahead. Long, black hair fell over a face cast in darkness. He wore a rich black tunic framed by shadows that swirled and misted around his frame. His eyes were downcast, presumably at something beneath him, but Adam was blocking my view of whatever he was looking at.

Was that the wolf? The one the alert was about?

"What did you do to him?" Lukas asked, defiant, directing the stranger's attention away. It seemed to work. Almost.

The dark-eyed stranger snapped his fingers, and a plume of silver dust erupted. It shot to the sky, parting in a great explosion of particles. Like delicate snow, it fell, dusting the ground with a pearly powder as white as bone.

The dark-haired one's black eyes snapped up. One second—that was all. One second to learn that he was pretty, in a way that stopped hearts. Sculptured, from the chiseled cheekbones to the glowing complexion. His face had a legendary beauty, one more often seen in high-fashion models than in everyday civilians. Full, kissable lips, dark, haunted eyes, and a tall, imposing frame.

He was more gorgeous than a painting.

He was more beautiful than the sun.

He whirled toward me in a flurry, cutting off my admiration.

My blood pounded as my view cleared—a blur of dark color shimmered before me. Neck cracking, hair flying back, he flew until we were face to face. His eyes were wholly black, posture rigid, when he hissed, "Silly demon beauty. Whose heart—or shall we say, hearts," he inclined his head to my companions, "Did you eat this time?"

Demon. Black eyes meant demon, not man. That was what Mom warned me about. *Man-shaped demons were some of the most handsome of all, designed to seduce and deceive.*

"Eat?" I questioned. "Hearts?" I jumped back, narrowly missing the silver blade he swung at my throat. There was a heavy, dark pain pressing against my mind. It was constricting and too tight, wrapping around every limb of my body, trying to hold me in place.

Was that what the other boys were feeling? Why they were frozen in time, unable to move?

The stranger kept moving me forward, backing me further away from the edge of the clearing. My movements felt as if they were transpiring underwater, weighted by some imaginary force. What kind of dark magic did this demon have?

I needed to strike him before he killed me.

"What kind of demon are you?" I breathed, darting forward. I whacked him with my camera, and he knocked it straight out of my hand. The click sounded.

I grinned.

I got the shot.

Gaksi's chiming laughter filled my head. *"Good thinking, silly girl."*

"A little help, maybe?"

"This is top-tier entertainment, kid. I can't pause this."

"Don't act like you don't know, *gumiho*," the stranger rasped. He rushed forward again. I jumped back. He was fast, but I was faster. Tension passed through his body. Faster than fear, wilder than excitement, he struck again.

"What's a gumiho? Who are you? And why—"

I shrieked, ducking under the continuous barrage of jabs he sent my way. "Are you trying to kill me?"

The demon gave me a razor-sharp smile. "I must say, your disguises have become more and more impressive. You've got these men absolutely salivating over you. Their bodies are frozen, but they can't keep their eyes away."

Shadows coalesced around him, blocking out the warmth of the summer sun with the chill of nightmares instead. He moved forward faster, backing me into a tree, hand jutting out to press me roughly against the bark. Before I could even process what had happened, the cool kiss of his weapon pressed into my neck.

His dark eyes swirled with tendrils of smoke and shadows, light and dark churning into an intense and pointed glare. His dark hair hung forward, highlighting his sharp jaw and angular frame.

At six feet tall, I rarely looked up to men. But right now, I was fixated on a beautiful creature that was taller than my wildest dreams.

The wolves rumbled and growled in warning but were fixed in place. Adam had started to crack, fissures forming along the lines of his body, but only broken shards of him could escape his containment. He stared at me with a pained, vengeful face, chipped away but unable to move.

"Pretty gumiho," the man purred. "Even my own heart fluttered when I saw this model."

"*GAKSI!*" I screamed into my mind. "*Help me!*"

"*Why, though? He's even more handsome from this angle.*"

"*GAKSI!*"

"*Fine, fine. Tell Reaper you're not a gumiho.*"

"I'm not a gumiho," I whispered.

"Don't lie to your prince," Reaper growled. "I can sense your demon energy even stronger up close."

"That's just my pet goblin!"

"*Do something, Gaksi!*"

The blade at my neck burned bluish-white, causing the man to drop it and yank back his hand.

"Quite unceremonious to drop me, Reaper," Gaksi said aloud, "and even more so to accuse my dear Luna of murder."

"Gaksi Goblin." The man—Reaper?—cracked his knuckles and balled his hands into fists. "Why," he grated out tersely, "have you possessed my sword?"

"I enjoy a good field trip," Gaksi answered, "and I had nothing better to do. I've been immortal far longer than you, boy. I have to take my entertainment wherever I can find it."

Reaper's face flicked back to me with a sneer. "Possessing the mortal is entertaining for you?"

"Not as entertaining as watching you fawn over your 'heart-fluttering' gumiho, your cursed nine-tailed fox, the most beautiful ripper of hearts you had ever seen—"

"Enough!" Reaper boomed. "What is your relation to this suspect?" He drew his sword back into its scabbard, huffing.

I collected my breath against the tree. This... demon... talked a lot. I always considered demons monsters, not humanoids that could hold conversations.

"What is a gumiho?" I demanded.

"*Hehe*," Gaksi chortled in my mind. He jumped back into my head, forcing Reaper to turn around again, only to retrieve his weapon.

"Is this how you've been evading capture?" he snarled. "Becoming a goblin's pet."

"Pet?" Where did this medieval-looking guy get the nerve? I stood up taller. Pretended I wasn't out of breath. "I am no one's pet. And you will release my friends."

He chuckled darkly. "I will release them when I deal with you."

"Coward!"

His posture went preternaturally still. "What did you just call me?"

"A coward." I used all my willpower to stand my ground. Demons valued cunning, loyalty, and valor. To insult a demon's intelligence, devotion to the dark, or bravery was to incite a death wish. "And you will explain what you did to the body before I slay you."

"*Ooh, spicy*."

"*Shut up!*"

"You and I know full well I am innocent," he said, his voice a deadly rasp. "And I am busy trying to catch the being that isn't." He spat out '*the being*' like it was a curse of the foulest kind.

The being that isn't? What did that mean? I was so high on adrenaline I could barely pierce together his sentences. Were these the effects of the whispering woods? You heard things that made little sense? Was this conversation even real? Was he even real?

"So you didn't just turn a wolf into dust," I accused.

He cursed. "Of course I did, you stalling fox." His gaze raked over my body. "I cannot believe you have turned a goblin into a protector."

"Why?" I asked.

"Why did you rip out his heart? I've had enough of the obvious questions."

"Then release my friends, and let us finish you." I managed. My voice was surprisingly steady despite my trembling heart.

He threw his head back and laughed. "You and I both know you have never had a friend."

Why was he talking to me like he knew me personally? Demons truly were insane. "Why did you kill the wolf? Answer me!"

My mother always told me I had a self-destructive streak. The stranger's withering glare directed at me was almost an exact replica of hers. He stepped forward, and I braced myself for sudden death when he paused.

Suddenly, a set of coal-colored wings materialized into a bird on his shoulder. It glanced down, then up, then squinted at me. Like it judged. It flicked its beak to Reaper and gave an almost imperceptible shake of the head. Like I'd failed some imaginary test.

"Return home, Sam." Reaper hissed to the crow. "Let the King know there's nothing—" he glared at me—"I can do about the gumiho right now, given her current protector."

The King? Who did he serve? And was he some sort of demon knight?

Or worse—maybe he was a mercenary from the other side. If he was responsible for killing a turned wolf and strong enough to freeze three men, his magic must be exceptionally potent...

"Go home, GAKSI!" Reaper thundered, making me flinch. "I will destroy this creature, whether or not I have to take you out with it."

Adam let out a low growl, shuddering in place. Xavier yelped once before freezing too.

"Stay away from Gaksi," I snapped back, hands on my hips. I strode forward, high on the defensive. No one threatened my family. In the Deokhye clan, we lived together, we died together.

"Demon!" Lukas interjected, walking, hands raised, from his hiding place. "Take me instead—"

Tar-coated vines coiled up from the ground, silencing him.

The three-legged crow squawked. "Light and dark, Sam, do you only arrive to criticize my magic skills?" Reaper growled, addressing the bird again. If my heart weren't thundering, I'd laugh. He stepped around Lukas casually, like a man writhing in vines was an everyday occurrence to him.

"What is your problem?" I asked. Slyly, I slipped my hand behind my back. The only thing close to a weapon I had left was my water bottle, which might have been enough to distract him. Since Gaksi was being useless, my best course of action was to flee. Talking to this demon any further felt unwise.

"My problem?" he snapped. "My problem?"

"He's about to blow," Gaksi sounded off in my head. *"Release your shadows."*

My reserve was almost empty from this morning. But I inhaled deeply, letting my darkness rise to the surface.

It glimmered a dark violet, encasing my flesh, coating my body like a caress.

The demon halted, rigid as a statue. His face froze,

panicked and wild, like he was seeing a wild animal. Terror flashed across his eyes, which widened to where I could see the white beyond the storming back.

"You're cursed," he said.

"Absolutely cursed," he repeated, before he stepped back into a void and vanished.

CHAPTER
THREE

THE ORACLE MUSINGS

Do you believe in soul mates, fanciful reader? The universe does. At Aether University, they're affectionately termed "starborn souls," souls fated in the stars to be together. However, the universe demands balance. Which is why, to be a starborn soul, one must also encounter a spirit saboteur. Someone who hates you with their whole spirit, enough to sabotage any and all attempts at happiness you pursue.

Watch out, dear reader! I spot demons, naked men, and curses! Is this still Aether University or a secret dungeon? A path toward your starborn soul or a trap laid out by a spirit saboteur?

THUD. Adam and Xavier collapsed on themselves, crawling off the mossy floor. Lukas whimpered as the vines retreated into the ground, cursing as he removed the blood-coated thorns embedded in his skin.

I rushed forward to catch Lukas first. Xavier and Adam

sauntered forward, still in wolf form but looking relatively unharmed.

"Are you okay?" I asked him. "Are all of you okay?"

"Yeah," Lukas grunted. "But that was… bad," he muttered. Xavier and Adam nodded.

"Are you well? I saw him encase you in a violet haze," Adam said. Alpha energy radiated from him, compelling me to answer.

"I'm fine." Thank heavens, that was his interpretation.

"I'm also fine," Gaksi added from wherever the hell he was.

"Curse you! Why didn't you do anything?" I yelled at the sky.

"I'm not the cursed one," Gaksi replied. "That's you, sweetheart."

I launched my water bottle up at him. It froze midair, meaning he must've caught it.

"Where was this energy when Reaper was trying to kill you?" Gaksi asked.

"Reaper?" Lukas rasped, pushing himself off the ground and leaning on my shoulder.

"The Reaper helps guide souls to the afterlife," Gaksi stated matter-of-factly, like a professor leading a lecture. "He was probably here to collect the boy's."

"What is he doing beyond the veil?" I asked my water bottle. Which moved its way back to me at an infuriatingly slow, casual pace, considering I almost died.

"Collecting souls, probably." My bottle tingled in my hands, like Gaksi was laughing. "Or just messing around. That's what I do."

Adam's hand landed on my shoulder. I whirled around, Lukas in tow, only to whip back around when I realized he'd shifted without backup clothes.

"Stars, Adam! You could have warned me!" I cried, face heating. Lukas groaned beside me.

"Apologies. Wolves are often nude." He was rather composed, considering our ordeal.

"Put on some clothes, man," Lukas said.

"Can't, siren. They exploded when I shifted." He spoke to my back. "Are you intact, Luna?"

"Fine," I said. "So this Reaper—he collects souls?"

"Unclear," Adam answered. "What are you?" Adam's voice asked next.

I knew immediately who he referred to. Stars, I hoped I could hide it longer. "Gaksi is... an unhoused demon that has allied itself with Aether."

"I have allied myself with you, Luna," Gaksi corrected aloud.

"You have an... alliance with a demon? That is forbidden." Xavier's voice said, wavering.

At once, the wolves stepped toward me.

"Principal Consta already allowed it!" I blurted. I heard a collective gasp of shock.

"The Beyond, he didn't," a sinister voice called.

A sharp-eyed, cruel-mouthed boy with a mop of brown hair emerged from the trees. "I'd know if my father approved any unregistered demon activity."

My heart lurched to my stomach. Hunter Consta. Trust fund baby extraordinaire, son of Principal Consta, and sole heir to the Fae King's throne.

Could the prince fight? I hoped not.

He sprinted forward, long strides covering an unholy amount of space.

Oh no. He definitely could.

"Finding a traitor to humanity so early? It must be my lucky day."

He paused abruptly like he wanted to savor the moment. Lukas tensed beside me.

It was against the rules to kill another member of the school, right? Definitely against the rules.

"*Get out of here, Gaksi.*"

"*Not when it's getting this good.*"

"Never thought we'd discover a demon lover so early, huh?" He clapped Xavier on the shoulder, who flinched. He was barely a breath away now. A pink and purple dagger waved in the air, taunting me. "Isn't it kind of ironic for a demon's whore to be killed by her own weapon?"

"You're late." I retorted, squaring my shoulders to stop from trembling. "The real demon already disappeared. And considering you were ahead of me when you stole that, you must have hid this whole time. The only demon you discovered was your own fear."

He hesitated. Anger flashed in his ice-blue eyes.

"Meanwhile, Gaksi was here, fighting for the good of the students," I continued. "What was that line of the treaty again? The one that separated the good magic users from the bad? 'Any demon who wishes to harm humans must be extinguished or sent back to their realm. But any demon who wishes to join the House system is permitted to do so, given that they have humanity's best interest as their motivation.'"

"Gaksi is allowed to be here just as much as any other mythical being." I looked pointedly at Lukas, Xavier, and Adam. Their faces were blank, revealing nothing.

The tension was thick enough to cut with a blade.

Lukas broke it by ripping my blade out of Hunter's hand and holding it out to me.

"Luna's right. If Gaksi is willing to behave, he can be here just as much as anyone else."

Hunter's withering glare could have melted metal.

"We need to update your father, Hunter," Xavier said behind me. "You didn't see it, but that poor guy was—" he huffed in a breath, "mutilated."

"Yeah," Lukas responded, nodding. "Probably better that you didn't see it."

"Are you really going to talk about a demon that's disappeared when there's one with us right here?" Hunter demanded.

"Rude," Gaksi responded. I gritted my teeth to stifle a smile when our phones dinged.

HYDRA ALERT! Classes are canceled for the rest of the day. A student has been murdered, and a series of unidentified demons have appeared on campus grounds. Return to your dorms immediately. Curfew is in place until the threat is neutralized.

"The Underlord works hard, but whoever runs the university alert system works harder," Gaksi noted to nobody in particular.

"Why was he talking about curses, Gaksi?" I asked, ignoring Hunter's crazy eyes as he tried to identify where the sound came from. He didn't make any progress, although my dagger glowed faintly as I zipped it back into my backpack.

"You'd have to ask him that, star shine."

"Worry not," Adam interrupted. "Demons always spout nonsense. Like that pet of yours."

"Not a pet," Gaksi said.

"He's family," I told them, "although he is really annoying."

"Take Lukas to the infirmary," Adam commanded. At Hunter's stutter, he said, "You have no power yet, fish. I'm in charge of this situation. You want to act like an Alpha, become one." He shoved Hunter away from me and moved under Lukas' other shoulder, who redistributed his weight to the Alpha. I tried not to look at the sweaty, naked body across from me.

A force yanked me by my backpack before I could take a step.

"Just remember, girl," Hunter growled, "the punishment for aiding an unallied demon is death."

CHAPTER
FOUR

THE ORACLE MUSINGS

What's a school for fighting demons without an attack on day one? Aether never fails to disappoint! Worry not, incoming freshman: the in-school training will be just as difficult as what you face outside the classroom. University will be the first time many of you have been challenged. Weed-out classes, toxic frenemies, and internalized self-doubt cause many potential legends to falter.

By the time all is said and done, this year's class of 1000 hand-selected first years will dwindle to an even 600, the most brutal culling in over one hundred years of Aether.

Where others might despair, the strongest among us find resolve.

Imposter syndrome, who?

After being interrogated by university police all night, I was relieved to have a quiet morning routine. Or so I thought.

"*Look outside, Luna!*" Gaksi said.

Lukas flashed a pretty grin, waving at me from beneath my window.

"I came to walk you to class today!" he called.

"*You'll be beating off the men at this school with sticks,*" Gaksi said affectionately from my doll collection. "*What did I tell you?*"

He opened the window with his fat little doll hands and waved at Lukas, who recoiled like he'd been slapped. "She's coming!"

I threw on another coat of foundation, attacked my face with setting spray, and ran down the stairs at breakneck speed.

"Stay out of my way," I warned Gaksi. "You too," I repeated to the swirling shadows on my palms. They dissipated.

I was relieved none of the boys mentioned the shadows I drew yesterday in the woods again. Reaper must have blocked their view of me, save a faint lavender haze. It was for the best. One of my secrets was already out. The last thing I needed was a second.

This would be a good second day. I was giddy with excitement.

In the past, boys I tried to flirt with thought my skin was "contagious," so they avoided me. This was the first attention I'd gotten since, well... ever.

In the sun, Lukas' skin gleamed. He had a chiseled jaw like a superhero and was muscular like one too. Exactly the kind of man you would find in a magazine. Or a fantasy.

And I was walking to class with him!

"I figured I'd walk with you, in case you were scared of any other demon encounters along the way," he said. We began a pleasant stroll. "What's a girl like you doing at Aether, anyway?"

"What do you mean?" My heart dropped. Was it because of Gaksi? Was it because of my shadows?

I raised my palms without thinking to look at them. Nothing there.

"I mean," his eyes roved over my arms, where I didn't bother to conceal my itchy patches, "you're cute, but you also look a little... sickly. Are you sure you're up to be here? Students sabotage each other all the time. If you've got an obvious weakness, someone—demon or human—is going to try to exploit it."

I wrapped my arms back around myself immediately, embarrassed.

"My skin doesn't prevent me from fighting," I said, "nor does it affect my grades."

"The Houses tend to be a bit superficial with that stuff, though," he said, noting my awkward posture. "Aw, that was mean. I shouldn't have said it like that." His shoulders shrugged. "Just—be careful, alright? I was worried Hunter would harass you today, so I thought I should probably give you an escort. But there's worse than Hunter out there."

"Understood," I said, processing what he said. Gallant to protect me from Hunter, but nasty to point out that I looked disadvantaged here. And that was not even acknowledging what lay beneath my skin.

I sat away from him in class, discouraged.

"All of your lives are forfeit," Professor Ansi announced from the massive lecture hall, her cropped hair matching her cropped temper. Chairs encircled the speaker, rows and rows of seats and desks, allowing her threatening voice to rage to all simultaneously.

"500 years ago, a group of faeries—specifically, a group of faery godmothers—became disgruntled that their most vulnerable human children were at mercy to the creatures of the Beyond. So, they established a wall—a veil to divide mortal and immortal, human and other."

"Faery godmothers can't be real," Hunter interrupted. "I've never seen one before, and I come—"

"Likely because you're a spoiled brat. Minus 10 points from your total," Dr. Ansi bit.

My watch buzzed, and I glanced at it.

New photos released from the night of freshman Tallum Forge's death, The Eternal Times, our school's newspaper, read. Beneath it, three photos resided.

In one, there was a massive, pale white shadow that was so blurred it must have been moving too fast for the camera. Besides some trees in high definition in the background, it was impossible to make out what it was.

The above photo was taken by university cameras on North campus five minutes before the alert went out.

Beneath it, another blurry white shot of nothing. Below the white, though, were two skinny legs peeking out from beneath, with muddy white sneakers at the ends. With a start, I realized those were Tallum's legs—whatever the creature was, it was big enough to cover the rest of his massive body. What a gruesome end for such a strong wolf.

Photo taken by university camera on South campus five minutes after Tallum was supposed to start class.

South Campus? If the background trees were where I

thought they were, that was a forty-minute jog from the tip of North Campus to South. The creature was quick.

Lastly, there was a photo of Reaper. Not my image, unfortunately, which disappeared with my missing camera.

University cameras must have taken this one right before his final exit because he was glowing in violet, like my shadows had reflected off him.

The above photo has been identified as a potential 'Reaper,' according to students who survived an altercation with him. President Consta warns not to be fooled by his handsome appearance. He has attacked before, and it is best to notify university police immediately if he is spotted on campus.

To join the University Press and get the latest news, submit an application to join The Eternal Times' student reporters.

"Is this the guy you saw?" Cordelia whispered to me.

"Yeah," I whispered back.

"He's kinda hot, though," Cordelia said.

"You're the person President Consta's warning was for," I teased.

Around me, I heard chittering and chattering, more than usual for this class.

"FOCUS," Dr. Ansi roared. "You can thirst over the fancy demon OUTSIDE my classroom!"

Some students (mostly male) laughed, while others shrank in their seats. Cordelia was a shrinker.

"What should we do if we encounter a hot demon, Professor?" a male student shouted.

Dr. Ansi sharply raised her hand, throwing the boy's body fifteen feet into the air. "I don't know. What will you do?"

The class fell silent. Even the boy in the air stopped talking. But by the frantic rise and fall of his chest, I knew he still breathed, even as the temperature of the room heated.

"This is Aether University. This is not a joke." Dr. Ansi said. "The worst thing to ever befall humanity—magic—is all concentrated here. If you don't take studying seriously, a demon—or an immortal, or even a classmate—will use their power to take you out." She waved her hand, shaking the student in midair.

He clutched his arms, drawing inward to himself, terror clear in his eyes.

"As a freshman, you are the weakest of the weak. The lowest of the low. You, of all people, should know that, Zain, as this is your second time taking this class." She flicked her hand down, slamming the boy back into his chair.

A repeat! He must be one of the many students that failed last year, coerced to try again with a new cohort.

"Ughhh," the boy—Zain—groaned.

"What was that?" In a flash, Dr. Ansi appeared in front of the student, ten rows back from her podium.

"I'm sorry, professor," he apologized.

"That's better," the professor said, taking a step forward and finishing the step back at the podium. She straightened her necklace.

"Usually, the brats come out in week two, but it seems like recent events have made you lot even more immature than normal." She brushed invisible dust off her shoulder and turned to write on the board. The chalk screeched, making students flinch.

YOU DO NOT BELONG HERE.

"I haven't forgotten how many of you ran when the last hydra alert went out." Disappointment and distaste laced her tone.

"Nobody is born with the rights to a house, or a magic system, or even access to the knowledge that this place exists," she said coldly, turning back to face the class.

"And if you fail out of this school, your memories will be erased, and you will return to being the most ordinary, mediocre person you always were before."

Several of the students gulped. For most of them, their parents told them to apply to Aether University with something generic: "It's where we went! It's an elite school! They have spectacular scholarships and athletics!" It was only when they got admitted that they saw magic was real and they could get a taste of it. The first post-admission campus tour was why Aether had a 100% matriculation rate.

I was a little different, though. I always knew Gaksi was real, so I assumed there had to be some good magic to balance out the little devil that he was.

"What is the first rule of surviving an encounter with a demon?" Dr. Ansi asked.

I raised my hand. "Never show weakness!"

"Correct!" She assessed me with a nod. "Any potential weakness can be exploited."

"Look to your left!" Dr. Ansi commanded. I turned my head obediently to the left, getting to look at Cordelia's side profile as she rotated her head as well.

"Look to your right!" I swiveled right, getting a good view of an empty window.

"1 out of 3 of you fools won't make it. From now on, assume that whoever you just saw on the left is a goner—or worse, your competition."

Yikes, I thought. I liked Cordelia. She also seemed bewildered, glancing back at the sweet-faced girl sitting next to her. Hyacinth, I think she said her name was.

"While you're carving out the competition, remember

that 90% of magic—blessed individuals will marry someone associated with Aether University. Some of you will marry the person you just saw on your right!"

Figures, I thought. I got a good long look at nothing through the window. Cordelia tapped my hand. Her text showed up on my watch.

Cordelia: *Besties for life?*
Luna: *Absolutely.*

The professor's booming conclusion jumbled my thoughts.

"For your homework, memorize the history of the Houses: Wolf, Siren, Fae, Vamp, Angel, and Rose. You'll need it when recruitment season begins in one week."

One week? I hastily checked my calendar app. It usually began at the end of the semester, and we only just started.

"Do we all have to memorize Rose House?" Hunter groaned.

"Only fools wouldn't." Dr. Ansi fixed him with a deadly stare before moving on.

Hunter squirmed in irritation. Being a nepotism baby wouldn't help him in class.

"The university has decided to move recruitment season forward to better prepare you Houseless freshman for the demons crawling out of what is likely Reaper's portal," Dr. Ansi continued. Your first House quiz is in one month—come prepared. Grades are assessed by all houses when deciding on new candidates."

She changed the PowerPoint slide to a student ID card of the recently deceased.

"We're already down one student. This is not a game. Hunting demons is a matter of life or death. By the time you've graduated, you won't have the shelter of this university to protect you. You should be able to fight them all alone, wherever you may be."

She clapped her hands, and golden, high-pitched bells chimed from the ceiling.

"When it comes to the undead, you're either the hunter or the prey."

"CLASS DISMISSED!"

CHAPTER FIVE

THE ORACLE MUSINGS

It's the most frightful time of the year for people-pleasers: Family weekend! Nothing discombobulates the new class more than the return of their own flesh and blood. Time to cut the umbilical cord, children: you're in college now!

"Hey! Sundress!" A white-haired girl with pristine features and a beautiful smile chased after me. "You seemed like you knew every answer in class today. Even when you weren't raising your hand, I saw you write it down before someone else responded."

I let her catch up. She was shorter than me, so her strides weren't as long. I always felt bad walking too fast for short people.

"Thanks," she said, holding a manicured hand with pointed white nails out. "Aubrey."

"Luna." We walked back to the dorms together.

The freshman dorms were the furthest from campus,

parallel to where the Houses sat, and made of the same worn brick material. Covered in leaves and ivy, they looked like they were about to be overtaken by the University Gardens just beyond.

"What did you use to study before class today?" she asked.

I felt a twinge of guilt. "My mom went here, so she filled me in on most of the introductory material."

"Oh!" Her high-pitched voice dropped a little. "I don't have parents, so I never know how to navigate new situations like Aether."

When I glanced at her, she was wiping a tear from her cheek.

Pity bleated through me. Sometimes I forgot how lucky I was to have parents so invested in my future. I debated saying something but wasn't sure what to say. This school frowned upon vulnerability, and comforting wasn't much better.

We passed the Cornucopia, our dining hall, shaped in an elegant spiral upwards, with the mouth being the buffet. The sugary smell of pastries and the savory smell of bacon wafted out.

Feeling awkward, I suggested, "Do you want to grab breakfast together? I can show you my notes if you want to look at them?"

"No, thank you." She shook her head. "I already ate recently. But I'd love to study with you again some other time?"

"Sure," I said, exchanging numbers.

Relief washed through my chest. This was how I could help her.

"We are going to be best friends," she promised, waving as she left for her next class.

Joy filled my chest. Maybe making friends here would be easy, after all. She didn't even glance at my skin.

"YOUR NEMESIS HAS ARRIVED," Gaski warned. I jerked off my bed, landing unceremoniously on my behind. I pushed myself up, side-eyeing the bird that innocuously perched itself on my window. Stupid pigeon. Let a goblin roam around in its head and wake me up prematurely.

Despite the ease of my days, I had a hard time sleeping at night. Nightmares from the night of the Whispering Woods haunted me.

I wanted to take my eyes out of my head, wash them clear of any memories, then re-install a new model.

The wolves frozen in place. Lukas constrained by vines. University police interrogating us behind steel bars. Sickly sweet sirens who coerced us into telling the truth. The poker-faced psychiatrist who determined that nothing we said held logic. Especially Gaksi.

The Whispering Woods were strong enough to make grown men see demons and for girls to be possessed by them. Or stricken by unusually handsome ones. Reaper's face seared into my mind like a burning kiss. I'd never seen anyone else look or sound like that. I wondered if I ever would again...

A crisp knock vibrated on my door, followed by my father's deep baritone of a sigh. "We know you're in here, Luna. I pay a lot of money on your cell phone bill to see where you are."

"Are you engaging in illegal, immoral, or improper activities?" Mom's shrill voice echoed through my room.

"No, Mother," I said, pulling the sheets back up on my

bed. My father opened the door, eyebrows raised at the mess that was my room.

It wasn't much, but I still struggled to keep it together. My books were balanced precariously on the edge of my desk, the bed was unmade (although, granted, I just got out of it), laundry needed to be done, and my phone was uncharged somewhere under the covers.

I always got my homework in on time, had my makeup done, and looked presentable on the outside, but my inner room was a disaster.

"For the amount of money we pay for this place, you'd think you'd take better care of it." He opened the door wider for my mother, who'd already made eye contact with Gaski. The pigeon Gaksi possessed blinked once in acknowledgment.

"Pet," she noted, scanning the rest of the room. She marched to my books first, throwing them back into their right position on my bookshelf with vigor.

"Coo!" Gaski responded. Whatever that meant. Mom and Gaksi's relationship had always been a little... tense. Once upon a time, he used to be close to her, but supposedly, he jumped ship to his new victim the day I was born.

"How is school going, child?" Mom finished putting back the last book and moved toward my bed instead. On the way, she smoothed down her straight, dark hair as if being in my room alone caused it to frizz. "All A's? Putting the rest of this school to shame?"

"No, just failing out, doing drugs, meeting boys, and spending time with my emotional support animal," I answered with a smile.

Beside her, Dad was sneaking crackers out of his pocket and into a beak. I wondered if Gaksi could taste food or was just keeping his current pigeon body happy. He caught me staring and winked, eyes twinkling.

"Focus!" Mom scolded. I swiveled my head back to her, throwing up a hand in a fake yawn to hide my smile. "Have you signed up for recruitment already?"

My face fell. House recruitment was coming up this weekend, and I dreaded it like I dreaded my injectable medication dose every two weeks. Unsettled, dark energy pulsed under my skin, shifting and writhing at the thought. If I didn't suppress the family curse, I'd be dealing with my shadows my whole life.

Just like what the handsome demon said. "You're cursed," he'd repeated, like a benediction, like a prayer. I'd shown him my darkness, too. Gaksi had asked that of me. And then he had dissolved into nothing, and I was getting hauled away by police, wondering how much of that was real versus imagined...

"You know, I was never into that whole 'which House do you belong to' kind of nonsense," Dad remarked. He was now holding the bird in his hand, petting it absent-mindedly. He dropped back onto my bed, taking up the entire space. "Back in my day, we just studied. We were too broke to do anything else."

"That's because you knew how to work," Mom said, pacing to my laundry next. As she folded, she continued. "Houses can give even the most derelict opportunities. You know I wouldn't be where I was today without it."

Folded over my laundry like that, you can see the evidence in place. Her ears slanted up into delicate points, fashioned by the ladies of Fae House itself. It was commitment on a new level, to cut off the tips of your ears for fashion. The ones who didn't do it were restricted from the benefits of being Fae.

It wasn't that being Houseless was ... bad. It wasn't like being outside the university, where you had no idea that magic existed. But losing out after recruitment meant failure. The unhoused may have worked harder than they ever had before, but the ones who got initiated were simply better. At least, that's what my mom said.

"Eugene, can you go get her present out of the car?"

"Of course, honey." Dad pecked me on the cheek on the way out. Mom's lips turned down. "She's too old for that."

"Please," Dad laughed on his way out.

That was why I'd always be closer to my dad than my mom. He wasn't so... competitive.

Mother yanked my wrist up to her eye level. "I can see it in your veins," she threatened. "You used too many of the shadows recently, and they've re-gathered."

"I've only been practicing distilling them in the morning," I said. If I didn't use them at all, I'd go insane. I had to dispel their energy, lest they dispel themselves. In bursts. Publicly.

Spewing black fear onto everyone, labeling me as a freak. A dark magic wielder. An Other.

"This is why you're here." Mother gripped my wrist tighter. Domineering over me like this, she looked positively feral. Demanding. Unforgiving. Fae.

"Ouch," I mumbled.

"You need light magic to replace it. That's what Fae house will give you."

Mother didn't even show her own dark magic anymore. Not when she went 'Full Seelie.' The Fae saw magic as Seelie and Unseelie. Light and Dark. Life and Death. Of course, other Houses had different names, but the concept was the same.

Light magic was beautiful, wonderful, and filled with

creation. Dark magic was tumultuous, predatory, and prone to destruction. While light magic made flowers bloom, dark magic stole their life away.

"Do not let anyone know what you really are," she said. "This is the only way you can start over."

"Not my fault I was born," I reminded her. "You chose to bring me into this world."

"I was hoping you'd be more like your father."

I flinched. There had always been a nagging suspicion in my heart that if I was innocent and shadowless like Dad, she would love me more, but she'd never actually said it. Until now.

"Powerless." Her grip loosened. My hand fell, limp, onto my lap. "No magic at all. Completely and utterly normal."

"Early bid day present?" Dad reappeared, eyes wide. I raised mine in return.

"I checked with your mom to make sure it fits." He held up a gauzy, lacy white dress.

An initiation dress. The same one you wore on the day you officially became Housed. White for rebirth. For a new life. Not for marriage, as much as the similarities existed.

"Thanks, Dad," I said, hugging him.

"Keep that as motivation," Mother said, pulling a duster out of her purse to attack my drawers. As if she didn't just insult me and tell me how much she hated who and what I was. "But may I remind you, dear, that you need to put in the work from now on."

"Do you have any plans now that curfew is lifted?" Dad asked hopefully, ending Mom's lecture. "Have you made any friends?"

"I might go to the candlelight vigil later today." The wolves sent out the notification that they were hosting one for their fallen comrade. Usually, the first week of college was filled with parties, but in light of recent news, the campus had been lifelessly silent.

"Meet me in the car, Eugene." Mother turned to him. "I'll just shoo away this *bird* and meet you there."

Dad left. Mom grabbed the pigeon by its neck. "Stay away from my daughter," she growled.

"Love you too, Jae," Gaksi cooed. "But you know as well as I do that I won't leave this world until my bloodline does."

"Keep your secrets secret," Mother said to me. Annoyed, I let my shadows run out, slamming the door after her.

As much as I hated it, she was right. My family history needed to stay undercover.

Because dark magic was forbidden at Aether University, and it was all I was.

CHAPTER SIX

THE ORACLE MUSINGS

Is it too soon to swoon? Below, from the camera footage of a firsthand witness: the prime suspect for the wolf murder! Isn't he dreamy? I do love a good mystery.

Speaking of swoon-worthy: if it weren't for Lukas' mediocre pickup lines, he might actually secure himself a girlfriend, as Siren House desperately needs a strong female leader.

In other news: who will be the star pledges of the upcoming recruitment season? The candidates every House fights over? My money's on the fearless one who played hooky to chase a demon: if that's not someone worthy, I don't know who is.

I FIDGETED NERVOUSLY in my frigid chair, watching air puff out in front of me. It was uncomfortable, much like myself, in a frosty room made from bricks of ice.

The door was a frost-coated blue. The walls were semi-translucent, filled with perfectly preserved flowers amid the ice. White mist swirled around the floor. Cold, desolate, and snowy, it resembled a wintry prison.

When I first got the email today, *'Thanks for applying to work at The Eternal! Schedule an interview time!'* I was jumping for joy. But now, sitting in the waiting room, I couldn't focus. I wanted so badly to pull out my phone, just for a little stimulation, distraction, or excitement, but I felt it would be unprofessional.

For such a well-regarded student newspaper, you'd think that they could afford some candles. I didn't even have Gaksi to entertain me today—he was off with his "buddy," whatever that meant. Shudder. I couldn't even imagine who would want to be friends with him outside my family.

At least me and my friends were alive. Yellow tape roped off another victim of demon slaughter from last night just outside the Whispering Woods.

"Come in," a brisk voice called from behind the door.

They wouldn't even greet me? Weird.

I cautiously opened the door myself, brushing snow off my fingers, finding a sharp-eared Fae waiting for me.

She sat on the edge of a pristine white desk chair, typing into a shiny new computer. The windows were drawn open behind her, bathing her in soft light. Unlike her rod-straight posture.

"Luna." She inclined her head, eyes still on the computer. "Sit."

"Let me work for The Eternal," I started.

Her typing ceased. "Hmm? No, 'good morning, how are you'?"

"Fae get to the point, don't they?"

She lounged back in her chair and swiveled toward me. "You're rather bold for a freshman."

"Thank you."

"Wasn't a compliment."

"Wasn't a lie, either." I smiled. I was a mastermind at faking it. *"You have to intimidate them,"* Mother had warned me before school started. *"Faeries respect power. Never let them see you as weak."*

"Faeries never lie, do they?" I asked.

The faery drew her hands together over a sparkling crystal table, risen from the ice floor.

"We offer positions to promising students. Fish do not simply invite themselves."

"Your newspaper, your rules." I copied her posture, leaning back in my arctic chair like it wasn't horribly uncomfortable. "You could let freshmen demand positions if they wanted to."

"There are other students on this staff."

"But none of them are the leader of Fae House, are they?" In this brief conversation, I'd figured out who I was talking to. Faeries loved to control the narrative, which included controlling the press. So much so that they'd convinced most of the world that they were harmless garden sprites and not capricious, cruel masterminds. Faery godmother propaganda and all that, erasing all the times they made medieval serfs dance until decomposition.

Flora surveyed me. She was a thin, bronze-skinned woman with piercing blue eyeshadow and perfectly styled hair.

"Shall we make a deal?" I asked.

Here we go. Everything with faeries went this way. The trick, however, was to make sure the deal always ended with me on top.

Flora's perfectly manicured brows raised. She looked

like she was wondering who was mad enough to make a deal with the Fae. Me, apparently.

"I'll work for the eternal," I proposed. "In exchange, you owe me a favor."

She tilted her head. Laughed, like icicles rattling in a snowy breeze. "You're not the first to offer me information for a favor."

"But you need info," I said. "Nobody knows who the campus murderer is. Even with your staff at it, you can't figure it out. Not only that, you're being outsold by the oracle."

"It is rather difficult to compete with one who can tell the future, yes."

"Did you see the picture I sent the oracle? I can figure out who's doing this."

That morning, I'd opened my mail to a $20 bill, my camera, and a copy of the oracle's gossip column. She never asked me for my footage. Nor credited me. But at least she paid me. Nobody else would know she stole it.

The tips of her lips turned up. "You had one lucky shot," she said. "What will you do without your camera? You'd be just as useless as everyone else."

"I would improvise," I said. "I'm crafty."

"What's the favor?"

I took a breath. Admitting that I needed something in return was a liability. Flora's gaze seared into my soul. I hesitated. A fatal mistake.

"Let me guess... Flora, I want into Fae House? I'll get you whatever you want in exchange for the pretty pointed ears?"

"No!" I exclaimed. "I want the freedom to choose."

"To choose?"

"My House."

"You already have that. It is a mutual selection system."

"But it isn't, is it?" I leaned forward. Flora sat back. Opened a drawer. "I can write down whatever House I choose, but they have to pick me back. It's only an illusion of choice."

"And you are worried you will get dropped by a desirable House." She pulled a shiny object out of the drawer. Cleared her papers off the desk. "And that you came to this university for nothing."

There it was. She'd found the crack in my defenses. Good thing I knew hers, too. Time to deflect.

"As worried as you should have been. With a name like Flora, I doubt it destined you for anything other than Rose House."

The room chilled, icicles biting like needles against my flesh. Flora flipped the knife she held once.

A knife? Surely she wasn't planning on drawing blood. Causing pain was an inherent Unseelie practice. "You're rather insolent for a mortal with no power," she said.

My guess was correct. Only intuition drove me, but I suspected that 'Flora' was not a very Fae-like name from the first time I heard it.

"And you're rather insecure over something that was settled last year when you pledged Fae. Is that why you dabble in blood art?"

The knife stilled. "You were raised by a faery." It was a statement, not a question.

"Yes," I responded. "The original Faery godmothers banned dark magic from this university. What would President Consta do if I said you pulled a knife out every time you need to make a deal?" I gave her my best smirk.

She sliced the knife against her wrist. Blood dripped down her arm, sizzling into the ice.

"Slit your wrist, girl."

I took out my pocket knife and ran it across my pointer finger until a drop beaded. Flora gave me a look that could cut glass, eyeing my un-slashed wrist with distaste. The drop fell.

"You owe me your time, House mouse. When I say go, you ask where. When I say fight, you say how long? And when I say slit your wrist, you *slit your wrist*."

The moment my blood hit the wood, my body recoiled.

Ice. An aching freeze, ancient and otherworldly, devoured me. The blizzard swarmed, overwhelming my senses, anchoring me in place.

The cold consumed. Then paused. Held me in its grasp for a moment more. Ached.

Then it vanished, flushing warmth to my bones. I collapsed forward, breathing deeply.

"First rule of working with me: strongest Fae always wins. You never reveal the dark magic I use to anyone, or I will rip out your mouth for trying."

I peeled my chest off my knees. Despite having the warmth knocked out of me, energy bristled under my skin. Knowing that the Fae leader hid her darkness revitalized me. I wasn't alone here, after all.

"Second rule: I give orders, not requests."

She pointed at the door, and it flew open.

"Third rule: your life is demon hunting from now on, starting with the handsome one. I don't care if it's unusual for freshmen to be so involved in the hunt. When you hear of his whereabouts, you follow. When he asks you a question, you answer. I don't care if you live or die."

A glacial gust of wind shoved me out the door.

"That handsome devil owns you now."

CHAPTER
SEVEN

THE ORACLE MUSINGS

It's Halloween, degenerates! Fae House is throwing Under the Mountain again, of course. That is if you can get an invite. Notoriously exclusive bastards—they only invite their own and the few potential new members they think are suitable for membership. Don't worry, though! The unwanted and unlovable are always welcome at Wolf House: that pack of animals keeps invites open to everyone. Riffraff and mutts included!

Show up or get out pledges! Tonight will make or break your place in the social hierarchy of Aether: dress to impress, or you'll never get invited back again. Just remember: this isn't high school anymore. May the most vicious and beautiful win!

HALLOWEEN WAS MY FAVORITE HOLIDAY. It was where the dead came alive, and the living got to play dead.

My mother wouldn't wear some ridiculous hairstyle or hat to cover her pointed ears. I could eat as much candy as I wanted without worrying the sugar would feed the bacteria that feasted on my flesh. Gaksi would join my schemes and make me the best-dressed girl in town.

In fifth grade, I won "best dressed" at my neighborhood's Halloween parade when Gaksi played the strings of the guitar for my "Haunted" Taylor Swift costume. He played the song all night without me even having to strum.

"It's haunted," I told fascinated kids and mildly concerned adults.

"It's just pre-programmed," my dad told his friends with a wink. "Luna has been learning about engineering!"

I wasn't.

In middle school, Gaksi used his power to make me a giant, glittering tiara. It was so extravagant one of my school bullies called me a 'rich, spoiled brat.' I took that as a compliment.

I wasn't cool enough in high school to be invited to parties. But I stayed home with Gaksi instead, handing candy to the children who stopped by. To please my mother, I'd have on a Renaissance corset dress, with Gaksi lighting fae lights that danced around my head. "I'm a faery!" I would tell the little ones. And even though I couldn't see it, Mom beamed behind me. I could tell by how gentle she was when handing out her own candy. And I was always happy because I made my mom happy, which made it the best day of the year.

This year would be different. I had goals to reach, alone.

Bass shook my dorm room as I got ready. Excitement painted the air. Around me, I heard the whooping and hollering of drunk revelers. It was hard to sit patiently and apply my eyeliner when such spirited music played. My foot tapped to the beat, eager to shimmy and dance.

Behind me, giant, arched feathers sprouted from my

back and extended high into the air. My dress was dangerously cute, white, and short, and I'd paired it with thigh-high lace socks and platform heels. Gaksi fluttered my feathers with the wind, making me look like a descendant of the heavens, wide enough wingspan to topple any man.

No gossamer faery wings tonight. Let me show these houses just how fallen angel I can be, instead.

Curling the last coils of my night-black hair, I sent a last-minute text to Aubrey.

Luna: *Ready?*

My phone buzzed, and I looked at it, only to find a message from Cordelia.

Cordelia: *Xavier invited me to a cookout with the wolves tonight. Want to come? He said everyone's invited.*

My brow furrowed. I already made plans with Aubrey, but I felt bad excluding Cordelia. I couldn't invite her Under the Mountain, either. Aubrey said it was hard enough as it was getting us on the guest list.

Luna: *Sorry, can't tonight!*

Probably best not to let her know I was going to a different party. I didn't want to hurt her feelings.

There was a pit in my stomach as I shifted between my feet, watching the last three dots of her response. I already told her I loved Halloween and couldn't wait to party tonight. What if she knew I was going somewhere else? What if she thought I was a rotten friend?

Cordelia: *Next time, then! :)*

I let out a sigh of relief. No worries there.

Aubrey: *Meet at 5 at the Andromeda Observatory?*
Luna: *Sounds good!*

I threw my eyeliner onto my cluttered desk and careened out the door. Shoving the door open, I hurtled across campus with vigor. In minutes, I'd arrived at the Andromeda.

"You look amazing!" I told Aubrey.

She'd dressed in a flower crown and sage-green dress. It brought out the shiny blonde of her hair, making her look like a delicate forest sprite.

Her face froze. "You too!" She smiled, quickly recovering. "The wings look great! How'd you make them?"

"Gaksi helped me!"

"Ah." She nodded, almost to herself. "Shall we get going then?"

We walked toward the mountains on the far side of campus. Gangs of freshmen moved in chaotic huddles around us. Between halos, glittering scales, and witch hats, there were enough costumes that I could barely stay focused on the walkway in front of us.

The alcohol I was draining in sips probably didn't help with that, either. I snuck some of the soju Dad packed for me into a flask to carry along. It was legal to drink at eighteen in Aether University since it was technically its own ancient country. I was too nervous to show up sober, so it felt necessary.

Boys in a sleek blue car decked with a trident whistled at us. "Looking good, angel wannabe!" I flipped them off. "Love the catcalling, Siren House!"

Audrey cackled next to me. "They act so superior for such a mid-house."

"Mid?" I glanced back at the car, which honked once before driving off. "What do you mean?"

"There's a house ranking system. Have you read The Oracle? She goes into it every year."

"Yeah, but what do the rankings mean?"

"It means who's invited to what!" Aubrey exclaimed.

"The best houses, the most successful alumni, the craziest parties, everything!" She pushed me playfully. "That's why we need to get into Fae or Angel house!" She leaned in closer. "I heard they even have answer banks for exams."

"Shouldn't the school ban those?"

"Principal Consta is Fae. Everyone important is. That's just how it is. They don't have to worry about consequences."

Something clicked in my brain. Maybe that was where my mother's entitlement came from. The attitude that she was better than everyone else. But if we got into Fae House, were we, too?

"Your mom was Fae, right?" Aubrey asked. "I saw her in one of the fae composite photos in the library while researching. Your mom is in it—you look just like her!"

I'd heard that before. Everyone said I looked just like my mom. Maybe that was why I was so resistant to focusing on just her House.

I looked like my mom. Did cheerleading growing up, like my mom. Worked diligently at school, enough to get into Aether, just like mommy dearest.

Which was why I decided not to audition for the cheer squad here. And not to tell people about my legacy connection unless they explicitly asked. I even left my mom's vintage hoodies at home.

Forget being in her shadow. I was ready to step out into my light.

We reached the entrance to the massive cave on the west side of campus. Two vigilant, identical fae men guarded the door as we approached.

"An angel costume to a fae party? Bold," the one to the right commented.

"I figured you must have gotten sick of the options already here." The alcohol had hit, and it made me brazen.

A wicked smile greeted his face. "Who do you know here?"

"Flora," Aubrey answered.

"How do you know her?" the one on the left grunted.

"She met me under the mountain," Aubrey answered. That must have been the password because the faeries stepped aside.

"Welcome, girls," they said in unison.

Synchronized lights flashed. Psychedelic music played ahead. Whatever noise bubble was off-limits to us before burst.

"Let's go!" Aubrey said.

Two shots later, Aubrey and I were dancing on an elevated surface deep in the mountain. The black dome of the cave above was painted in elaborate murals of Fae and Angels dancing in unison. Angels themselves flew above us. The Houses must have combined to throw this one.

So much for being bold. I fit right in. The guard must have been saying all that to make me squirm. How fae of him.

I kept sipping from my acorn filled with fae wine. Moth-sized pixies played in my hair, bouncing it about happily.

Hips swaying to the beat, I let myself loose in throngs of partiers. I was glad Gaksi was controlling my wings because otherwise, I'd never be able to swing them out of the way of the crowd.

They made me very popular too. Multiple fairies and angels alike commented on how much they loved them. I'd never been this pleased before.

"Angel dust?" Aubrey grabbed my shoulder, holding out a straw.

"I'll pass, but thank you," I laughed.

"Your loss!" she screamed over the music, inhaling the rest.

I hadn't been this free in years. This must be why everyone wanted to be in a top-tier House. Parties soothed the soul.

Hacking and coughing next to me broke me out of my harmony. A boy abruptly jumped off the railing, rushing to the dark of the cave out of sight.

I recognized that sound. When my youngest brother Joseph was about to throw up, he sounded exactly the same.

"Hey Aubrey, did you see that guy?"

"The what?" It was hard to hear. Music too loud. "The guy throwing up. Do you think he's okay?"

"Probably." She grabbed my hands, and we jumped and twisted around to the beat. I was a little too sober not to be worried. "I'm going to go check on him. Wanna come?"

She shook her head.

"Be back soon!" I hopped off the platform and forced my way through the crowded bodies. Gaksi pushed my wings harder behind me, using wind gusts to move me a little faster. When I moved past the majority, I heard a kid hurling.

I located him throwing up in a dark corner of the mountain, surrounded by two bigger, brawnier guys. He clutched the trash can like a lifeline while they berated him.

"You're banned for life, man."

"This is pathetic."

"Can't handle your alcohol, huh, fish?" The biggest one

reared his foot back and kicked the kid in the stomach, who grunted and collapsed.

"Hey!" I shouted. "Leave him alone!" The two guys' heads snapped up.

"Party is the other way, pretty angel. We're just taking out the trash here." He bulldozed toward me. Scars lined his bald head, extending down his neck to his tattered clothing. "Come on, girly, party's this way." I slid past the blusterer and kneeled to the boy on the floor. I brushed his shoulder.

"Are you okay?"

He only moaned.

"He's wasted," the other guy said. Or maybe the biggest one. I didn't care. I was angry drunk now. "What's wrong with you? Beating up a little kid?"

"He's little, but he's not a kid," the one closest laughed. "He's just as old as you."

The one behind me grabbed my collar and tugged. I got pulled back, thrashing. "Let go of me!"

"Go back to Halloween, fish. Leave this to the seniors." They exchanged a look. I noticed the winged insignia on their shirts.

"Very angelic of you," I gritted out with clenched fists. "To beat up someone for being sick."

"He's a liability," the smaller one said. "Ruins the party to have puking, drunk people everywhere."

I heaved my wings back, forcing myself free, and made my way back to the sick one. I brushed his hair back with my hand to check his forehead. He was feverish, eyes closed, and clammy.

"Consider my party ruined, then. I'm taking him back to the infirmary."

One of them moved to grab me, and my wing snapped out, knocking him flat on his behind.

"Thanks, Gaksi."

"Back off," I growled.

"You'll pay for that!"

They both rushed me, and I panicked, covering the boy with my wings. Gaksi was so connected to me, he did what I wanted intrinsically. Was I strong enough, or sober enough, to take out two?

"Listen to the lady," a rumbling voice called out from the shadows of the cave.

No.

My spine tingled with recognition. I'd know that voice anywhere, in any universe, at any time.

"Who—"

Snap.

The boys toppled.

No. Not now. Not so soon.

The boy in my arms was warm just a second ago.

My wings blocked us like a shield as I heard the soft steps of the Reaper.

"You're supposed to carve out and eat men's hearts, not heal them." His deep voice echoed off the walls of the cave.

"Perhaps I'll start with yours." I flexed my wings, faking bravado. "You wouldn't get that close," Reaper retorted.

"I'm close now, aren't I?" Stall. I had to stall.

Reaper couldn't be here right now. Because he came to collect the dead, and this kid was alive just now, just mere seconds ago...

"Move aside, little seraphim," he whispered. I shuddered, feeling his hot breath against my neck. How could he feel so... warm and human? Weren't demons dead themselves? Shouldn't he have been cold?

His hands brushed the tip of my wings, sending a quiver through my soul.

"You are not wanted here," I breathed. "Get the hell out."

"Wanted or not, I am here nonetheless." His touch vanished, and he appeared in front of me.

"If this is a ruse, it is a very good one," he said. "Gumihos get more and more clever with every staged death."

"Staged?" I roared. Without thinking, I grabbed the knife from my garter and hurled it at him.

It froze midair.

"Your aim needs work, however."

"You think this is a ruse? That I just staged a kid dying?" My voice cracked on the last word. The alcohol was making me hysterical. I felt too panicked to breathe, to think. I just needed to fix, to fix this situation I was in right now…

His gaze hardened.

"He's not even dead," I said. "You need to go away. He was alive just a second ago; I just felt how warm he was. I'm about to take him to heal him. I mean, he's barely any different from my brother in high school, you can't just take him away."

My rambling cut off when he closed in, hand over the body. He had a look on his face that I couldn't place. Like he was deep in thought.

"This school has been good for your acting ability. You are almost making me sympathetic to a sad little girl right now." His gaze locked with mine. "Let's say I entertain this little charade." His lips turned into an acrid, gloating smile while he held out his hands to demonstrate. "On one hand, I've never thought of the gumiho as a creature to feel bad for her victims. When you were having your little meltdown over the boy, it was almost believable. On the other hand, you claim you are not a gumiho, and yet, whenever there is a dead body on this campus, you are never very far away."

I glared.

"Let's make a deal then: if you are not the gumiho, prove it. Catch her for me. Then I will never have to visit this cursed universe again."

My eyes squeezed shut in frustration.

Never make a deal with a devil.

That was one of the first lessons of Aether.

But if I did this, would I never have to see him again?

"Let's catch her together, you beast," I said. "Because I certainly won't be accused of being one."

I blinked, and he was beside me. His soft lips pressed to my neck, lingering for only a moment.

Heat rose from my toes all the way to my flushing face.

"Until we meet again, wicked seraphim." His kiss burned like a brand.

He teleported back to the boy, hands centered on his chest until they both illuminated with cloudy gray. I felt his absence more than his presence, like the aching withdrawal of an addictive drug.

The haze dissolved sharply into dust, taking my deal-maker with it.

My shadows rioted in response, revolving around my neck like a collar.

What had I done?

CHAPTER
EIGHT

THE ORACLE MUSINGS

You heard it from me first, dear Oracle Fan Club: the entirety of the Aether University Police Force will resign tonight. After losing three of their own last week and losing two today, they plan on announcing their resignation to President Consta after a blowout fight that leaves President's Hall demolished. How do I know? I'm the Oracle. I know everything.

NOT who's committing the murders, though. Obviously, I would have spilled the tea first. Don't you fools know me at all?

While we're at it, you investigative journalists can slide right OUT of my DMs with the accusations. None of the death threats against me have ever landed. (I can see right through them, fools!) And threats to reveal my true identity? You'd have to know it first (and that's saved for my starborn, which you ugly wannabes are not!)

Finally, could hazing happen so soon in the recruitment season? A freshman has been found dead in the aftermath of the

Fae/Angel rager. Will this hurt their reputation? Who would join a House that could haze a student to death?

THE LECTURE HALL was silent as a corpse today. As silent as I was regarding the events that transpired last night. I had been so embarrassed, so ashamed of what I agreed to, that I told no one.

I dove back into my studies like it never happened.

Despite that, the weight of my shame pulsed on my neck all night, an intimate reminder of the most velvety kiss I'd ever received—and it wasn't even on the lips.

There was a mark on my neck in the shape of two dark, black wings, and I had to throw on a choker before class to cover it.

Students had their notes pulled out on tables in front of them, scanning readings as Professor Ansi took to the podium.

"Welcome to your first oral exam, slackers," she said, letting the insult hang in the air. "First to answer each question gets the most points. I've used magic to ensure that only one of you gets heard first—whoever started speaking first. Even if you have the right answer, I will silence your mouth if the magic senses you are too slow or unconfident. You'll also be prohibited from answering the next question as punishment. Points will still be added to your final tally, however, if you are correct on the second question. If you guess nothing, your mouth will be closed for the rest of class."

She glared at us like a mother scolding her overgrown children.

"It's always better to answer something rather than

nothing. There's no easier target for a demon than a kid who won't fight back."

So, answer quickly. Hope for correctness. That was the lesson she tried to impart here. The hidden curriculum mother warned me about. Speed over content, at least for inexperienced beginners. I supposed that made sense. If I were to encounter a monster tomorrow, I'd be better off staying agile and running away, not dwelling and plotting an offensive strategy.

"Questions get harder as we go. Brace yourselves."

Cordelia clasped my hand. "We've got this."

"Silence!" Dr. Ansi said. "Any more interruptions will cost you points." Thuds sounded from students forcibly sitting upright in their seats.

"And remember: if this classroom is stressful, you have no business fighting real creatures of the night."

She waved her hands, whamming the classroom doors shut. Late students would be locked out entirely.

"First: which House has the highest GPA?"

"Fae House!" Hunter shouted. I had also moved my mouth to respond, and a tally appeared on a slip of paper in front of me. I was right, even though I didn't get the credit for the first answer.

"Correct," Dr. Ansi said. "Although we are using points for this oral exam, written exams covering the usual college curriculum will be calculated into GPA, a separate measure at this university from point totals. Faeries have long prided themselves in selecting only the best and brightest."

"Which House has the highest retention rate?" Dr. Ansi asked next.

"Wolf House!" I yelled. In the corner of my eye, I saw Xavier and Adam's almost imperceptible nod of approval.

"Wolf House protects members of their pack, so they have the lowest fatality rate of any House."

Hunter shot me a glare. Two black tallies appeared in front of me, so I didn't mind. I bet he didn't study any of the Houses besides Fae. As the Fae crown prince, other Houses must be background information to him.

"Which House has the most demon kills?"

"Vamp—" I almost said before I felt a force constricting on my neck.

A tally vanished from my paper.

"Angel House!" Hunter said. "They're deceptively innocent, so demons let their guard down." He smirked at me. So he did study other Houses. Beneath the pretty boy facade, he was quick with his answers. I stewed in my frustration, eager to snap back with the next question.

"Very good, Hunter. Angels are opposite to demons, so their opposing magic is double effective." Ansi scanned the room. "What's the minimum score to pass?"

I held my tongue. The class, too, was silent. She never told us...

"Five," Dr. Ansi said. "Any less, and you're withdrawn from the recruitment process, effective immediately."

Cordelia squeaked in fright. Others shifted and shot panicked glances at each other. My eyes roamed the room. Two tallies for me, three for most of the room. How long was this exam?

"Deokhye women never fail, Luna," Gaksi murmured in my mind.

"Besides, if you do, that annoying loser wins." As if on cue, Hunter's paper slipped off his desk. He reached under to retrieve it, knocking his head on the desk along the way.

"What percent of incoming freshmen will make it to the end of recruitment?"

Two in three, I remembered from our first class. I wished I could answer, but my lips were sealed shut with minty, sticky magic.

Which also meant nobody could hear my scream when my chair toppled and slammed me into the ground.

Pain ricocheted through my side, but I lifted my head enough to see what happened.

From the floor, I saw that someone tied a rope to my seat. At the end of it, Hunter and his surrounding pals, including Zain and his buddy Brayden, were high-fiving. Jerks.

"For those who didn't answer—no, that was not in the assigned reading. But it was in the mandatory first day of class, and your inattention is your own fault." She jerked her head at me. "And you should be paying attention to all your surroundings. Especially the seat you reside in."

My lips turned down into a scowl because she was right. How long ago did Hunter trap my chair? I sat in the same place every day, so it was an easy target. Foolish me, assuming I'd be safe and secure anywhere on this campus. There were no rules about cutting down the competition to get ahead.

I dragged myself onto my desk, making me even taller than the rest of my classmates.

You want to make a spectacle out of me? Go right on ahead.

"*That's my girl!*" Gaksi encouraged.

"Which is the least popular House to pick during recruitment?"

"Rose House!" I shouted. Anyone that hadn't noticed me before now saw me sitting tall on my desk. That was the one House my mother told me to avoid at all costs. "They're the smallest and known for gardening, sisterhood, and baking. Although they are imbued with magic, nobody has ever seen them practice it."

Four tallies.

"Absolutely right, Luna," Dr. Ansi said. "As a female-only House, they automatically restrict membership to only half the students. Despite their willingness to admit any woman, they remain the least popular, year after year. Which House succeeds the most in demon capture after four years of university training?"

"Siren!" I answered again. "They can go the furthest in the human world because of their persuasion, so they have the most opportunity to reach resources hidden from others."

Lukas caught my eye and winked. Shameless flirt.

Dr. Ansi nodded.

There was only Vamp House left. I wondered what she'd ask.

"What machine determines your future?"

I heard a cluster of "V" sounds, abruptly choked off. Eyes widened in panic.

"The Antikythera!" Hunter answered.

"To all of you who answered, Vamp House, your attention skills need work. Demons love using wordplay to trick you into believing you know their next move. At the end of recruitment, you can choose which House you believe will give you the best attributes to fight them. However, the Antikythera machine will guide you along the way, adding and withdrawing as it sees fit." She clapped her hands together. "Count your points!"

Seven. I passed! Cordelia patted me from the side. She had exactly five, so she was safe.

Behind and around us, students held up papers to their faces as if staring at them longer would make more points appear.

"If you failed, pack your bags. You can continue taking general education courses, but any Aether unique classes, as well as access to a House, are banned until next year. I hope you shape up along the way because you've just blown your shot."

After class, I went to the Cornucopia for lunch with Mother. She insisted on a visit to congratulate my progress on passing the first hurdle.

When I arrived, she captured me in a tight, crushing hug. Overjoyed, convinced I was finally in her good graces, my heart twisted when she whispered her true thoughts in my ear.

"I know you've been cavorting with the Reaper."

My blood pumped. "What?"

She dragged me by my ear to the nearest table. It was lunchtime, and students from all classes and Houses had moved to the Cornucopia, eyeing my maternal showdown. My ears turned pink, and not just from the tugging. Everyone I knew was watching me get scolded. Two girls from my Pills & Potions class pulled out their phones to record.

She waved her hands, forming a sound veil around us. It didn't hinder visibility, leaving me on display for communal scrutiny.

"Do not forget your mission here, Luna Deokhye," she commanded, her voice carrying the authority of a thousand suns. "You have sins to erase and a legacy to live up to."

"I didn't choose to be born this way." I crossed my arms, teeth clenched. "You have no right to judge me, Mother. You sired me, after all."

"Do not make me regret that."

We stared off. Youth and daring on one side, experience and tradition on the other.

"Do whatever you have to do to break your contract with the Reaper. He's danger in a pretty package; a persecutor disguised as a saint."

"Or what, Mother dearest?" I couldn't believe her. Did she really think I entered this contract willingly? Or that it what would be easy to extricate myself from it? I didn't think I could escape now, not with my double deal with the Fae House leader.

"Or you will not be my daughter anymore," she said. The words sliced through me like a blade, cleaving my soul in two. "No money, no legacy acknowledgment. You will simply exist as an orphan, and I will never contact you again."

My mouth dropped open, stunned, as I let the weight of her declaration sink in. I always knew Mother resented the demons of the dark, but not enough to dishonor me by casting me aside. The implications of her ultimatum devoured me.

I wouldn't get the legacy ceremony in Fae House and the Aether college experience. Without tuition money, I'd have to drop out, with nowhere to return home to and nowhere to run away.

"What about Dad?" I asked weakly.

"Dad doesn't want you cavorting with the devil, either."

A single tear rolled down my cheek. "I don't know how to break it, Mom."

"Figure it out." The sound barrier dropped. My bracelet tightened around my wrist as Gaksi's form of reassurance.

"Make me proud, not humiliated."

CHAPTER NINE

THE ORACLE MUSINGS

What's worse than the terrible twos? It's the terrible three! Brayden, Zain, and ringleader Hunter will spend tonight chasing pretty dryads back to the Beyond. They'll be having a bit too much fun, if you ask me! Harassment has never been my cup of tea.

Speaking of tea: Beautiful, dark creatures will be roaming the campus tonight. Not as beautiful as me, of course, but pretty close, and a tad jealous, too.

MY NECK WOKE me early almost every day, concentrating my shadows into a perpetual, aggravating force. I couldn't stand it. Two days and two bargains? Mistakes etched into my skin? What was next on the third day? Selling my soul?

I had to walk. Pace somewhere that wasn't this tiny dorm, where the shadows in my soul might jump out and suffocate me.

It was past curfew, so only a few figures lurked in the darkness outside. Because demons were more active at night, we were ordered to remain in our dorms after sunset until being Housed. But with Gaksi bobbing along in my hair ribbon, I doubted any significant harm could befall me.

The only nighttime figures on this campus were darting between bushes and up balconies for late night hookups with one-night stands and starborn souls.

At least some of us had a starborn, true love. My only companion for these lonely nights was Gaksi.

"*Incoming*!"

A tawny-brown wolf darted in front of me, growling faintly.

I held up my hands and backed away slowly.

"Hush!" a familiar female voice sounded from above.

"Cordelia?"

She waved out her window, holding a finger over her mouth. "Shh!"

The wolf growled.

"Hey, Xavier," I said, holding back a giggle. Cordelia and Xavier! Xavier and Cordelia! I was *so* getting the full scoop from her later. "I'll keep your secret if you keep mine?"

He blinked.

"Goodnight," I said lightly, walking in a different direction.

Thankfully, he didn't follow.

THE MOON SHONE high in the night, illuminating the sky over the library. Stone arches lined the entrance to the massive building, taller than the tree line. The inside was all brick and stone; it was one of the first buildings built on campus.

Only candles lit the inside, giving it a warm glow on a quiet night.

Arched semi-circles cut rays of moonlight into the otherwise stony stacks. My feet shuffled across ornate rugs as I perused the oak wood shelves for something to entertain me.

Flora: *Wake up, house mouse!*
Luna: *Already up, your highness.*
Flora: *The oracle claims a beautiful creature will roam tonight. Wander around at midnight and find him. I need more info. What is he? How do you get rid of him? The safety of our campus is at risk. As is your place in it.*

I gritted my teeth. Was that how all leaders lead? Exploiting young people's hard work for personal gain?

My fingers burned, each throbbing at the tip, like I'd drawn blood from each during my bargain with Flora. That must have been her way of encouraging me to get on it.

A marble statue of Athena stood in the center of the grand reading room, a tribute to the University's location off the coast of Greece. She watched over me as I sought her level of wisdom among the supernatural tomes.

Where would one find a book on basic demon identification? I couldn't exactly go and ask the late-shift librarian for help. I could hear my mother's warning now.

Stay away from the dark side of magic. The unhoused demons remained on the other side of the veil for a reason. Only the corrupt and cowardly ran from justice.

My hands browsed through the tomes. All I had to go off were my memories. A three-legged raven. A ghastly pale man with dark eyes and darker shadows. What kinds of creatures were those?

Demons of the Sky. Demons of the Earth. Demons of Ancient Times. New-Age Demons. Demons Resembling Men. Aha!

I ripped it out, then slid deeper into the archives. I should read this in a secure location where I wouldn't be easily spotted. It wasn't forbidden to read it, but public distrust of the unhoused was at an all-time high following recent attacks. No need to shine a spotlight on me as a potential suspect. I'd already survived one interrogation with university police. I'd rather not go through another.

"Consider yourself prey," my freshman orientation advisor had told me during move-in day, "because if any unhoused demons find you, you're fresh meat!" She'd jumped close to me, trying to scare me, and I had laughed. Didn't age well.

When I reached a dusty, isolated part of the library, I sat down and flipped through the pages. Sirens were still in it, which marked it as an ancient text. Sirens only became Housed recently.

It was a good thing, too, because they were causing problems before they did.

"Never date a creature that hasn't allied with an Aether-affiliated House," Mother warned. *"Unhoused demons will drag you to the other side, and you will never return. Like sirens of the past, dragging their lovers into the deep."*

Aether University had banned romantic relations between the Others and the students after too many had gone missing. Or returned in pieces. Or they returned, warning others that their love had never been reciprocated, broken and bruised.

"Think of all the sailors that have drowned. The drained bodies of vampire victims. Before they became civilized, they, too, were monsters."

"You're just an insignificant doll to them," mother had emphasized. *"Demons are pretty and charismatic enough to feign love. Too savage to ever feel any."*

After sirens, there were chapters on centaurs, ghosts, and then a section called *Death Carriers*. The first was a grim reaper, sickle sticking out. He was oddly familiar but not from the night of the attack. Just general folklore. I admired his figure longer. The long black cloak matched, although the face was shrouded by shadow. Could this be him?

Curious, I eyed the illustrated sickle. I ran my finger along it, jerking back when I felt a prick.

A drop of blood welled. "Ouch!"

Did the book just... cut me?

I whipped my head around, as if someone could have seen that. Surely not. It was just a paper cut. From the middle of the page. Not from the sickle!

Using my uninjured finger, I cautiously turned the page.

Froze.

Took a breath.

Calmed my racing heart.

It was him.

Jeosung Saja. He had the same long black hair, clothing, and hollowed eyes.

The Jeosung Saga is a fearsome creature. He often appears in dreams of the accursed before their death. His pursuit of the dying is relentless and unforgiving, and he is not often perceived by the living. It is thought that he leads the dead to their final resting place. But is that heaven or hell?

I glanced down at a buzz from my phone.

Cordelia: *Luna, I saw a photo of you and that demon guy at the Halloween party. He's hot!!*

Luna: *From where?*

Cordelia: *The Oracle Musings! You know she knows everything about everyone!*

That checked out. My mother read *The Oracle Musings*

religiously, so she must have found out about the bargain through that.

Luna: *He could be a murderer!*
Cordelia: *Hasn't murdered you yet, though, has he?*
Luna: *Yet?*
Cordelia: *How old do you think he is? 100? 200? 2000? I bet he's ancient. And he's been wandering all alone this whole time, desperately waiting for some companionship...*
Luna: *He is off limits.*

I wished we were in person, so I could be firm with this conversation.

Cordelia: *Is he as good-looking in real life as he is online?*

My fingers hovered over the screen. It felt foolish to describe him. I'd only conversed with him twice, and both times were under duress.

A strange ache felt its way into my chest. What would it be like to talk to him outside of a murder scene? Would his eyes flash as dark? Would his mane of hair flow behind him when he moved?

Snap out of it, Luna.

Luna: *He's Other. He's demonic.*

And just as beautiful as you would expect any demon to be.

Luna: *He's dangerous. Strong enough to freeze three men solid.*
Cordelia: *You're swooning! Everyone loves a strong and mighty man!*
Luna: *Go to bed, Cordelia.*
Cordelia: *We'll revisit this convo tomorrow.*

I smiled inwardly and put the phone away. Filtering through the stacks, I searched for "gumiho" next. I had absolutely nothing to go off of. I could start with the Gs, but

I didn't think that word came from English. The last book I read didn't give country identification per demon, either.

Stars! This was horrible. I dumped my pile of books on the shelf.

An entire stack crashed to the floor, my pile having unbalanced it. I staggered back as the books replaced themself gracefully, fluttering as if my mishandling offended them. I rushed forward to help them along.

"*Smooth,*" Gaksi's voice mocked.

"Curse you!"

"*I'm not the cursed one,*" Gaksi replied. "*That's you, sweetheart.*"

"You're supposed to stay hidden!" I shouted at the roof.

"*The yelling is helping with that, I'm sure.*"

"You've seen me run around these stacks for so long, and you haven't helped me at all!"

"*It is important for children to learn their independence. And to self soothe.*"

"Go to hell, Gaksi."

"*Already been and wasn't much impressed. Reaper and I much prefer this realm.*"

"Do you think he killed that wolf?" I asked, sitting. "I'm serious, Gaksi. Not joking."

"*Unlikely. I've never seen him kill anyone. Torture, sure, threaten, absolutely, but murder just isn't his job.*"

"How do I stop him, then?"

"*You can't, any more than you can stop death.*"

"Well, then, how do I stop the murders?" I asked, exasperated.

"*That is not your job,*" Gaksi says, "*it is Reaper's. His responsibility is to stop the gumiho.*"

"And what is the gumiho?"

"I would show you, but it appears she has already stolen any mention of herself from this library."

"Then just tell me."

"The gumiho is the creature likely causing most of the murders on this campus. She must have crossed the veil somehow. Her presence is likely causing other creatures to follow the massive pull of her energy, causing more mortals to perish. She uses her beautiful face to trick men before she slaughters them."

"Well, how do I eliminate her?"

"You don't. Reaper will."

It clicked.

Is this how you've been evading capture?

"That's why... Reaper... wants to kill me? Because he thinks I'm this gumiho thing?" A grunt in my mind confirmed. "Why would he think that?"

Stone creaked behind me. "The gumiho is said to seduce vulnerable men with her beauty," a gravelly voice said, distant footsteps echoing nearer.

Reaper.

Ice shot through my veins. My pulse throbbed in my neck, where his mark sat.

"Did you come here to burn all the books mentioning yourself?" I asked.

Broad hands landed on my shoulders, twisting me around. I kept my chin up to face him. The sharp angles of his face were even more prominent when illuminated by candlelight. If I wasn't so indebted to him, so angry at him for forcing me into this bargain, I could admit that my toes curled when he put that kind of light pressure on my shoulders. Feather-light, despite his hard gaze. Despite my trembling soul.

"Must you insist that I'm the gumiho? It is a vulnerability to admit attraction."

"Indeed," he rasped, leaning down to kiss his brand. The shadows thrummed beneath my skin. They were pleased. I'd never felt them so strongly. I'd never felt my heart beat so vividly in my throat, either.

"Indeed," I repeated, desperately searching for my reasoning abilities. Anger ignited in me with the audacity of his kiss. How dare he return and kiss me again? After locking me into a demonic bargain? Reinvigorating my shadows?

"Blaming me is perhaps the perfect cover for yourself and your own wicked deeds," I said, voice as resolute as I could make it.

Silence stretched. Then, tenderly, his hand moved to grip my chin between his thumb and forefinger. He held me tightly, like a seal. "You know how I could solve both our problems, bold seraphim? I'll just take you away," he threatened, face darkening. "Take you to the other side, permanently. Collaborating this way would be beneficial, don't you think?"

I jerked back but couldn't move far, not with him holding me in place. Even my magic had died, sputtered out from shock. Like it knew an ancient force had bested it. A primal, dangerous one.

"You couldn't pull that off with Gaksi defending me," I stuttered.

"He's not always around, lonely seraphim." His hand moved upward. Caressed my face with a soft, inviting touch.

"You wouldn't dare," I continued. Heat brushed my skin. Dark, swirled tendrils coiled from his clothes through my hair. Each contact renewed my magic, creating a cloud of static around my head. He smirked.

"I could, and I would." He brushed the shadows down

to my scalp. My head buzzed with energy. "And I would even like to."

He snapped, and I fell backward.

I shrieked, collapsing into a void, convinced he was taking me to the Beyond.

The place where no mortal was supposed to go.

The place where demons emerged.

The place where no mortal had ever returned.

For a moment, I was suspended in space, seeing nothing, free fall.

THUD.

My behind landed on a soft surface. I opened my eyes. Slowly. Cautiously. Petrified of what I might see.

Gaksi winked at me from the computer screen of my dorm room.

"DEMON!" I screamed into the sky.

CHAPTER TEN

THE ORACLE MUSINGS

There are demons, and there are Demons. Many of you came here to fight demons, low-level creatures that are as easily extinguished as they are forgotten.

But to make an impression? Cavorting with high-level, high-beauty, and high-energy Demons will spell disaster indeed.

Time to make like a siren, fishies: Sink or Swim!

P.S. My long-awaited House Ranking is coming up, don't worry! Pre-order the next edition to learn which Houses stayed on top!

ONE OF YOU IS AN IMPOSTER.

Professor Ansi, zealous as ever, left that encouraging note on the blackboard.

"I must make amends to the above note." Her keen gaze combed over the class. "There's room for multiple of you to fail out, actually. We could always use more janitors."

"This is coming up in her end-of-year evaluation,"

Cordelia whispered. She'd written 'One of You is an Imposter' in curly pink handwriting in her notebook. She wrote everything the professor said, even if it sounded ridiculous. "Every fish plays its role in the ocean."

"The ocean?" I asked. What an interesting phrase. "Did you grow up by the beach or something?"

"I—," Cordelia began, clearing her throat. "I love the sea. There's nowhere else I feel I belong."

"Interesting." Why didn't she answer the question? "So, you want to be a siren, then?"

"More than I've ever wanted anything." Her eyes glistened so fast I thought I might have imagined it. "I used to despise them, but lately, my options have been limited..." Her gaze fell slightly before gesturing to the front of the room.

"Hey, check out Lukas," Cordelia said. He'd fallen completely asleep in the front of the class. Xavier was sitting next to him, trying to sneak a picture of him with his phone.

Cordelia eyed them instead of the professor until a student plopped down next to me.

Aubrey, dressed in a matching workout set, waved. "Hey, girl!"

"Hey!" I said, moving my stuff aside for her. "Aubrey, this is Cordelia," I told Aubrey, gesturing to my friend.

"Are you like a hometown friend or something?" Aubrey asked Cordelia.

"No, we met on the first day of school," Cordelia answered.

"Oh, very nice," Aubrey nodded.

"Hey, where were you during the first exam?" I asked Aubrey.

"I got attacked by a demon, so I was in the infirmary."

She held up her arm, where gauze covered her from shoulder to wrist. "I'm lucky I survived. Luckier still that I survived the interrogation chambers."

"Ouch," I said in solidarity. "Guess we have that in common."

I didn't question her further. I was sure the campus leaders had done that already. I did, however, sneak her consolation candy during class. She smiled at me before throwing it in her backpack.

The professor resumed talking, and we quit chatting to write notes frantically. The pace had increased every day, and it was a pain to keep up.

"What's the number one rule of Aether?"

"Don't use dark magic!" a raucous member of the terrible three answered.

"Good!" Dr. Ansi said. "Rule two?"

"Don't date it!" the same voice said. The class laughed.

"Absolutely right, Brayden," Dr. Ansi replied. "The reason we ban dark magic at this university is because it is often practiced by demons, who commonly use it for seduction, and it destroys the user or the surrounding environment as fuel. It strips the surroundings of energy, taking away what makes it unique." She went on about the different ways demons could lock you into an unhealthy relationship.

Bargains were #1.

Unfortunately, I already had two.

"I bet he's a gunner," Aubrey said to me.

"A what?" I responded.

"A gunner! You don't know what that is?" Aubrey questioned.

I shook my head.

"A gunner is someone who is always trying to outdo the

competition," Aubrey explained. "Gunners want to be at the top of the class and stop at nothing to get there. I suspect everyone in the terrible three is a gunner. They're practically falling over themselves to answer questions before anyone else can. Ready to gun down the competition at any moment."

"Aubrey!" I hushed.

"They do all this to get into a top house." She sulked at me. "We have to be on the lookout."

"Got it."

"Speaking of gunners," Dr. Ansi glared straight at us, "What is the easiest thing a gunner can do to get ahead of their peers?"

My pen fell to the desk. How was her hearing so good? She must have been a vampire. They were known for extraordinary hearing. When she leaned down to draw on her sketch pad, fangs peeked out of her smile.

"Get hot!" Zain yelled, and the class broke into laughter.

The professor sighed. "Yes, the halo effect applies everywhere, but especially at Aether. Every House wants residents who will fulfill their image. Doe eyes look best under halos. Shiny hair makes glowing werewolf coats. Glowing teeth carve into the best fangs. Full lips sing the best praise at sea. Immaculate skin conveys the spotless nature of faeries."

I cast my eyes down to my skin, which was far from immaculate. I'd need more skilled makeup artistry and clothing choices to cover my inborn flaws going forward.

"Forget superficialities," the professor continued, "for the rest of this lesson, we'll focus on immediate problems: demons you're more likely to encounter soon."

Her hands moved over her charcoal sketch, and Reaper stepped off the page.

Professor Ansi was an artist. Every Housed member gained a special ability, a pearl, in addition to the basic magic and abilities that came with their House. Sirens gifted each other literal pearls when they earned their pearl, hence the name. Dr. Ansi's pearl was that she could draw images that magnified into bigger ones. This one was large enough to cover a two-story building.

"Who is this?" she asked.

"He calls himself the Reaper," Cordelia quipped.

"And where is he from?"

"The Beyond," Hunter scoffed.

"Obviously. Minus one point for pointing out what we already knew." Dr. Ansi scolded.

"Hey!" Hunter complained.

"Better question: why is it relevant to know where he's from?"

"Because other demons will follow his path here," I answered.

"Correct, Luna. Five points to you for being less annoying than Hunter."

Hunter's shocked expression was worth the vengeance I was sure he'd try to deliver later.

Professor Ansi swiped her sketchpad, and the image changed to a dog, flaming and burning off the page. It barked smoke and fumes. "This is the Bulgae, a folklore creature from Reaper's domain. Why is it important to recognize it?"

"So that you can bolt," Aubrey answered. "Bulgae incinerate everything in their path."

The fire dog shot sparks into the sky. I watched with rapt fascination as they exploded like fireworks, searing students caught in the crossfire.

"Yes, the Bulgae has never crossed over before, but it is

rumored to be strong enough to melt planets. Should you see it, the only thing on your mind should be escape. Speaking of melting…"

She flipped the paper, and a three-legged crow flew up. It was as small as a regular-sized one, though it flapped its black wings menacingly.

Sam. That was what Reaper called that creature.

"What does this creature represent?"

"The sun," Aubrey answered again. "The sun god."

Sun *god?*

"Yes, the Goguryeo Dynasty of Korea thought that the three-legged crow, the Samjoko, had powers mightier than dragons."

"How would we take it out?" Hunter asked.

"You can't. These are warnings against worst-case scenarios. These are not everyday demons that can be killed, only evaded."

"But if we wanted to try, which would be worth the most points?" Hunter asked.

Professor Ansi's eyes narrowed. "To engage in that task would be recklessly foolish. We only know of one mortal who has attempted to evade Reaper's, the strongest's, capture, and he died twice."

All heads whipped toward me.

Thank you, oracle, for planting a shiny red target on my back.

"For all those who survived the Reaper's first encounter, see me after class."

Despite Professor Ansi's warning, I daydreamed about Reaper for the rest of the lecture. Why didn't teachers say how beautiful demons could be? How they clawed themselves into your thoughts, even at the most inopportune times?

Bells chimed from the ceiling again, merry notes filling the air, lulling me out of my thoughts. Students shuffled out, but slower than usual. I moved against the wave, forcing my way down to the professor.

Xavier and Adam spoke to her only briefly before departing. I didn't know what Hunter said after, but I heard something like "your funeral" before she waved a hand, and a wind gust shoved him out.

My question was ready by the time I reached her podium. "How did he die twice?"

Concern flashed over her features, but resolve filled her voice. "A man tried to escape death by setting traps to confuse Reaper. It didn't work. After death, he fought off demons on the other side to make it back to his home. But his family had already buried him six feet under, so he died twice upon his return."

"So it's hopeless, then? If you've already seen him once?"

She shook her head. "Fate is a fickle thing. The man's problem was that he couldn't accept that he had already died. But you, Luna Deokhye? You are very much alive."

I shifted on my feet. "As of present, yes."

She sat back in her chair, erasing her crow sketch. "The first round of recruitment is coming soon. You may find that your association with the Reaper causes you problems being taken seriously."

"I'm more worried about my image than my reputation right now, Dr. Ansi. Gossip can't cover the heinous state of my skin." My hands balled into fists at my side, desperate not to scratch.

She eyed my hands with pity. "All freshmen coming in think the same things. That they get selected solely on grades, or beauty, or eagerness to fight evil."

"Are they not?" I asked.

"The Antikythera of this school surpasses our expectations every year. Despite input, both by new and returning students, those who trust the process always end up in the House where they belong."

Darkness tingled under my skin, upset at the idea of confinement. "What if I don't belong?" I asked.

Her eyes drilled into mine. "Your competition may look healthier, Luna, and they may be crueler, but they are not as tenacious. Nor are they braver."

She unfolded her earlier page of Reaper, and an image of us launched out of the page.

Of him, ferocious, glowering over me.

Of me, brassy, hand poised on my water bottle like I might bludgeon him with it. In her image, I wasn't covered in rashes. Nor was I aghast at the mythical being dominating my space. I was drawn like a warrior, like a fighter. Like I was a formidable opponent to a beast beyond this earth.

"You're the first student I've had encounter a death god multiple times and live, Luna. Never forget that."

The next day, I woke up in an inferno.

"Gaksi!" I screamed. "I'm on fire!" I raked my arms down my face, my arms, my legs, my body, my everywhere.

I dropped and rolled onto my carpet, but that only scorched me further.

"I'm burning alive, Gaksi!"

A water bucket dumped itself onto my head, soaking my pajamas and bed sheets. "I don't think it's fire, sweetheart," the bucket rattled.

Itchy. I was so, so itchy; I wanted to just pare off my skin with a knife—

"None of that!" Gaksi chided.

"Do something!" I wailed. Heat bit every movement of my face, every scrape of my nails against my skin.

I ripped off my clothes like I could take my skin off with it. The bucket flew out the window.

The last time misery consumed me like this, my mother had just switched up my laundry detergent to one that wasn't hypoallergenic.

Wait. I did laundry yesterday.

Did someone tamper with my laundry?

I ran to the bathroom, dousing myself in freezing cold shower water and soap. It eased the burn for a moment.

Pain ripped through my system again, making me howl in agony.

After minutes of scrubbing through, I still used my fingers like talons to scratch up and down my body. Ugly red lines followed my streaks. How was I supposed to go on like this? I was so itchy I couldn't even focus!

Maintenance alert, my phone voiced out. *A student has snuck poison ivy into the laundry machines. If you had any exposed wounds before re-applying recently washed clothes, please report to the infirmary.*

Exposed wounds? I pounded my fist into the shower wall, spraying water everywhere. Half my flesh was exposed when I was flaring up!

Useless, pointless, malfunctioning skin barrier!

I sank onto the floor of the tub. Water blasted at my back, stinging the worst of my splotches. It didn't matter. It was nothing compared to walking out in public in this state.

This had to be aimed at me. I should have never shown

my hand in class. Everyone that saw it knew that, one, I was smart, and two, I was easily felled by my own autoimmunity.

Argh! *Any potential weakness can be exploited.*

I clutched my head in my hands. My shadows moaned in agony, desperate to jump out of my skin. I let them encircle me in misery, succumbing to a vortex of dark.

I EMERGED from my blackout in a pair of brawny arms, cradling me to a warm chest. Flames licked weakly up and down my skin. Sea breeze wafted through the air.

"Lukas?" I asked.

"And me, too," Cordelia said. She sat in the same cot Lukas did, holding me. "I dressed you and got Lukas to bring you here since I couldn't carry you myself." Harsh white lights blinded me. Hospital beeps indicated I was, unfortunately, still alive.

She knew, I realized with a start. She saw the shadows.

She knew, and she was going to tell, and all of this will be for naught—

"It's okay," Gaksi reassured. *"I said it was me, protecting your privacy."*

I exhaled.

"As soon as I saw that message, I knew it was probably, well... aimed at you." Cordelia patted my hand. "Gaksi let me in."

A sea foam haired girl popped in shortly after, examining my skin.

"Are you a healer?" I asked. Her green eyes roamed my red skin. "Yes, I'm Aloe, from Rose House." She extended her hand, using magic to wrap aloe leaves around my torso and lower body like a cocoon. Lukas released me for her to do so.

"Fitting," I muttered.

"Yes, my parents had excellent foresight," Aloe said gently.

My cocoon pressed in tighter, relieving the worst of the burn. With a start, I realized they contained my shadows comfortably as well. They swirled around the aloe gel, comfortable.

"Are you still rushing a House?" Aloe asked.

"Yeah," I said, trying to look dignified in my new enclosure. I heard Gaksi chortling in my head.

"You should consider Rose House," she said mildly, tying the wrapping tighter. "The best plants bloom at night." Her hands pressed down, and my shadows concentrated on meeting them.

Aloe knew about the shadows.

How many people knew? This went from bad to worse.

She handed gauze to Cordelia. "Make sure she takes this pack with her." To me, she nodded. "Stay in there for an hour or so. The leaves will fade away on their own."

She left.

"I like her," Gaksi voiced in my brain.

"She knows about my shadows!" I screamed internally.

"Yeah, and is she calling you out on it? Or blackmailing you? Some people are just nice, Luna."

"She might come after me in the future."

"Nobody knows that for sure. Focus on how you feel in the present."

"I'm itchy at present," I replied.

"I know, sweetheart," Lukas said. Did I say that out loud? My cheeks flushed. How embarrassing.

He turned to Cordelia. "We think it was Hunter.

Supposedly all the dorms had students reschedule their exams today—which has already been taken care of for you, so don't worry—except his."

"Let's kill him," I mumbled. Lukas chuckled.

He must really like me. The sun had nearly set, meaning he'd been with me all day. Were students allowed to date their T.A.s? Probably not.

Which meant he was risking trouble to be here for me.

"As much as I wish that was allowed, you have to get back at him some other way. You can only harass fellow students. Killing them takes away points," Lukas said.

"How do I get power over someone whose dad owns this University? I mean, isn't he immune to consequences?" I moved my hands to scratch, and Lukas caught both wrists with one hand.

I ignored what that move did to my imagination as he squeezed a little tighter, smug.

Cordelia cleared her throat. "Maybe you should try to beat him at his own game?"

"Sabotage?" My voice hitched in excitement.

"Not necessarily," Cordelia said. "If you become the most alluring candidate for recruitment—which ultimately, is what I think he wants for himself—then you can beat him at his own game without stooping to his level."

But I was already doing my best for recruitment. That wouldn't satisfy me.

"Lukas?" I asked.

"Sabotage is only frowned upon if you get caught, Luna," he answered with an impish grin.

An idea festered in my mind.

By the time the next exam came up, the wheels were set in motion.

Lukas "accidentally" left a practice exam on Dr. Ansi's desk after her office hours.

The oracle released a column saying her favorite freshmen were about to have the luck of their life. (At least, it looked like the oracle's column, preprinted on the same desk.)

Hearsay promoted that the terrible three, laundry-tampering fiend included, landed an authentic copy of our next written examination.

$100 if you wanted a copy from them. $200 if you wanted the detailed, written explanations on the back.

And from the shock on my classmates' faces when Dr. Ansi handed out our next test, I knew my scheming had worked.

Half the class failed.

Spirit saboteurs, indeed.

CHAPTER
ELEVEN

THE ORACLE MUSINGS

House recruitment has begun! Who will rise above this year and recruit the best class? Will it be the charming Siren House or the elusive Fae House? Will Angel House give out enough fake halos to convince the potential new members they deserve wings? Will Wolf House find enough lone wolves to make a functioning pack? Can this year's Vampire coven put the blood in bloodthirsty? Only one thing is certain—the recruits of Rose House are just as prickly as they are pretty.

I SPENT ALL NIGHT STUDYING, eager to find my place in this University and be best prepared for round one. Fae House, like my mother, was known for trickery within honesty. Wolf House, like Adam and Xavier, was recklessly brave and loyal. Siren House was beautiful and secretive, always persuading others to give them what they wanted.

I rummaged through my drawers, throwing clothes left and right. My room was slowly becoming as unorganized as my middle brother Jason's. Which was kind of embarrassing, considering he was a teenage boy and I was a sophisticated young woman.

Fated stars, where was it? The drawer slammed; I yanked another open. I just bought new nail polish for recruitment, and it needed time to dry, and I was already running so late—

"Missing something?" The sleeve of a jacket wrapped around my wrist, halting my frantic search.

"Obviously!" I shook Gaksi off.

The sleeve rewound in a flash. *"Your phone is ringing, Miss Disorganized."*

Underneath the pile of haphazardly strewn clothes, my phone vibrated. Pushing the laundry aside, I answered.

"Want to walk over together?" Aubrey asked.

"Sure, Aubrey. Meetup between our dorms at Curie hall?" I asked, tossing junk aside.

"Perf!"

Cordelia met up with us when we got there. "There are so many people here!" she said, awed.

The entire Colossal ballroom was filled with seats. The sickly sweet smell of hairspray permeated the air. Compacts snapped open for last-minute touch-ups, and lip gloss popped back into containers.

"Even the boys dressed up," Cordelia mentioned. They wore grey and black suits with bow ties. Like prom.

"That's because it's not just four years of school," Aubrey said. "It's for life. You can never change House once you're initiated. And they can never remove your magic, either."

It was a permanent bond and show of faith. Once you

earned magic, it lasted until death, where it burned through you before returning to the University.

"Come on, let's sit for the speeches," Aubrey said, dragging us to our seats.

Each House had a brief introduction, and then we divided into small groups to physically visit each one. A housed student acted as a guide to each small group but hid her identity so there wouldn't be any bias in advising. Ours found me and Aubrey within minutes of arriving. Cordelia was swept away into a different group.

"Ladies." She hugged us both. "I'm Melody. Can't wait to advise you two." I shifted uncomfortably. I was never good at physical contact. When she released us, her pastel pink ringlets bounced. "I'm not a regular mom. I'm a cool mom. Contact me for anything."

"Come on, let's walk over," Melody said to our small group. "If you can't find me, ask Hyacinth."

The short, dark-haired girl strolling beside us smiled. I recognized her from class. When she looked down, I felt a nudge of sympathy in my chest. She wasn't in any of my regular freshman classes, only my magic-related classes, which meant she was a second-year trying to secure a place in a House again.

All upperclassmen were required to have magic to continue, which meant this was her last chance.

"Don't you think it's weird to start all over again?" I whispered to Aubrey.

"She must be weird for not succeeding the first time," Aubrey responded. "We mustn't be like that."

I nodded but reached out to tap Hyacinth on the shoulder.

"Good luck," I told her. Her eyebrows raised in surprise. "You, too."

Aubrey shot daggers at me with her eyes. Melodramatic diva. Before she could say anything, we arrived in front of my first bargain maker.

Flora and Fae house were our first visit. She avoided eye contact, standing in front of her storybook-style castle.

"Fae are first, always," she said by way of greeting. "We never lie, and we always end up on top. I know Aether's best and brightest will end up here. Come, welcome to the faery cottage."

Apple-sized pixies led us on individual tours of the pastel-decorated, woodsy home of the Fae. Enchantments made the whole house glow faintly.

It was more magical than I could have ever imagined. From the glimmers of reverie I saw when I returned to the entrance, I wasn't the only freshman entranced by the estate.

Marble columns of Angel House marked our next stop. Their House leader fluttered her snowy white wings behind her at the entrance. Aurora, of Angel House, had glowing dark skin and curly hair braided across her head like a halo. I couldn't tell if her beatific smile was filled with kindness or fakery.

"We have wings waiting for our angels," she purred. "Claim your halo and join us."

Cherubs decorated the upscale Angel mansion. Statues, paintings, and encased jewels from medieval times contrasted with modern checkerboard floors and floor-to-ceiling glass windows.

If an angel dropped from heaven today, I could see her living in a house like this.

Vampire Manor came next. The entire house was painted black, save for scarlet accents. Vivienne of Vamp House launched herself off the roof to greet us, dark hair flying as she landed. With severe features and a blood-red smile, she exuded the confidence of someone who could never be toppled.

"Why slay your enemies when you can bleed them dry?" she asked rhetorically. "I'll see the ruthless and unforgiving here soon."

I had to hold myself back from laughing at the gargoyles, coffins, and blood-filled chalices inside. They were shameless about their gothic aesthetic, and I respected that.

Lukas, leader of Siren house, showed up with nothing but a massive golden trident and a speedo with an even more massive... well, it's not polite to stare. He basked in the whistles, then talked up the freshmen like we were old friends. I didn't even remember everything he said because he spent so much time cracking jokes and rambling. I was pretty sure he oiled his chest, too. Not that I was looking, of course.

"He's built," Gaksi mentioned.

"I'm trying to focus here," I told him.

"You and me both," he sniggered.

Sirens built their villa against the beach, and water flowed in rivers through the property. A dolphin jumped out at me mid-tour. I almost died of happiness. I wished Cordelia was in this group because I would have loved to see what she thought.

I shook the sand off my feet as we moved to Wolf House. Their House was built into a cave on the far edge of campus, string lights decorating the inside.

Howls greeted us as Adam received our group.

"Join our pack," was all he had to say. Wolves trotted beside us on our tour, which comprised a confusing labyrinth of cave tunnels and dens.

Wisteria, of Rose house, introduced us to her home last. She wore a dress made of curving wisteria, which matched her short, lilac hair. "What makes Rose House unique is that it's an all-female House."

"Of bitches!" Hunter shouted from the back of my group. Aubrey shoved him.

Wisteria beamed and continued. "That would be the female side of Wolf House, actually."

The male recruitment guide scowled beside her. "Hey," he gutted out. "Not cool." So he was a wolf, then. I wondered where Melody belonged. She was so lovely, I'd bet Angel.

"No offense, of course," Wisteria said to him. "Just taxonomy."

"She's kind of rude," Aubrey said to me.

"Kind of iconic, I think," I responded. "Also, am I crazy, or do almost all house leaders have names that use alliteration with their houses?"

"You're not crazy. It's considered good luck, almost like a tradition. Especially with the women," Aubrey told me.

"Are you gunning for Angel house, then?" I asked.

"Absolutely." Her smile lit up her face. "We have to strategize, right?"

"I can definitely see it," I told her. "You have angel energy."

"Thank you!" she gushed.

Rose House resembled a greenhouse, all flowers and vines. Flower fragrance wafted from all angles, and relaxation flooded my blood. I loved vegetation. It made me feel like I was transported to my backyard at home, growing fruits and vegetables with my dad.

After the tours concluded, we divided into classrooms for interviews.

The conversations went by in such a blur it was hard to remember them. Unfortunately, most of them carried the same topics.

"What heritage do you have here?"

That was always the starter question. I knew exactly what they were looking for when they asked: "Yes!" an enthusiastic pledge always piped in. "My mother, grandmother, great-grandmother, aunts, cousins, and sisters all became sirens!" The active members, or actives, would excitedly nod along, listening to her laundry list of loyalty to one house. And then the active would turn to me, and I'd have nothing to say. Unless I was in Fae house, of course. But whenever I was stuck in a double interview with a double, triple, whatever level legacy? I was all but forgotten.

"My mother's Fae. Father is a Houseless human engineer. Grandparents never went to a magic college." That became my line.

The actives would scribble down notes, and the frantic questioning would continue.

"Do you plan on living in the house?"

"Yes, absolutely."

Sophomores had the option of living off-campus, but they rarely did. Magic was better wielded on campus, and stronger bonds formed from living amongst your own kind.

"What's your major?"

"Zoology of earthly and mythical creatures."

That was why I brought my camera to campus. Thanks to my mythical family friend, I'd always been interested in animals that weren't human. As a side quest, I wanted to make an encyclopedia of all the creatures out there someday.

"Why do you want to join our House?"

There came the hard question. I battled between answering honestly and telling them what they wanted to hear.

"I believe in the values of Fae House, including academics, cunning, and ambition. Given the privilege of joining, I will devote my life to becoming the best Fae I can be."

On the inside, I didn't know what I believed yet. But I knew that I wanted a community. And a new form of magic would swallow the dark shadows within. So, I'd work earnestly to prove myself in any situation I ended up in.

After finishing the same conversation five times, I was nearly freed from talking. My head pounded. I had an overwhelming urge to hide from humanity for a few hours, but I still had Rose House left.

"How's it going, Housemaster extraordinaire?" Lukas' voice chased after me before my last round. He was still in a swimsuit. I couldn't help but giggle.

"Okay," I answered. "I think I'm exhausted, though. They spent a lot of time asking about me, and I got little time to ask about what makes their House special."

I only got the bare minimum. Fae couldn't lie, but they were masters of deceit and cunning. Angels could fly, but not all the way to Heaven. Wolves were strong as a pack, though not alone. Vampires had super strength at the expense of drinking human blood. Sirens could sweet talk, but they were no stronger than a regular human—as evidenced by Lukas pulling my arm with all the strength of my youngest brother.

"Yeah, the facade of choice is kind of misleading." He pulled me into a hug against his bare chest, surprising me. "Be careful," he whispered in my ear. "Houses build a ranking list based on who they think will make the strongest pledge class. But if they feel like your identity is based on deceit, they can drop you before the final initiation."

Choked gasps rang out around us, causing Lukas to drop me. The temperature dropped quickly enough to kill.

"I always knew this process was predatory," a cruel voice sounded, "but do you really have to force your half-naked body on impressionable freshman girls?"

At the hilltop, cloaked in shadows, stood my dealmaker.

Fear bolted through my veins. My heart pounded against my chest. There were so many people here, running around and scampering back home in heels and suits. Would he really try to act on his bargain with me? Now, in public, with witnesses?

The hairs on my neck stood up as he studied me, eyes swirling with mischief.

I should have run, but I couldn't hide. And neither could any other freshmen here, many of whom were petrified.

"Let me guess... you, humans, would call this... hazing?" He stepped forward.

"Get out," Lukas ordered.

"Now, Luna! Run!"

He shoved me.

I bailed, sprinting like my neck didn't burn with each breath I took.

CHAPTER
TWELVE

THE ORACLE MUSINGS

Our mystery murderer is a shapeshifter! Despite my best attempts, all images I conjure shift between forms. No amount of bribery—nor carnal favors from Siren House, thank you very much—can clear up my visions.

One thing is certain, however: The Houses have been slacking and will reap the consequences of their own incompetence.

Our human-slayer is aiming big this time. The long-term effects of this future killing will take out one of our illustrious House leaders. The future is fickle and undecided—whoever it will be is a surprise even I cannot predict.

But do not lose faith, dear reader! A heroic rescue may be upon us! One lucky reader will have a chance with our local heart stopper. And that story is only just beginning.

I can't wait until our damsel in distress picks up her skirts and learns to save herself!

HYDRA ALERT! HYDRA ALERT!

Run, Hide, Fight! Another student has been reported missing. A mysterious otherworld demon has been spotted carrying a mutilated body through the Whispering Woods.

My phone buzzed, waking me. A week passed since Reaper's last appearance, and campus had been quiet—too quiet—ever since. "Stars," I breathed, reading the latest alert. Through the thin walls of the dorms, I could hear everyone else's devices popping off, too.

My phone tolled again.

Flora: *Get on it, girl!*

I gave her all of one text yesterday: *'His name is Reaper'* before she blew up my phone and forced me to come in. My fingers had turned so purple on the way in I thought I'd lose them to frostbite. Could she send that chill all the way to my neck? Then maybe the necrosis would kill off Reaper's deal, too.

Luna: *On my way!*

I threw on my boots and coat and ran down the stairs.

"Off to see your crush?" Gaksi asked.

"Off to get intel," I told him. I took off running to the Whispering Woods. The air felt so cool on my skin I had to remind myself I was on a stealth mission.

There was something so spontaneous about a University campus at night. Stars shined as bright as all the futures built here, and the dreams waiting to come true.

Focus, I reminded myself. Just take some photos. Don't get discovered. Maintain a distance to avoid detection. Get my one clear photo and scramble home. Avoid Reaper noticing my presence. Fulfill Flora's bargain for now.

What did the police force see that was so horrible they

all quit? The group boasted strong alumni. They'd never backed down from a challenge before.

Screw this annoying deal. I could only handle one catastrophe at a time.

Rain poured from the sky. It had been cloudy this morning, but the clouds irked me with their torrent as I ran. The thump-thump-thump of my feet on the ground matched the splatter of rain against dorm rooftops.

When I reached the woods, the trees had deviated from their usual location. The arched sign had been ripped in two jagged ends cutting off right after BEWARE.

I kept hustling. This time, the flickering lighting above the tree canopy hurt my eyes. Rain bounced off my eyelids, and lightning flashed over my vision. My run slowed to a walk. The near—darkness consumed me, and muscle memory alone guided me to where I found the last body.

My foot caught, and I catapulted, hard, onto the wet ground. I pushed myself off, wiping the mud off my hands. Gross. But... hot. Wait, hot?

Lighting struck, illuminating my hands.

Blood-red.

I gasped, shaking my hands like it would get rid of the steaming fluid. My whole body was wet and dripping, but from what now? Rain, mud, or flesh? What did I run into?

I pulled out my phone light.

Gore lined the walkway. Flesh, blood, and unidentified bits of bone lined the forest floor. Little skin-colored pieces of fur littered the ground, covered by puddles of steaming blood.

Wolf.

Shaking, I wrapped my arms around myself. I covered my mouth with my hand, only to gag at the smell. The foul, coppery taste.

Mangled trees surrounded me. I hadn't noticed before, but the roots had been upended from the earth. Branches were down, trunks slanted like some terrible beast had gone through here.

That miserable scent—decay—struck, forcing my steps back.

This was a mistake. I had to get out of here. Flight kicked in, and my leg instinctively moved back. But before it did, I closed my eyes and swiped up, then pressed down on my camera. The camera clicked. I couldn't look.

Voices sounded from the side. I staggered into the nearest bush—was this the same one? Didn't matter. My head was down. I needed to get out; I needed to go home; I needed to go—

"*Stay still,*" Gaksi ordered. "*Danger is near. Help isn't.*"

I wished I could tease him. But I couldn't.

You're a scholar, mother always said. *You should always study first, and save fighting for when you have real skills.*

I should have listened.

How much time had passed? The tree canopy obstructed the moon. I refused to pull out my phone again. The light might alert the hellion to pursue me.

Home, I thought. I should go home. Quietly.

CRACK! The sound of breaking glass came from behind me. Woods didn't have glass, but dorms did. Never mind. That escape route was out.

The trees grew and shrank, branches popping and breathing in and out. What was happening?

The wailing got louder.

I blinked. Breathed. And begged myself to stay quiet as shrill screams lit up the night.

∼

"*Save this,*" Gaksi commanded. Time had passed, but I didn't know how much. Gaksi had popped in and out of my head, alternating between finding my escape route and soothing me. Something pushed into my hand. A rectangular metal piece brightened as soon as my fingers brushed it. The lock screen flared.

Friendly eyes glowed through the screen.

Alpha Adam.

The phone clattered out of my hand. I couldn't be standing in...

"We meet again," a dusky voice called.

Limbs moved. Instinct won.

I struck. With all the desperation of a human, all the viciousness of a fae.

I sank my knife deep into Reaper's chest.

The petals painted on my knife glossed over with black blood. Almost as black as his eyes.

"You!" I screamed.

"You did this!" I moved to sink it in deeper, but Reaper seized my arms.

"Relax," he said. "You look... disgusting, mortal." His voice resembled his face—shocked, appalled.

"You're a murderer! Murderer!" I kicked my feet at him, which he deflected with his shadows. Warm figures pushed my legs away from him. Humanoid apparitions surrounded him—like he'd made his shadows into soldiers, and they'd all swarmed us.

"You need to get cleaned up," he said. "This was not meant for mortal eyes."

"Mortal? Not gumiho? Not today? No, 'this is a rather impressive act' or 'what an ingenious plan to make it look like some other force injured you today!'"

I shrieked into the sky in frustration. His shadows

thickened to coat me, pulling my arms away from him. "Fight me, Reaper! Let's just get this over with! You want me dead, don't you? The feeling is mutual!"

He pulled the knife from his chest, shaking off his onyx blood.

"You cannot kill me, hopeful seraphim," he said, eyeing me with displeasure.

"But if you really are a mortal, my responsibility is to care for you."

The world went dark.

I AWOKE where the sky above was covered in a lifeless, never-ending gray. The air felt cold and damp as if winter was approaching, but the sky lacked the energy to produce snow. Dense gray clouds swirled and rotated, moving the sky in a dreary kaleidoscope.

I wasn't cold, though. A warm arm cradled my back, and another held my hand in his. I was sitting against a body in an unknown location.

I jolted to awareness. Was this the Beyond?

Reaper sat beside me, crossing his legs. He dipped one of my hands in a tub of water, and gore floated off. I reeled.

"Sorry," he said, jaw tight. "I am frustrated."

"With what?" I could feel the earth beneath my body. At least, I thought it was earth. It felt soft and vaguely damp, like soil.

"I could feel your fear and confusion through our bond. It took me too long to find you, and when I did, you looked horrible."

He could feel me? Like my emotions?

"Have we teleported to the Beyond?"

"No," he answered, "We are in the Barren Fields, East of the House system."

"Why did you bring me here?"

My thoughts had slowed. Each came through a fog before it reached my consciousness.

He materialized a rag out of shadow. "You were having a breakdown. I thought removing you from the environment was best. These fields are devoid of magic or life. Nothing will bother us." He dragged the shadow cloth up the length of my arm. The blood had stained the straps of my dress a rich scarlet. "Don't look," he commanded.

"For once, I think I agree with you," I breathed. I avoided thinking about what I just saw. Of what I was covered in. How I'd get home. I was in denial. Free and ignorant of my current life circumstances.

The shadows brushed my collarbone. I shivered. Closed my eyes to darkness.

"Are you cold?" His voice embraced my skin like the shadows had.

"No," I murmured. He shifted so that his arms wrapped around me from behind. The shadows dripped down my legs. Soft. Warm.

"Where did you acquire the dokkaebi?" Reaper asked.

"The what?" I was on my way to slumber.

"Your goblin. Where did you acquire him? The black market? A shady merchant?" His shadows slid around my body in a soothing cocoon.

"Wouldn't you love to know, lover boy," Gaksi huffed.

"Lover—what? I did not invite you here!" Reaper stuttered. For once, he actually sounded a little flustered.

"It's a barren wasteland. Nobody is invited here," Gaksi said.

"How did you cross over, goblin?"

"I've been between realms longer than you, boy." Gaksi's creaky chuckle echoed in the howling wind.

"Seraphim—" Reaper started.

"Seraphim? Not gumiho this time?" I questioned.

"It's rare for a gumiho to seek vengeance for others," Reaper said. "You were also crying over that boy." His chin pressed down against my hair, head rested on mine. He smelled good, like jasmine and chocolate. "Did you love him?"

Why was he continuously asking me questions? I was tired, the dregs of sleep calling to me. So tired. Yawning, I replied, "Mind your business."

Adam and I had been stuck in the university dungeons for 24 hours while the police interrogated us. Due to our inability to explain Reaper's incomprehensible rambling, the questions persisted. The picture saved it from being labeled as walking woods hysteria.

The police were extra hard on him because of how adamant he was that he heard the sword talk. But he held his tongue when they asked him if the sword spoke more or less after interacting with me. I would always be grateful to him for hiding that.

For hiding Gaksi, even if he couldn't hide my interaction with Reaper.

"If you collect the dead, how come nobody's ever seen you before?" I asked.

Energy sapped out of me every second, and I had limited time to question him for Flora before I passed out.

"You could try reading a book about me some time," he said dryly. "There's multiple in your library about me."

Arrogant demon. "You could try with politeness," I slurred out. My tongue felt so thick in my mouth. "Most of the books barely mention you."

"There are multiple messengers on the other side. The Grim Reaper, Thanatos, I am one of many. My recent visibility is because we all take care of our own messes. For instance, the Grim Reaper would greet the ones who were to die at a vampire's hand. Anyone slighted by the fickle threads of the Fates would be greeted by Thanatos. But the gumiho? She's an escapee from my universe. So she's my mess to clean up."

"Hmm," I groaned out. I was dizzy and drifting away.

The shadows crooned around me gently until I was gone.

WHEN THE DAZE CLEARED, I was back in my bedroom.

Alert. Awake. Alarmed, because I was sitting in a demon's lap, over my bed. Reaper nestled me like a lover in his arms.

"Get off!" I screeched, pushing him away.

"Better?" he rumbled.

"You just kidnapped me! And before that—Adam was murdered!"

"Not by myself," Reaper said. He kicked up his boots on my bed and lay his head on my pillow. Closed his eyes and exhaled. "This room smells of you."

I almost stabbed him again.

"What the hell did you do to me in the Barren Fields? When you were—"

I shuddered. "Cleaning me?"

"Well, Gaksi supervised me getting the worst of the carnage off you, so it was a chaperone-approved cleaning," he explained matter-of-factly. "And the forces that work on the Barren Fields are not under my control."

"So what the hell happened to me?" My voice dropped dangerously low as I turned my head to face him.

"Your energy, including most of your fear, was devoured by the forces that drain magic out of the Barren Fields."

That was it. Why I was so exhausted, why I let him run his shadows all over me... we even had a conversation! Like companions! I jumped out of his arms, swung my legs over his chest, and wrapped my hands around his neck.

"You should face your fears with this level of zeal," Reaper said, eyes blown wide.

"What's that supposed to mean?"

"You threaten demons every day, but you can't let your skin breathe without makeup?"

Humiliation washed over me at the accuracy.

"If you can't die," I exhaled into his face, "can you still feel pain and suffocation?"

His eyes blazed.

"No, my dear seraphim. But I do enjoy being straddled by you in bed."

I moved to slap him, but he caught my hand in a tight grip.

"Everything that has gone wrong in my life since I got here is because of you," I raged.

"Your universe. Your inability to keep your own residents contained."

He said nothing, eyes cold.

"If I were a fool, I would think that the way you held me in the Fields is proof that a demon could actually be gentle." I stroked his neck with my free hand. He made a sound that could only be interpreted as a whimper.

"But I am not a fool, and you are a worthless immortal."

With the raging disgust I dripped from my voice, he finally dissolved.

The lanterns blurred my vision as they drifted off into the night sky.

Wolves howled in agony, in tandem.

I'd always thought of nighttime as a place of solitude, of rest.

But it was a place of sadness, too. It felt wrong to be so attached to this man when I thought of him the most at his end. At his mutilation.

I let a tear fall at Adam's memorial. When I smoothed it away, a patch of my skin came off with it, leaving an ugly, exposed red patch. The next tear stung when it fell, and I let it hurt, too.

I didn't even read The Oracle Musings column that morning. I already knew what it would say. It never struck me before how cruel the Beyond creatures could be until I saw it firsthand.

I strode through the Diamond, the diamond-shaped grassy area in the middle of campus, as midnight approached, looking for a tree to rest under and collect my thoughts. Nearly a month had passed since I arrived, and I finally realized the danger I was in.

The danger we were all in. Humanity couldn't rival the nastiness of the abyss.

But I'd stayed here, all the same, refusing to run. To hide. To cower. What did that say about me?

They are not as tenacious. Not braver.

Professor Ansi's flattery echoed in my head.

She believed in me. So why didn't I?

Seeking solace, I climbed up the tree, eager for the familiar comfort of hanging from branches like a child.

Swinging from them always made me feel better growing up.

A cacophony of wicked laughter disrupted my peace.

"Wolf House must be as feeble as a newborn if their leader gets taken out that easily," Hunter jeered, contempt dripping from his voice.

"They're bottom-tier magic, through and through," Zain snorted.

"Yeah, and I bet they're all bottoms, too," Brayden joked, eliciting cruel laughter from the trio.

Those disrespectful brats—

I dropped from the tree, using shadows to cushion my fall. In the dead of night, they were invisible, and I reeled them in with the force of my rage.

I was tired of hurting today.

I was ready to hurt someone else instead.

Hunter paused mid-step, slowly rotating his head toward me.

He saw me. Good.

My shoulders went rigid, but instead of wariness, red-hot anger lit up my skin. Who mocked the deceased on the day of their memorial? How dare they?

I hurled a dagger at his boot, slicing the corner of it off and nailing his boot to the mud. Before he could react, I nailed the other boot down, too, immobilizing him.

"Don't be so disrespectful, prick."

"You." Hunter's glower only ignited me.

Brayden ran up at me from the side, but I dodged his punch, spinning low to kick him behind the shins. He toppled, and I aimed a kick between his legs for good measure.

"You'll pay for that!" he shrieked, grabbing his crotch.

Zain moved to tackle me, but I sidestepped, letting him

slam headfirst into the tree I jumped from. He crumpled to the side, clutching his wounded head.

"How could you make fun of someone who died at a demon's hands when you're so easily subdued by a mortal girl?" I taunted.

"Does your demon control every blade you strike?" Hunter asked, dangerously calm in the spot he was rooted to.

His accusation hit me hard enough for my steps to teeter. "No. My mother taught me to throw long before I came to this school."

She'd insisted on teaching me how to defend myself with blades. I thought she was being ridiculously overprotective, but I appreciated her now.

"Cute. A demon slaughtered my mother," Hunter sneered, disdain dripping from his voice.

The admission faltered my steps. "I'm sorry, Hunter."

And I was. I'd be nothing without my mother.

"Not sorry enough to stop associating with hellions." He tried to step forward but blanched at his stuck feet.

I crept slightly toward him. "If I remove the knives from your feet, can we call a truce?" Hunter watched me with hungry, angry fascination. Would I have been this ferociously angry if I had grown up without a mother figure due to demons? Was poisoning my opponent justified if she posed a danger to humanity and my family?

He laughed, head thrown back with the force of his own derision. "Do I have a choice? I'm unarmed, and my friends are imbeciles."

Swiftly, I yanked both knives out of his feet at once. We both jumped away, maintaining a safe distance.

"I will destroy anyone that supports demons, Luna.

Don't say I didn't warn you." His vindictive tone promised death.

"I think we're on the same side, Hunter," I said, hoping it wouldn't come to that.

He threw his head back again when he laughed, a humorless sound. "You're going to regret letting me go, liar."

With a firm grip on his friend's shirt collars, he started dragging them away, a visible display of his animosity written on his face.

"Unlike you, hideous, I could never forgive."

CHAPTER
THIRTEEN

THE ORACLE MUSINGS

*V*irgin ghosts will be visiting the campus today! From the ancient kingdom of Silla, they haunt places where young girls like to reside. Stargazers, coffee enthusiasts, hopeless romantics: all of those will get a special visit today. It was thought in ancient times that they appeared as reminders of what you would become without love: deserted and drifting.

I caught my first demon today.

Well, Gaksi helped me catch one.

I was walking home from class yesterday, admiring the autumn leaves falling, when Flora assigned me a lead in the observatory.

Not a lead about the notorious one, who haunted me daily with the mark on my neck. Not the one Cordelia's so besotted with and Gaksi so captivated with.

This one was a lost little girl. She donned a long white

dress and a dead, unmoving stare. Her body floated aimlessly, legs hidden under her gown, figure flickering between a solid and transparent state. Long black hair swayed with the unmoving wind around a ghost-pale face.

"HEY!" I called out. I braced myself for an attack, blades drawn.

No response.

Should I ambush? All my blades were on me. I could earn an easy amount of points from taking down this demon. I could see the clock tower leaderboard change now: my name would rise to the top, and everyone would know I had a successful kill. That I was one to watch out for. Houses, students, and faculty would see that I'd proven myself and that my admission to this university was far from a mistake; in fact, I was thriving.

The spirit floated around me. Now or never. I raised my blade, and her head turned.

Uneven eyeliner lined her wide-set eyes. Like a middle schooler, unsure how to apply her first product, her face looked uncertain and bewildered. Her face was almost exactly like what mine looked like a few years ago.

I lowered my hand.

She sailed aimlessly past.

"Are you lost?"

Foolish, foolish behavior, trying to reason with the undead. This farce could end any minute, and she'd have the upper hand.

"Do you want to use the telescope? I can help you look at the stars."

We were in the Andromeda, surrounded by fancy machines, but she lacked interest in all of them.

If this was a trick, it was consistently executed. Nothing

came out of the demon. No whistle, moaning, groaning, or even following. She was just...aimless.

I followed the ghost for an hour through various hallways, cautious enough not to get too close. We passed countless constellation maps, and despite me hounding her with clues, nothing seemed to jog any memories. It was as if I didn't exist to her.

How could she not attack? Why would she want to cross over to this side if not to wreak havoc?

I was starting to wonder if she existed when I told Cordelia to meet up with me, and she screamed in terror and ran away. I'd apologize for that later.

Eventually, I got close enough that I tried to reach out and touch. She only hovered higher up so I couldn't reach her and continually moved away.

"Let me help you go home," I said gently. Perhaps I could just relocate her rather than slay her. "Gaksi, help me out here."

"She must have spawned in this building," Gaksi said, *"because she doesn't seem to know where she's going or what she's looking for."*

"I figured."

"Call your favorite demon," Gaksi suggested. *"This one's from his realm."*

"What, do I just shout at the sky? Hope that he comes tumbling out?"

"No, press on your bond, silly."

"Isn't it treacherous to call upon a demon that could kill me?"

"You thought this was a malevolent spirit, and it was not. Perhaps you misjudged him."

"He already tried to erase me!"

"Do you want to get rid of this spirit or not?"

My blade glimmered in my hand. I could kill her if I wanted to. Gaksi lighting my blade was his approval to do so.

But she'd been so harmless. It felt immoral to destroy something so disoriented.

Against better judgment, I pushed down on my bond with two fingers, one on each wing.

"I knew you'd make the right choice," Gaksi said. It didn't erase my guilt.

Not only did I fail to destroy a lower-level demon, but I invited another to meet me.

No wonder Hunter hated me.

The room gleamed faintly, briefly illuminating the room before light coalesced into my captor.

"What is this?" I asked him before the light settled, pointing at the lost ghost. He looked at it dubiously.

"How did you contain this creature?" he asked.

I put my hands on my hips. "You're welcome."

He sighed, shoulders drooping. "This is the gwisin. It's a rogue ghost from my realm. A reborn version of someone who once was. Scary, but harmless." His gaze rotated to me. "Like you."

"You owe me," I said. "I contained this for you."

He paused, back turned. Took a deep inhale. "This was not part of the bargain."

"No, this was just the right thing to do! I couldn't just leave whatever baby spirit this is alone!"

His face softened. "What do you want in exchange?"

"A favor," I said.

Please say yes. This could work out perfectly. If I could piece out information from him as my favor each time I caught one of these little ghosts, then I could have a continuous stream of information for Flora.

"A favor," he repeated, rolling around the last word like it was a foreign concept.

"I have been thinking," I continued, eager to jump in and ease his hesitation. "For the first favor, you could give me a piece of truth."

His eyes narrowed. "Truth." He strode toward me, ghost forgotten. "Do you think me a liar?"

"No, but you barely say anything!" My words tumbled out. "And I've only been chasing down this thing for an hour, and I'm tired, and I would like to know more about the demon who forced me into a bargain. Is that so bad?"

He towered before me. He glowered, like a dark and vengeful prince, deciding what he wanted from his subject. I refused to be intimidated.

"I would like to expand on our deal," I forced out. "For each demon I catch for you, you owe me a favor. Anything I ask."

"That is a horrible deal," he stated, shaking his head.

"Consider it a favor from me too. I do your job for you."

"Why would I offer my enemy my good graces?" His face contorted. Black clouds swarmed around him, shadows crowding out the white lights of the room.

His lips were so close from this angle. I wondered what it would be like to press into them.

"What if I offered you the choice?" I suggested.

"Of what, little seraphim?" *Seraphim.* That word made my stomach flip and my toes curl. For someone who was convinced I was his nemesis, he sure loved to compare me to an angel.

The air shimmered. Behind him, the ghost shimmered as well. He was about to disappear again and take my catch with him.

"For this favor: Truth or dare," I said, resolving my

nerves. "For the truth: Why do you call me seraphim? And don't tell me it's because I wore an angel costume. Because that's way too basic, and I know you put more thought into it than that."

He winked. Winked! I didn't even have time to reveal my dare before he answered.

"Because you're beautiful enough to pass as an angel, but wicked enough to fall into the arms of a devil."

I caught another gwisin the next day. The appearance was the same. Long dark hair and a pale flowing dress. This one was in a coffee shop, knocking over bags of beans.

I brewed some before I called Reaper. "Do you want some?" I offered. She peeked at me, and my soul soared with hope, but then she went back to knocking stuff over.

"Gaksi, can she hear me?"

"*Yes, but she's not from this era, so she's confused. She doesn't speak your language.*"

"Oh."

I took a sip of the coffee mournfully. I wondered if she missed coffee so much she spawned here out of nostalgia. Did she meet friends in a coffee shop? Work in one? Go on dates and feel excited for her future in one?

I pulled my lace choker, and Reaper stepped in through the nearest wall.

"Favor," I demanded.

"Impatient, are we?" he mentioned. He reached out his arm, sending a trail of shadows to wrap around the gwisin. They coiled around her like a snake, pulling her in like a lasso.

I knew what I should ask him. What my mother would

ask him if she were here. She'd ask him how to get out of the bond.

But I was not my mother, and recruitment season was coming. Which meant any thoughts on escaping this bond must come after Flora got me all the way through to the end.

"Truth: where are you from?" I asked instead.

His face was smug when he answered, "The Beyond."

Wow, so verbose. Next time, I should be more specific. "Very helpful."

"You're welcome." His gaze fixated on my neck. "You covered my mark."

I rolled my eyes. "It looked like a hickey. I couldn't just show it off."

He grumbled and drew the ghost closer.

"Can I quote you for an article?" I asked.

His brow furrowed. "For your newspaper?"

How did he know I was connected to the school newspaper? Was he keeping tabs on me?

"No, for the oracle's gossip column. Yes, for my newspaper."

Please say yes, I hoped.

We might actually outsell the oracle if he responded favorably. Everyone wanted to know who Mr. Hot and Mysterious was. And then Flora could give me a break for a while.

He scowled. "No."

Damn. "Okay then." He was doing the air glow thing again, but I desperately jumped in with, "Your fans will be disappointed."

The air rearranged. "My what?"

He sent back the gwisin already. He waited alone.

"You have a fan club. My friend Cordelia is the leader.

They think you might be a murderer, sure, but you're very handsome." Handsome enough that Cordelia thought we would look good together.

"Why did you choose to be an interviewer," Reaper said, "when in most situations, you're talking about yourself and your own friends?"

"What am I supposed to do when my interviewee is so solemn and silent?"

"Listen," Reaper suggested. A tendril of shadows moved forward, wrapping around my ankles in a light brush. I should step out of them, but I had nothing to tell Flora. I needed solid information, or she would follow through on her threat to wear my severed hands like a necklace. Reaper's shadows stabilized, anchoring my feet to the ground. I had no choice but to stay.

The shadows tickled. I almost laughed. But I kept my face serious. He smirked.

"Why did you keep calling me cursed when we first met?"

I saw a flash on his face I couldn't recognize. "I can sense Gaksi's energy on you. It made you appear demonic."

And he was that afraid of Gaksi? More than he seemed to be of his original target?

"What are the consequences if you don't capture the gumiho? Besides the loss of human life here. Humans aren't your subjects, are they?"

The shadows swirled up, brushing my knees. I swayed them away.

"I cannot return home with any of my dignity if I allow her to escape," Reaper said. "There is too much at stake. My honor is at risk."

"Why is your honor at risk?"

"Because my father expects this of me."

My eyes widened in surprise. He had a father? I thought he was immortal and created out of energy, not descended from another being.

"You owe me three truths," he instructed, holding up three long, elegant fingers. "But I am a kind and generous god, so I will start with just one. What is your greatest fear?"

I swayed with surprise. Shadows immobilized me; I couldn't step back or fall. That was why he restrained me. Because he was so desperate for this answer. How invested was he in frightening me?

I should have never invited him here. Demons were exactly what I was warned about: deceptively calm and innocent until they waited to strike you with your worst nightmare.

I inhaled. Could he tell if I lied? I supposed it didn't matter.

"Demons like to trade in secrets," my mother had warned me.

"And they feed on lies, growing stronger every time. Lies, deceit, crime... all of those are hallmarks of demons at play."

"I'm afraid of never being enough."

There. Boring. Honest. Truthful. Something he could never possibly care about when he was busy doing whatever demons did all day.

"To who?" he asked.

"My mother," I said first. The shadows compressed me like a vise, urging me to continue. I wasn't going anywhere. "The Houses. My friends. Myself. I feel like I keep chasing the best because I've convinced myself I belong there, but I'm wondering whether I really belong anywhere." The shadows relaxed, letting me breathe.

A pregnant pause entered the room. For once, it seemed like Reaper was struck silent, not purposefully quiet.

"What does she think of you engaging in a demonic bargain?" he said after an eternity.

"That's your last question," I pointed out. "And she's furious."

For the best, too. If it would work, she would perform an exorcism to get rid of him, even if it nearly killed me in the process.

"Well, then." He brushed a speck of dust off his shoulder. "Perhaps you should inform her how often we communicate."

Bzz Bzz. My phone vibrated. Caller ID: **Mother**

"You little snitch!"

The green light pressed without me.

"Evil bastard!"

"I'm the firstborn, actually," he bemoaned as he departed, "much like yourself."

I glimpsed his sarcastic smile last.

"Tell mother dearest I send my regards." He faded out, so only his voice remained.

"Unlike you, I am not afraid of her."

CHAPTER FOURTEEN

THE ORACLE MUSINGS

Who pissed off our ice queen? Our favorite queen bee, Flora, will spend tonight thawing out the four sophomores of Fae House she froze solid in her rage. As the only sophomore serving as House leader, is the pressure of her responsibilities finally getting to her?

Speaking of pressure: Xavier, junior Beta of Wolf House, will be initiated as Alpha tonight. Anyone invited to witness the spectacle will be able to watch how this wolf handles his pack: will they grow as one mighty pack should, or flop like a group of motherless puppies?

And in freshman news: The first rounds of cuts are here! Time to face reality, fish: some people have it all, and some people have nothing. Especially not a House!

THE MOST BRUTAL round of recruitment was coming. I stayed up all night with anxiety, tossing and turning in the sheets.

Would the phone call come? Would my world end overnight? I could already hear Melody's singsong voice.

"I'm sorry, Luna! You have been dropped from every house during recruitment. However, you can stay on this campus as an unaffiliated, and try again next year! It was a pleasure to get to know you!"

In my nightmare, I didn't even make it to Rose House, the House that took all women. Reaper's disruption cost me that interview, and now I'd get to see whether they really took everyone—even those they hadn't met yet.

It was almost noon. We expected to get our invites to the next round as soon as the clock hit twelve. Until then, I waited. And paced. And stress-cleaned my bedroom.

I had such a frightening meeting with Flora yesterday I was worried she wouldn't uphold her end of the bargain. After a month of chasing demons around, I only got two pieces of information: that the gwisin was from Reaper's territory and that he had a father. I tried telling her he had shadows, but the tattoo had constricted so tightly around my neck that I couldn't breathe out the words. She kicked me out with so much vigor I was sure our bargain was over.

"Perhaps instead of worrying about your House, you can return to fretting about your love life," Gaksi suggested. He lit up my phone screen, sending off a happy little ringtone. *Love Story* by Taylor Swift. My favorite.

"Get out of that thing! I need to know if I've been dropped!"

"Please. Flora's a fan of yours, too. I can feel it."

"You feel all sorts of things!"

He jumped into my stereo, playing classical music instead. *"You need to relax."*

"Relax? With what? Not my recruitment status! And not with my personal problems from yesterday either! He called my mother! That's like kindergarten tattletale behavior. If this were colonial times, I would have just challenged him to a duel. Scratch that. I would have just beheaded him! I bet you can infuse enough magic into a guillotine to do it."

Gaksi only laughed.

I flopped down on my bed in frustration. 11:00 A.M., my stereo said. I hopped out to my bookshelf and picked a book to read. Maybe *Pride and Prejudice* would calm me down. My comfort characters usually did.

Tap. Tap. Tap. A pigeon tapped its beak on my window.

"Shut up, Gaksi."

Tap. Tap. Tap.

"Isn't me, child." His voice sounded from the stereo.

Shoving the window open, I got a good look at the creature. A little brown bird carried a bottle on its back. A messenger pigeon!

I darted over, unclasping the wine-red bottle, and read the inscription on the back.

Regards from Vamp House. Enjoy your first taste of power, on us.

It was early! They could get in trouble for breaking recruitment rules by sending out invites early. I was about to text Aubrey and Cordelia but waited. What if they didn't get the favor? I wouldn't want to rub salt into the wound.

I guessed it didn't matter, anyway. When you were as old and wealthy as vampires, a little recruitment fine was no big deal.

Rotating the bottle in my hand, I read the description on the back.

1000-year-old wine. Cellars of Vamp House.

Not blood, then. I took a hearty swig, then coughed. It was revolting and sour. Much stronger than the seltzers I preferred.

Gaksi snickered. At least I got one invite back. Maybe Flora did like me after all.

A crisp knock hit my door. Another favor? I scurried to open it.

Outside, a butler awaited. He was dressed in a sharp tuxedo, hair groomed back, holding a black package topped with an enormous bow.

"For Miss Luna." He handed it to me, bowed, and left.

I undid the bow. Inside was a gold-embossed card. When I opened it, a white mask manifested. It was plain and unadorned, just one white stripe with two eyeholes.

Invite for one, to the Annual Fae Masquerade. Don your mask and become whoever you want to be.

I put the simple mask on and turned to my vanity mirror. The white morphed into two long, elongated moth wings. Wispy and lovely, they made my dark eyes glow with excitement.

"Look at this, Gaksi!" I angled my head, admiring myself. I grabbed my phone to snap a selfie for my mother. Would she even recognize moth wings? Before I snapped the photo, the mask transformed into bright orange monarch butterfly wings.

Much better. I sent Mother a photo. She replied within seconds.

Mother: *Beautiful, Luna! You will make such a pristine fae!*

I beamed with pride. Compliments from my mother were a rare and unexpected treat. I hoarded them in my heart like precious jewels. I usually only got praise from Gaksi.

"I like you better without the mask," Gaksi said.

"And most of the time, I like you better silent," I reminded him.

"That's why we always chatter like this," he teased.

"Check your closet," he prompted.

A white package emerged on a hanger. Beneath it, a white hoodie hung with silver angel wings hand-painted on the back.

Show off your new wings, the hanger read. *Work hard, and you can earn real ones.*

Like a cult, I thought. Wouldn't that be creepy to see the next day in class, all the ones invited back to angel house wearing the same outfit?

I'd probably wear it, though. It was cute. And judging from the size, they got my measurements exactly right.

At exactly noon, Lukas texted me.

Lukas: *See you soon.*

Luna: *Is that your way of saying I'm invited back to Siren House?*

Lukas: *Of course, gorgeous.*

Lukas: *And I can get you whatever you want in the meantime. That's siren power. See you next round (or sooner ;)*

Xavier texted me next.

Xavier: *Campfire tonight, Wolf House cavern.*

Luna: *Thanks.*

Xavier: *Sure, kid.*

I balked. He wasn't that much older than me to be calling me a kid. Only a junior. Having to step up from Beta to Alpha must be doing a number on him.

The last favor to appear was a set of chrysanthemums on my nightstand.

Hello, Luna, the vase read in elegant cursive. *We chose chrysanthemums as our gift for you because they signify Life in the West and Death in the East. It reminded us of you at the crossroads between your old life and your new one. Choose wisely.*

The vase rattled. "These are some nice flowers," Gaksi said. "I like these girls."

"I bet they're cheap," I retorted. "Aubrey said Rose house has the least money."

Immediately after, Aubrey called me.

She got invited back to her tops: Fae, Angel, and Vamp. Dropped from Wolf, Rose, and Siren. I was shocked. This round wasn't where I thought she would be cut. Her grades were perfect. The Houses must have been nitpicky, but on what criteria, I'd never know.

"I think it's a yield protection thing," she told me. "I'm a little above the cut for Wolf, Rose, and Siren, so they probably don't think it's even worth wasting their time on someone who's not returning."

"I see," I said. I owed it to Flora for not getting dropped from any house, unlike others.

My phone rang. Cordelia was also calling. "Call you right back, Aubrey."

Cordelia's voice shook through her sobs. "Siren house dropped me, Luna!" she wailed. I offered her a reassuring, "those witches!"

To be honest, I wasn't surprised. Cordelia was beautiful, sure, but she wasn't a massive, sneaky witch (excuse me, a cunning manipulator), so I never saw her as much of a Siren.

"What if I end up Houseless? I don't even like most of the remaining houses! I have nowhere else to go!" Her distress was palpable even through the screen.

I took a moment to gather my thoughts, desperately searching for the right words to say.

"It will be alright," I told her, trying to keep doubt out of my own voice. She had only two Houses left—Rose and Wolf House—and they were both considered bottom tier.

Wolf House lacked surprise for me. It was obvious Xavier had a thing for her, and was saving her a spot. Rose House took all women. It was almost worse to be in Rose House than Houseless. If you become totally Houseless, you could argue that you left out of your own accord. But if you ended up in Rose, it was obvious that you got rejected everywhere else. At least, that was what Aubrey said.

Cordelia's voice oscillated between frustration and envy. "Easy for you to say! Everybody wants you!"

Her words caught me off guard, as nobody had ever described me as desirable before. A surge of shame washed over me. Her plight would have been mine if I hadn't made this bargain.

"Melody told us to give all Houses a chance," I said, instilling hope in my voice. "And I know you'll make it. Have faith in yourself!"

The words slipped out of my lips, but I doubted it would repair her shattered confidence.

"But I only came here to become a siren! I took such a huge risk in coming here, and I don't know what to do next—"

"It'll be okay!" I insisted. "Fortune always favors the bold."

She hung up.

The dial tone felt as empty as I did.

THE NEXT DAY, I wore my angel hoodie with the rest of them. Campus was quieter than usual. The first round of cuts humbled people. Multiple people who told me Angel House was their top were not matching with me today. It was a somber day for everyone.

"Today is the deadliest day of the year for first-years," Professor Ansi boomed from her podium. "Why?"

"Because the presence of so much supernatural energy already draws demons to this campus, but the full moon, especially, will bring in extra," Aubrey answered.

"Halfway there. Elaborate on why it's deadly."

"Because first-years are eager to prove themselves and fight when they should run or capture," Brayden said.

"Correct. I recommend you all move in groups tonight if you're daring enough to slay demons and move up the leaderboard."

"Want to work together?" I asked Cordelia and Aubrey.

"No, thanks. I'm going solo tonight," Aubrey said. "I'm kind of messy when I fight, and I wouldn't want you to get caught in the crossfire."

"Fair," I said. "Cordelia?"

"I... think I'll sit this one out tonight. It would be foolish for me to fight with no powers yet," she added sheepishly.

"Last year, there were hundreds of demons spotted roaming the campus property," Professor Ansi said.

She scanned the room, noting our inhales. Some scared, some excited. "Choose your plans for tonight carefully."

Bells chimed, and Lukas caught up with us when the class dispersed.

"Stay in your rooms tonight." His voice left no room for argument. "Professor Ansi loves to rile students up, but it's mostly so that she has less to grade later when half her students die. It's not worth going out there tonight. You can match a House without being top of the class."

"Yeah, Siren House," Aubrey spat. "Some of us aim higher."

I didn't miss Cordelia's exhale. I'd tell Aubrey to watch her mouth later.

Lukas sighed, moving his hands through his hair. "Look, as someone who's seen this night go down... it's a bloodbath out there. You're just as likely to be taken out by another student as a demon."

"I'm not afraid of death." I said plainly.

Specks of gold swirled in his blue, concerned eyes. "What happened to the girl who ran away from the Reaper a few months ago?"

I stared him down.

"She grew up."

GAKSI WOUND around my choker like a beacon. It lifted up lightly, pulling me toward my next demon. Of his choosing, of course.

"*You aren't fighting today. Only moving them back home,*" he'd declared on our walk here.

I wouldn't think twice if they were anything like the lost ghosts. Easy points.

"*The other students are ready to kill tonight,*" I told Gaksi. Metal clanged in the air. Weapons were brandished across campus.

"*The spirits are restless tonight. I will not lose you to them.*"

I kept walking, and an ear-splitting scream echoed.

"*Another freshman felled by their own rashness,*" Gaksi said.

Terror gripped my limbs. "*Do you think the murderous one that killed all the men—*"

"*Yes, she's out. I can feel her here now.*"

The trees rumbled in front of me, and I hid behind a tree, preparing.

"Get back here, you pesky thing!" Ahead of me,

Hyacinth chased a ghost, who floated—rapidly—away from the portal.

I released a breath. False alarm.

A tug on my neck pulled me to Gaksi's choice of demon.

I should have known not to trust him.

CHAPTER
FIFTEEN

THE ORACLE MUSINGS

Questions, questions, and more questions in the stars tonight. So far, there have been 13 victims total, all male students. 5 wolves, 2 sirens, 1 vampire, 3 angels, and 2 faeries. Are these targeted attacks? Is the number relevant? Is any female deemed safe?

More male victims will come in the future. Rose House has been awfully quiet on this news. As an all-female House, is it not the least bit suspicious that they have been totally spared?

Lastly, is this a villainous murderer or a heroic vigilante? Latest news in: a wolf, who shall remain nameless, has confessed to me that our fallen comrade Adam took advantage of her under the full moon many months ago with his compulsion pearl. With all of our mysterious killer's murders consisting of men, it begs the question: why?

"Your mom is a real piece of work," Reaper mentioned mid-demon capture.

I'd followed Gaksi's lead to Reaper, and we chased a gwisin around the library.

"I don't know how she did it, but she snuck a cell phone into my palace. And I know she snuck a cell phone into my palace because it rang when I was trying to rest, and she yelled at me from across the universe."

"Good for her." Tiger mom for the win. Also, he lived in a palace. I'd make sure to tell Flora that. Mom had accidentally given me material to work with.

"Do all demons live in a palace?"

A mischievous glint sparkled in his eye. "No, only those related to the royal family."

Interesting. "How are you related?"

"I am the Prince of Demons, seraphim."

"What?"

Reaper, the impulsive, fiendish controller of my bargain, was the *Prince* of *Demons?*

His voice lightened, clearly enjoying my shocked expression. "Consider yourself blessed to be in my presence, darling subject. You may even bow if you wish."

"Never," I snapped. He had to be bluffing. There was no way.

"Speaking of local royalty, Luna, why does your school's gossip column defend a serial killer?"

That was an unexpected turn. Why wouldn't he elaborate?

"You mean The Oracle Musings?"

"The oracle seems to have more followers than I do these days."

He was so chatty tonight. Upbeat. Revealing secrets and conversing in a way I'd never seen him.

"*It's the full moon*," Gaksi said, "*It's like alcohol to a demon. Fuels them with energy.*"

"Is it you?" Reaper asked. "It would explain why the gumiho gets a favorable edit. You could have created that paper to save yourself from the scrutiny."

"What? Nobody knows who that freak is! And she's been around a lot longer than I have. All I know is she's never wrong. Even the principal mentioned she's one of the best oracles we've ever had. Which is probably why she hid her identity. So people wouldn't torture her for information on the future."

I herded a lost spirit away from the bookshelves. This one had glasses balancing unevenly on her nose bridge. My lips turned down. They were cracked and foggy. I doubted she could see anything.

I unzipped my bag and pulled out my own pair. "Reaper, do you know her prescription?"

He raised his brows. "Are you serious?"

"Tell her she can have my glasses if they match." I held them out in my hand.

The demon was dumbfounded.

"Don't tell me you've never seen glasses before. What, you're going to take her back to the other side, blind?"

"Why do you show empathy to the dead?" he asked. A tendril of smoke coiled around my glasses, lifting them out of my hand. Swapped them out with the ghost's in a flash.

She blinked twice, creepy stare unchanged. But her leathery hands opened the tattered book she held. Progress!

Reaper drew her to him with dark ropes of confinement.

"You aren't afraid of most demons," Reaper said, suspicious.

"It seems like many of them are lost souls, not beings of evil," I replied.

"Your school curriculum seems to think otherwise."

He wasn't wrong. Every mention of demons beyond the

veil painted them in the same negative light. Even Reaper's mention, though brief, cast him in antagonistic gloom.

"Well…" I stopped, unsure what to say next. "It could use some revising."

Between Gaksi and Reaper, if I left them alone, they left me alone. Neither was so inclined to murder me for my mere existence, as opposed to what I once believed.

"Truth of the day: what's your strongest memory of taking a soul to the other side?"

He flicked his wrist, and the ghost disappeared. "You've put some thought into this question."

"Yes," I said. Unflinching.

He stole a vulnerable admission from my last truth, and it was time to repay the favor.

I searched every corner of the library. Internet. Asked every historian and professor. All archives of his existence were destroyed. I knew they once existed because they were in the library catalog, but as soon as I went to retrieve them, they were nowhere to be found.

Was it the gumiho that stole the information? Unfortunately, there was nothing about that creature either.

So if I wanted information from him, it must come from the source.

Dark helixes entwined Reaper's hands. He looked away. "The first soul I carried over will always haunt me. I was young and foolish enough to approach her before death. I held her hand until she died and then brought her over."

Hand holding? Did he care for her?

"Why did you approach her before?"

He grimaced.

"Because I knew she was going to die."

He pulled a red cloth out of his pocket. "Every

upcoming death is listed in here." He waved it at me, a man tempting a bull.

"Why don't you prevent them?"

"I can't. It is impossible. I am the Reaper, not fate." A solemn look crossed his face.

The one I'd learned to recognize. It meant he was going to fire back with a different question for me.

"You owe me two truths today if we're doing an equivalent exchange of favors," Reaper said.

"Or," he held out his hand, "let me take you on a... dare."

"Dare?" He remembered what I said last time.

"Yes, dare. Truth or Dare, Luna?"

My hand locked in his. The practical part of me wanted him to keep talking. The dark shadows within me screamed with anticipation, craving an adventure. He pushed lightly in with his thumb, moving in light, maddening circles.

"Dare."

We vanished.

∽

REAPER RELEASED my hand in a wasteland that was colder, older, and more devoid of color than any place I'd seen before.

Broken, dead trees surrounded us, covered in so many cobwebs they resembled snow. Empty birds' nests dotted grey, ashy trees and jagged branches cut into the sky.

"We're in the Barren Fields again," I realized. His thumb brushed my hand in confirmation. Its warmth, in sharp contrast to the cold environment, made my own shadows flip in silly little joy. They loved his touch.

"Indeed." He tugged, and I stumbled along, "Although

this place is much farther from your University than the last place. Hence the trees and spiders. A bit of life remains."

I wondered why. Maybe the ocean nourished their growth.

As we walked, my traitorous shadows sang. They wanted to set up camp and stay here. This was exactly what school warned me about. That if I strayed too far from campus, I would go mad and never return.

Wind whistled. Icy air battered my face as I trod along, lids half-closed against the assault.

"Gaksi wanted to come. I could feel him trying to join in with you."

"But he didn't?" Usually, I felt his presence like a phantom limb. Now, I was uncharacteristically alone.

"I told him I wanted you to myself for an evening."

"Controlling."

"I could just leave you here, you know." He hauled me out of the way when I stumbled over a crater. It looked like the ones you saw on the surface of the moon. "Remind you why your university prohibits relations with demons."

I knew he wanted a reaction out of me. Fine, I'd give him one.

"Perhaps I would encourage a relationship if I didn't detest you," I proposed, pressing a kiss to our joined hands. "But you have to spend the night at my place first."

"Nothing would delight me more, spicy seraphim." He adjusted to brush his mouth against my bargain mark. It sent a wave of heat straight to my core, toes curled, breath heavy.

"But you have to make it back home first," his silky voice threatened.

"Excuse me?"

He traipsed away, fast now that I didn't weigh him down.

Waste of space. Annoying, arrogant demon. This—flirtation—we had would be the death of me. Literally, if I couldn't keep up with the demon and got left behind here. Alone.

I prowled after him. There had to be a way to kill him. Every creature had a weakness. One day, I'd find it and use it to destroy that imperious demon.

"I can hear your thundering thoughts from here," he shouted ten paces ahead, "it's almost as loud as your heavy breathing."

"I'm plotting your demise." I hopped over miscellaneous holes in the earth. Stupid potholes, slowing me down.

Ahead, a red-orange glow lit up the night sky. Reaper paused beneath it.

A heavy chuffing sound vibrated the air ahead. It sounded like panting. But it couldn't be Reaper, could it?

As I closed in, the glowing apparition drifted downwards. Each feature radiated energy, lighting up the surrounding expanse. There was a long, furry-looking tail. Four larger, muscular legs, each as big as I was. A bulking body as large as a horse. Two large, pointed ears, which swiveled toward me.

I lurched back when I saw the monstrous face. Burning red eyes, a drooling muzzle, and razor-sharp teeth growled at me.

"Bulgae?" Reaper commanded. The dog barked, a terrible, ferocious bass, at me. The sound waves pushed me a couple of steps back. The very air quaked.

Reaper just brought me here to die.

Think, think, think. I learned about this one when

Professor Ansi introduced it. The fire dogs were responsible for the world's eclipses. An ancient king, addicted to power, wanted to be able to control the light and dark phases of the day. So he seduced a witch to make the dogs of Beyond, whose job was to steal the moon and sun. They never succeeded, leading them to become more aggressive every year. Every time they tried, their hulking figure blocked the sun and moon.

The lunar eclipse was tonight.

"To escape my hellhound, Luna," Reaper taunted, "the exit to your home is that way." He pointed ahead, directing my gaze to a large, decayed tree with gnarled roots and a branching ruby canopy. Deceased, almost gone. Like everything else in this place.

Along the trunk, a mirror, gilded silver, hung. Its cracked surface revealed a dual reflection—below, Reaper's reflection took up the frame, and above, familiar red trees swayed. My home. The Whispering Woods. The colorful trees parted in the middle like they were waiting for me to jump through and come home.

So, I needed to run like hell to my salvation.

I could do this.

I was not dead. I did not belong there. I was life. I was going to go home.

Reaper arched a long arm toward me. "That beauty over there is my dear Luna. Please, go steal my moon!"

The dog pounced.

I screamed, avoiding the surging panic by rolling to the right. The beast's jaw snapped at me, tearing off my backpack. It exploded in shreds, but I kept running to the mirror.

The hellhound roared, sending a cascade of flames in front of me. Patches of frozen air sizzled and lit. My mind raced to strategize amidst the chaos. The dog toyed with my computer, shaking it back and forth with vigor. I tried not to think what would happen to my body in those powerful jaws.

If Reaper wanted to kill me, there were easier ways than this. He already knew who lived and died, according to his red cloth. This was just a trap. A torture trap. To trap me here, not kill me. Evasion, not survival, should be my goal here.

I was going to live, I told myself like a mantra as I darted between searing flames.

The leaves of my red trees grew bigger.

The rickety sign appeared.

My legs sprinted faster without the backpack weighing me down. Maybe all the walking I complained about during the first week of college was paying off.

I was fast. Alive. I was going to survive.

Details, like the lines of the tree bark, became vividly visible from my proximity.

I ran with flexed legs, arms whirling, fully prepared to lunge—

The dog jumped in front of me, smacking down in front of the mirror. It sat back on its haunches, howling triumphantly. Ringing dulled my senses. Residual smoke scorched my lungs, stinging with every breath. The air was burning, burning me alive—

Think. How did I get this damned dog out of my exit path?

If I didn't, it would lay waste to me here. Forever.

I rebounded left. Dashed right. Kept evading.

I gauged the distance between me and my backpack contents, now strewn about in a deep crater. Then between me and the mirror.

An idea flexed in my mind.

I was going to live.

And I was willing to take a risk, even a borderline suicidal one, to do so.

I sprinted to the crater holding my remaining belongings and jumped in.

Grabbed what I needed. Plotted. When I was done, I'd turn my wrath onto Reaper. I'd absolutely lay into him, put him in impossible positions just like he did me—

"Given up already?" Reaper barbed.

He wished.

And I needed to get out of here before I thought about torturing him with the wrong kinds of positions.

Hurtling to the ledge, I climbed out, ignoring my screaming chest. Smoke billowed within me. My shadows wailed, begging for release, but I couldn't let them out. I promised my mother. And I was stronger than that.

Where was the hellhound? In front of the mirror. Perfect.

Then I charged.

"Hey, doggy!" I wiggled my fingers. The ground was shaky, unsteady—fire had burned through the ice coating, making it slippery and sloppy. I pushed forward. *Be bold*, I told myself. Don't hesitate. You only had one chance to get this right.

Burning rubber and roasting flesh invaded my nose.

My mind went dark.

Black energy burst under my skin, raging through my head until I was limitless.

I got close enough to shove the knife down the dog's throat.

The beast roared, tearing its claws down my right arm hard enough to scrape out blood. Undeterred, my left hand swung up straight behind its head, using the force of my determination to hurl my projectile skyward.

Drawing back my bloodied arm, I circled, evaded, and rounded the beast, buying myself precious moments. This was it—the final gamble.

This better work. I only had one arm left.

A glint of reflected light descended. Perfect.

"Come get me, dog!" I yelled.

It reared forward while my other blade dropped from the sky.

The blade struck, nailing the beast, who roared at the sky in confusion.

Reaper clapped. "Mirror, mirror, on the tree. Who is the fiercest girl I see?"

While the beast was impaled, I leaped into the mirror, using my final surge of adrenaline to leave the hellhound behind.

I TUMBLED OUT THE MIRROR, gasping for breath in the cozy familiarity of the Whispering Woods. But there was no comfort, no sense of achievement. The fury burning through me consumed any trace of relief.

"Bravo!" Reaper lauded. I launched my third dagger at him.

"What was that?" He said, voice rising, betraying his surprise.

"I had three daggers in my backpack, demon," I staggered toward him. "One to pretend to kill it. One to actually kill it. And one to kill you!" I crawled to my now discarded weapon, my body protesting each movement.

"Ah, ah, ah." He covered it with his boot. "I think you've

had enough for the day. I am very impressed. You survived the dare."

His voice only fueled the venom in my soul. "You'll never survive me when I'm through with you," I promised, voice raw. My arm still bled. I held it against myself, slumping onto the mossy earth. The forest was almost as red as the haze in my vision.

"I'll haunt you forever," I vowed. My lungs were so raw, my voice cracked.

"The feeling is mutual," he crooned. He knelt down, pressing a hand to my forehead. Gentle energy flowed. The pain ebbed away. Bit. By. Painful bit.

"I'm proud of you, savage seraphim," he purred before dumping me through space and back into my bed.

Alone in my room, pain gone, but emotional scars etched in my soul, I simmered in my hatred all night.

CHAPTER SIXTEEN

THE ORACLE MUSINGS

It's finally here! My infamous rankings list!

In the top tier: Fae and Angel House will recruit the smartest, most vicious, and most notorious class for the future. In the middle tier, Vamp and Siren House will maintain their reputation and status. Wolf House, as usual, will form their pack of rejects and furries in the bottom tier. And Rose House? Well, you don't need me to spell it out, do you?

Finally: I have even better news. The hunt is over. One very swoon-worthy heroine has claimed our handsome devil.

Luna Deokhye, congratulations on seducing the Reaper!

I WOKE up with 125 calls and 50 messages. Gaksi laughed so hard the room shook with his glee.

"You missed everything," I accused.

The demonic mocking continued.

"You didn't even answer my messages while I was gone!" I usually made him do that while I was out. But where did he go? To do nothing! While my phone was blowing up! After a whole night of suffering!

He tossed the oracle's gossip column onto my bed.

I froze.

Reread.

Sank back into bed.

"We need to hunt down and kill this woman."

Stars and heavens. Heavens and stars. The whole campus would have seen this. How did the oracle know I saw him last night? And we weren't even dating? He tried to kill me last night! Again!

"I go through one day of hell from Reaper, and the next, the oracle decides it's her turn. She's going to ruin my life. Why didn't you do anything?" I accused. "Why didn't you wake me sooner?"

"Neither of us can control the whims of the oracle," Gaksi huffed, amused.

When I finished off Reaper, Gaksi was next.

I braced myself to sift through the onslaught of messages.

Flora: *You're sleeping with this man yet have so little information to deliver to me? Pathetic.*

Luna: *I'm doing my best! And we aren't sleeping together.*

Flora: *You make more work for me. I already had to pull strings to get you back to every House this round. It'll take a miracle to make you seem appealing after this.*

Luna: *Good thing we have a bargain!*

Flora: *Good thing I am a god.*

My mom didn't even text. She was the source of 50 of the calls. Starting at midnight, when the oracle released her latest column. Mother went to bed at 9 P.M.

The calls resumed at exactly 6 A.M. when she usually woke up. So not only did mother know that everyone knew, but she was also sleep deprived. I was *so* not poking that beast right now.

Cordelia sent me all of one text.

Cordelia: *Finally!*

Luna: *Unhelpful!*

Aubrey called several times but limited her texts to a couple of words.

Aubrey: *We need to take this girl down. This is a serious hit to your reputation. No House wants a "problem" recruit.*

She was quick. Her text arrived nearly 30 seconds after midnight. She must have been up and ready to go.

Luna: *You read my mind.*

Aubrey: *Anytime, bestie. I'll make a plan and report back. We will make it to the top together.*

Loved the loyalty. At least I had friends.

The only House leader that texted was Lukas.

Lukas: *Sorry, sweetheart. Rumors suck.*

Luna: *I'm nobody's sweetheart, but thanks.*

Lukas: *I bet it would dispel rumors if we made out in a public location.*

Luna: *Nice try.*

At least Siren House was still on my side.

Lastly, I checked messages from my father.

Dad: *Brace yourself. Your mother paid a werewolf personally to carry her to your dorm. She's arriving at lightning speed now.*

Luna: *Pray for me.*

Dad: *Get rid of your boyfriend, and maybe I will.*

I had class today. Mother wouldn't dare distract me from my studies, would she? I could avoid her that way.

I nearly slipped and fell when I exited my room. Crushed moonstone lined the entryway, with an "X" spray painted over the top of it.

Message received. I was dead to this university.

Students scattered on my path to school. Like a shark among fish, they fled as soon as I walked onto the same sidewalk.

Aubrey, ever the loyal friend, shot death glares at anyone staring.

When I sat down in class, there was a ten feet circle of space around me, save my friends. The usual students who sat around me had stolen other people's spots, leading to a chain reaction of grumbling. Especially displaced students glared at me from the back of the class, where they stood. Without desks. The entire length of class.

ONLY FOOLS DATE THE FORBIDDEN was written on the chalkboard.

"Now, class, why has this university banned dating demons?" Professor Ansi began.

"They're evil," Brayden piped from the front of the class. He had his angel hoodie on again today. I wanted to burn it. Gunner.

"It's embarrassing," one of the wall girls shouted. "If you had your own magic, in a normal, organized way through the House system, you wouldn't even be attracted to the dark magic they convey."

"It's unfair," Hunter shouted, "for your boyfriend to set up your kills and artificially inflate your score."

Stars. How did I reset the leaderboard? Who counted my gwisin banishment from last night? I didn't want that! It was a tag team effort, not individual.

"You'll be expelled," Cordelia answered next. I was about to pinch her when she continued, "but rumors of dating demons are as old as time. You can't punish someone over a rumor!"

She patted my leg. Nice try, but nobody doubted the oracle. She'd never been wrong before.

Professor Ansi agreed, then went into all the consequences of dating demons. Bodies disintegrating into a husk. Possession by a vengeful spirit. Girls that disappeared without a trace, pulled through the veil and into god knew where.

As uncomfortable as I was, I knew it could be worse. My mother was definitely at my dorm by now.

I shifted uncomfortably, just worrying about it.

"See me after class, Luna," Professor Ansi said after her lecture. The terrible three laughed obnoxiously. Great. Even more singled out.

Students shoved past me when I moved down the steps to the professor's desk. I stumbled more times than I could count, feet darting out more than usual to trip me. Students took off at Professor Ansi's glare.

"How badly do you want to be at this University?" Dr. Ansi's voice thundered before I even made it halfway down.

My voice wavered. "Badly. More than I ever wanted anything."

Every late night at the library, studying like my life depended on it. Every resume booster I suffered through in high school to get here. The demons I'd faced, internal and external. I fought through all of them to make it here, and I was going to stay, no matter the cost.

"Then you need to act like it," Dr. Ansi said. "Next time I hear about you and the Reaper's relations, you're expelled."

"Understood," I said, dismay gripping my worn-out heart.

∽

MOTHER HAD BLOWN my door off its hinges. Splintered wood lined one side of the hallway to the other. Trepidation coiled low in my stomach.

Mother brooded, ominous and foreboding, in the corner of my room. She blocked the window like a vengeful specter, and tremors coursed through her body, navy-blue shadows writhing in unsettling jumps.

"Do you want this to be you? Never in control, never free?" Smoke seeped around the room with every word. "Unable to contain your anger? Bursting into black with every emotional outburst?"

The smoke snaked around my waist, lifting me up like a tentacle.

"You'll never reach your potential if you continue down this path." The tentacle constricted, compressing my chest, making it impossible to draw air.

"Mother," I gasped.

"Don't talk back to me," she said, voice low.

"Mother, if you kill me, I'll just go back to the Reaper anyway," I rasped out. She released me at once, and I landed on my side. Yelped, feeling a future bruise already.

The pain radiated, making me curl up in a little ball on the floor in fetal position.

Was that how I felt in the womb, too? Trapped? Scared?

"You are already a liability, just from looks alone. Houses won't even let you in if you look weak. Have you applied your medications today?" She grabbed a wet wrap I fixed around my arm.

"You wore a wet wrap to class? This shouldn't leave the house!"

Wet wraps helped lock in moisture so my skin wouldn't dry out. I applied it hastily this morning to heal the worst of my skin before my mother showed, and upon realizing I didn't have time to let it soak before class, I decided to just keep it on throughout.

"It's not like it's a secret. I have hideous skin, Mom! People have already figured out I'm splotchy!"

"You look as malformed as you are on the inside when you go out looking like that. Only lazy people show their ugly on the outside."

My arm dropped to my side. Her words hurt worse than applying alcohol directly to freshly opened skin. Shadows shrunk within me, wounded by her acrid judgment.

"I cannot love a disappointment, Luna." She used a shadow tentacle to lift my camera from my book bag. "Is this what motivated all this? A quest for fame? For notoriety?"

With a cruel and deliberate twist, it shattered on the floor, exploding into pieces.

"Mom!" I cried. I fell to the floor, grabbing bits of reel, hopelessly trying to salvage the individual pieces. There was no point. It was ruined.

Books soared off the shelf into mother's open arms. "*Demons Resembling Men?*" She scoffed, and a wave of her power shredded the entire shelf into dust.

All my favorite books, including my childhood copy of *Pride and Prejudice*, fell like dull confetti onto the floor.

"Where's Gaksi?"

"You can't destroy me, you crazy hag," Gaksi growled from my doll.

Mother snarled, and they were all decapitated. Years and years of collector's items gone, severing the ties to the last of my innocence and memories.

"Do you know what the Reaper will do to you? It will be worse than this! He will destroy everything you are! He will take you so far away from who you used to be that you won't recognize who you've become!"

Her fury escalated, creating a tornado of shadows that whirled around her, spinning out of control. A torrential wind whipped through my bed, desk, clothes, and heart, until nothing was left of my room but my mother and a ravaged layer of black ash on the floor.

"You will not engage with the Reaper again, Luna." Her voice rang with authority, quenching any rebellion left within me.

"As you wish, Mother." My fingers combed through the ashes of my former possessions. Water dripped down my face, making a sort of paste with the floor.

When mother departed, she took the last of my dignity with her.

CHAPTER SEVENTEEN

THE ORACLE MUSINGS

What makes a great love story? Is it the looks? The passion? The adventure? I, dear reader, think it's about choices. Scholars debate whether the Goddess of Spring ever wanted her lover, the King of the Underworld. Was her betrothal to him completely involuntary? Was she a victim?

Or was it a power play, a strategic move to evade the gods and the forces above? Did she run toward the problematic option, not away, because she saw herself as his future queen and not as Demeter's daughter?

Make good choices today, readers! Today is the turning point for your own great love story. Hades and Persephone were only the beginning!

"Check your messages, Luna!" Gaksi's voice forced me out of my slumber. Why purchase an alarm clock when you can be disturbed by your own familiar demons?

He threw a phone at me. Where did he get it? I did not know. I didn't know how I woke up on a blanket or how a basket of clothing lay above the dust beside me, either. His night must have been busy, filled with stealing and compiling replacement items for me.

My eyes glistened. I didn't deserve Gaksi.

Lukas: *You. Me. Siren House Rager. Tonight. Be ready at 11 P.M.*

"A suitor!" Gaksi cheered.

His complete disregard for last night's events was exactly why I loved him so much.

"A slimy one," I muttered. Should I even go? My life had actually fallen into a pretty predictable routine lately.

Wake. Study. Sleep. Occasionally, chase down a ghost and tally more points to stay competitive. Travel to the campus zoo for the occasional school assignment. Get bullied by Flora, then go hunt down my nemesis. Acquire information from Reaper, convey said information to Flora, and repeat the cycle all over again.

Whenever I retrieved a soul for him, I could barely come up with new information. I was so angry with him that my questions were brief, and his lips grew tighter with each passing conversation, fueling my rage.

"Why did you try to kill me with the Bulgae?" I asked him.

"I was trying to see if an ancient prophecy would hold true."

A futile, ridiculous task, given that I was not the real moon, only named after it.

"How old are you?" I asked him next. That one was for Cordelia.

"Old enough to have a job. Young enough to be ruled by my father."

"How's your relationship with your father?" I asked at the behest of Flora.

"Much like yours with your mother."

"How do I even know you're telling the truth?" That one was for me.

"I do not lie."

Only tiny tidbits of information, nothing substantial. Meanwhile, I'd told him about my grades (which were stellar), my siblings, and my hobbies. When I asked him why he was so curious, he said he wanted to track the inconsistencies of gumiho lies.

Arrogant demon.

Gaksi threw a necklace at me. "Start getting ready!"

I paused. Were siren dates safe for an unpowered mortal? Sirens were inherently manipulative. Then again, Flora only promised she could get me invited back to every House. I never made her promise to give me a bid: the final invite to join after the last round of recruitment. If Fae House didn't work out, I should protect my backups.

I supposed it would be nice to be liked. Sirens were pretty. Even if all their charm was fake.

And after last night's debacle, I needed to escape this miserable room before I dissolved into dust with it.

Hmm. What would a siren wannabe wear to a party?

I shoved through the clothes in the laundry basket. Jeans? No, too pedestrian.

Pearls? They were from under the sea, right?

Indecisive, I texted some to Aubrey for approval.

Aubrey: *No to the pants. Yes, corset. But tighten it a little more! Sirens aren't modest! You want to blend in, not stand out.*

I compressed my body into a teal corset, tight enough to make my bust shine. It matched with a navy miniskirt cinched like a sarong around my waist. I'd never been the most slender, so I styled my outfits to show off my curves, not hide them.

I jumped into a pair of sneakers last. If I was going to dance, I needed comfort. I'd just hide my feet in pictures if I took any.

"Come out, future siren!" Lukas called from outside my door.

11 P.M. already? Did I sleep for nearly twenty-four hours? No wonder Gaksi had time to compile things.

I swung the door open.

"Wow," Lukas breathed. His pupils dilated. His gaze swept over me, from the long, curling hair to the revealing outfit. He even grinned at the shoes. I smiled inwardly. My outfit worked. He was bewitched.

I'd chosen it to make him want me. Men were ruled by their emotions, weren't they? If he wanted me to be his, he'd be more likely to invite me to join Siren House permanently.

Mother always told me that men can only think with one head at a time. And it usually wasn't the one between their ears.

We held hands as we hiked to the beach. Lukas kept stealing glances at me, lingering on my body for so long that I had to redirect him not to fall.

I elongated my stride a little with every step. My skirt rode up my legs, hugging my wide hips and showing off my long legs, which he nearly tripped over.

"Why haven't we hung out before?" Lukas questioned

wistfully. "Then maybe the oracle would gossip about our love life instead."

"That's not a good thing," I said. "In fact," I glanced at him, "why aren't you worried about the rumor I'm dating the Reaper?"

He rolled his eyes. "He's got nothing on me, fish."

Hmm. I stared straight ahead. He had confidence going for him, for sure.

I admired him in a new light. He was handsome, especially when the sun backlit his blonde waves. Would we be dating if I had never gotten caught up in my bargain? Would I be this happy-go-lucky?

"Admiring me, gorgeous?"

He flexed his muscled arms in the sky. "Like what you see?"

I freely laughed and said, "I think it would be even better if what I see is permanently attached to my arm. You're more pleasant than I thought you'd be to date."

Despite my half-insult, he radiated like the sun itself had risen for him. "I have never agreed more."

And I meant it. He was so carefree, so in tune with himself, that if even a sliver of that energy reflected off me, I could absorb his endless optimism.

My bargain tingled, agitated. I ignored it.

Blasting music boomed ahead. The sun was setting, and the ocean sparkled with neon colors. Sirens danced with colorful beads and bracelets, illuminating the dark beach.

Excitement spurred within me. After the monotony of the past few weeks, it would be nice to actually have fun.

I put on my most doll-like, innocent smile. One I had never used on a man, ever.

The tingling ceased. As it should.

Lukas looped his arm all the way through mine. "Shots?"

"Yeah!"

The flavor was sour and sinful, and I downed three at Lukas' encouragement. I deserved a break.

"Does pirate treasure ever wash up on this beach?" I asked.

He considered for a moment. "Only treasure I've ever seen on this beach is you." He smiled proudly at that.

He was kind of dumb cute, but cute all the same.

An embarrassing blush and three more shots later, I was gone. Bodies distorted along the beach, thumping up and down with the bass. The pounding music, the exuberant dancing, and the alcohol erased any kind of thought from my head. I was blissfully gone, twirling like this was my last night on earth.

Sirens pushed and shoved. I gagged when one of them spilled their drink on me. It smelled horrible, like anchovies and dead fish. Wait, was that a drink or vomit?

I stilled, sweaty and flushing. The bodies kept spinning, spinning, spinning around me, like I was the center of a haunted merry-go-round.

"Lukas?" I asked.

No response. Blurry figures swam around me. Where did he go? I caught a flash of golden yellow hair diving into the waves. Did he leave me to go swimming?

I sluggishly moved through the throng to the beach. What was happening? My head felt weighed down by lead. My steps were sticky and gross. Dizzy stars danced in my vision.

"Hey, fish," an older girl grabbed my arm. "Are you alright?"

"Fine," I sputtered out. I pushed past her, and thankfully, she left me alone.

At some point, I attempted to make my way back to my dorm. End this whole adventure. My stomach hurt. But the sea culled me back every time, the crowd dragging me back to the ocean. The chaotic haze enticed me to the ever-retreating shore.

Storm clouds rolled above. Thunder rumbled louder than the music.

When I thought I would surely collapse, strong arms jolted me to a stop.

"Woah, what happened to you?" Lukas shouted.

"Don't yell," I whispered. He had neon face paint on, and the glow hurt my eyes.

I moved to pull away, but he held me tighter. Waves lapped at my waist. Waves?

Something cold and slimy slid around my leg, and I realized it was Lukas' mermaid tail.

"Ew," I muttered.

I'd walked straight into the ocean. There were other sirens around us, and I could understand their leering even in my inebriated state. My face heated.

"You're drunk." Lukas snaked his tail back beneath him. I wondered where his pants went. His shirt had disappeared somewhere, so I got the full view of his hairy blonde chest. It was disgusting.

"Put some clothes on, siren," I said. My eyes closed. I paused. What was I doing here again?

"I would actually much prefer to take yours off." He tugged me deeper, all friendliness gone, replaced by a man I didn't recognize.

There was an intensity in his hold. A frightening one. I

recoiled, but he crushed me to his chest. My limbs shook, overexerted.

Breathe, breathe, breathe. I was about to hyperventilate. Panic. Thunder rumbled again. Lukas dragged me further into the depths. I was going to drown, or even if I didn't, I'd be electrocuted.

Why couldn't I think? Had I been drugged?

"Come on, all the other sirens are watching. There's a place much more private—" He grazed a repulsive kiss along my jaw.

What was Lukas' pearl? Was it related to what was happening? All sirens could make you like them, but if his special power was related to poison—

A giant wave crashed down, throwing us underwater.

I thrashed and floundered as water surrounded me. Where was the surface? All I saw was dark.

My leg got yanked in one direction by a meaty hand. The neon wristlet on it glowed, and I kicked it with a vengeance. Ugly neon!

Air. I needed air. My lungs wouldn't last long without it.

A current stole me away from the offending color.

It threw me into a hard, smooth body contained in familiar shadows, even in the depths of the sea.

The hands wrapping around me were gentle. I could push them off if I wanted to.

But where would I go? Back to the Siren leader?

I forced the haze out of my mind to decide.

If I went back to Lukas, I'd be a Siren. He'd drag me into the ocean, use me, and make me the next initiate of Siren House (ideally). I'd be under his beck and call forever. A figurine for decoration.

Women begged Siren House to take them every year in

defiance of their sleazy reputation. Cried their tears out like Cordelia when dropped.

And I wouldn't just be a siren—I would be *his* siren. The one that cherry-picked the next initiates. The starborn mate of the most charming man on campus. The head siren, who ran the recruitment process and built up the House into exactly what I wanted it to be.

I would be irrevocably, overwhelmingly beautiful and popular. And I would belong somewhere, and have a House designation that could never be taken from me.

I could even be like Flora and haze as many recruits and active members as I wanted.

Or I could disappear with another.

One who tried to kill me.

Who had no designation to offer me.

Who'd filled my life with fear and adventure. Who thwarted me at every turn. Who gave me the best distraction from everyday life I'd ever experienced. Who was entirely predictable because I knew how evil his kind was from the start, unlike the false naivety of sirens.

Someone who rescued me from insanity before and was back to rescue me again. A creature who was so far from this nonsense, a creature who called me beautiful without me having to dress like this, who offered me something Lukas never could: an opportunity to be myself.

And revenge. A chance to go against everything my mother taught me and make my own future.

Firm hands captured my waist, pulling deeper, and I let the Reaper drag me under.

We emerged on a cliff overlooking the beach. Revelers pranced below, some cavorting on the beach, others in the ocean.

"Reaper," I mumbled.

His arms pressed against my stomach, my back to his chest. I rested my wet arms atop his.

"How do you feel?" he asked softly into my ear. His nose brushed it lightly.

"Take me home," I requested.

"Very well," he said. His body shifted. One arm held my back, and the other held up my legs so I was being carried like a baby. I was a bigger girl, but he tossed me in his arms like I was feather-light.

The move sprayed water from me everywhere, but he was dry. His magic must have kept the water off him. He should teach me how to do that.

"Why not just teleport?" I asked, resting my head against his chest. Shadows wafted around us in a protective orb, so we were in our own private bubble.

"You're sick," he said quietly. "It would only disorient you more."

I narrowed my brows, focusing hard. "My head hurts."

"I know, sick seraphim." He pressed a kiss to my forehead. His voice dropped, filled with dark rage. "Trust that I will rip your abuser limb from limb for this."

His breath smelled like him, too. Cocoa and jasmine.

"I am not yours," I said. "You count as an abuser, too. I chose the lesser of the evils," I pouted.

"I had a purpose," he said. "I needed to test an old prophecy."

"What was it?"

He chuckled. "It will not come true if I reveal it to you."

His body moved as if supernatural sculptors carved it from obsidian. Hard, unrelenting, ancient.

"You're so gorgeous," I said, running my fingers along his chest. "You're strong."

"Indeed." I can hear how pleased he was. Vain demon.

"For this favor, I request a truth," he said between steps. "Do you hate me?"

His voice hitched. There was something young and chaste in how he asked that. Like he was afraid to hear the answer.

"I should hate you." There was a long silence, and he resumed walking. "But I can be a version of myself around you that I can't be with anyone else. I'm not trying to impress someone with you. I don't have to hold back my attitude and behave. I can be exactly as unhinged as I want to be, and you wouldn't be scared of it."

My shadows stirred in my chest. They wanted to come out. Reveal themselves. Show off to this man.

As if on cue, Reaper's own shadows broke off from the orb to sit atop my head. Like a little black crown.

"Does the bargain make me like you more?" I asked him.

He hugged me impossibly closer to his chest.

"No. Any hopes, desires, or dreams you have of me are entirely your own."

CHAPTER
EIGHTEEN

THE ORACLE MUSINGS

The second House leader has perished! Unlike past victims, this one was found dismembered in approximately 200 pieces, each cut in an organized, methodical fashion. Has our mystery killer become civilized?

Not only that, but our fearless Siren House leader left a lengthy confession list behind, naming every child he's sired and every heinous crime against women.

Very bottom-tier behavior, Sirens.

I FELT like a dragon had beaten me into a bloody pulp.

My head hammered. My limbs were too heavy. Even breathing brought with it a compressing weight upon inhale, and a stinging burn on the exhale.

"You were poisoned," Reaper confirmed, brushing a lock of hair out of my face. He sat on a chair of darkness, rotated toward me, one leg crossed over the other. The picture of nonchalance, sitting on a seat of his own power.

The sobriety, and embarrassment at how empty my room was, hit me all at once.

"Get out!" I pointed at the window angrily. "Do you see how open that is? Do you know what could happen to me if I get caught with you in here?" I moved to sit up, but a dizzy spell dropped me back on my blanket.

"I think I prefer you sicker," he replied. "You were much more honest about how dear I am to you." He gave me a sardonic smile. I sulked, covering my face with my hands. A thought occurred to me, and I yanked them back down.

"Peekaboo?" He tsked. "You're a little old for that."

"Did you stay here all night? Did anyone see you come in? How did I get into my pajamas?" The questions jumped off my tongue.

"No, I had Gaksi watch you. Shadows concealed our entry. And I dropped you off at your friend Cordelia's apartment first. It thrilled her to wash you on my behalf. I owe her a favor now."

I checked my clothes. No vomit covered me anymore; the coral reef pattern was definitely Cordelia's. I grabbed my phone to text her, only to be greeted by her usual messages.

Cordelia: *He's so much hotter in person. You struck gold. Share him with me sometime, will you?*

Luna: *I don't share.*

Red, fiery anger stirred in my chest. He was my bargain maker. Nobody else's.

I rejected that oddity and came back to my senses.

"You put her in danger," I told Reaper. "Do you know what the consequences would be if she were seen with you? Ruining my life is one thing, but destroying my friend's is quite the other."

"She didn't seem to mind." His eyes twinkled. "Perhaps I'll even hit her with her own bargain."

I threw my blanket at him. He held up a hand, pausing it midair, and floated it back around me like a cloak.

"You are reckless. Irresponsible and dangerous."

A self-satisfied smile crossed his face. "You forgot gorgeous."

I tuned him out. Flipped over on my side and started playing on my phone. Maybe then he would get the message.

His shadows roamed over my waist, tugging gently. *Come back*, they seemed to say. *Play with me.*

Despite their soft pressure, I remained facing the wall.

"Fine," he huffed. "Stay there. I enjoy the view from behind, as well."

Bastard.

I pulled the blanket up to cover my rear. He chuckled.

"You're not the only one that wants my backside," I muttered.

He snarled. The room temperature plummeted.

"I should have made his death more painful." His voice dropped to a rich and primal baritone. "I had to rip that predator limb from limb for trying to take you."

I was stunned into silence.

The vigilante watching me in bed was lethal. Cruel. And once the oracle named him specifically, infamous.

When he said nothing further, I decided the best course of action was to let the barbarian lie.

So, I read some emails on my phone, pretending like a masochistic demon wasn't simmering behind me. Checked on schoolwork as if it could kill me quicker than my dealmaker. Perused the oracle's gossip column, hoping for any new information on my companion.

The silence stretched uncomfortably.

Ping.

Mother: *"Don't disappoint me today."*

Suddenly, I felt too hot, my threadbare blanket too thin to shield me from the hard floor. Too vengeful about how blank my wall looked, staring back at me. Too furious with the world for leaving me possessionless, with a demon at my back. This had gone on long enough.

"If I thank you, will you leave me alone?" I asked.

"Why would you want that?" he teased. His voice sounded so light. Unserious. As if he hadn't dismembered a man last night and haunted me in the present.

"Because you can only ruin my life by being here."

"I—" Reaper interjected.

"No, let me finish." I spewed my rage to the wall. "Yeah, I know technically, you came here because you wanted to kill the gumiho. But you didn't have to engage with mortals. There was no obligation for you to bond with me. You're pathetic."

The air became static. Electric. Charged. Dust lifted from the floor, suspended in the air.

"You have such little opinion of me?" His voice was crisp, bitter.

His frame creaked wood as he rose.

"I have to maintain the veil between my kingdom and yours. When I don't, more monsters come through. Every day, I wake up to see which demons I have to return. Which names got added to my list. Which blood is on my hands for not keeping them safe."

I didn't dare breathe. His anger was palpable, hot enough to burn what was left of my frozen heart.

"In the end, I have to face them and the pain I caused. Recognize that I let them die. That I am responsible for their death, with my incompetence. For centuries, I have worked tirelessly to keep the natural state of things in order. Take dead souls back home. Keep the creatures of my universe at bay. When the gumiho escaped, my kingdom dissolved into shambles. Demons are attracted to power, and they all wanted to climb after her, follow a new leader into a new world. My father, Yunma, ordered me to solve this mess. And do you know how he did it?"

He stepped in front of my face, pushing up his shirt sleeve. A sleeve of inked tattoos glistened in the largest bargain mark I'd ever seen. He laughed darkly. "Taking demons back with me is one of the only ways I can get home, save an impossible miracle happening."

"So I have to be here, Luna." He said my name with fervor, like an enchantment or a curse.

"And I have to maintain my bargain with you because you radiate so much demonic energy. You are either the gumiho, the most powerful creature from my realm, or one of my strongest subjects, which makes you my... responsibility."

He took a deep breath, then placed two fingers on my neck and—ever so softly—pulled them away. Inch. By. Inch. With each retreat, he pulled a piece of my inner shadows out, weaving them like rings around his hand.

I watched in fascination as my shadows harmonized with his.

He thrust his hand forward, merging a fraction of his shadows into mine, pushing all the energy back into my body at once.

My thoughts frenzied, electric, as his energy pulsed in tempo with mine.

"I see your shadows, seraphim. And I am not afraid of them."

CHAPTER NINETEEN

THE ORACLE MUSINGS

Who's in which clique? That, in essence, describes the function of our House system. A social stratification ritual where the machine—the notorious Antikythera—decides where and to who you belong. You are who you surround yourself with, right?

FALL BECAME WINTER. Classes thinned out. Extra seats abounded, even for those avoiding me. I spent my days studying, capturing demons, arguing with Flora, and conversing with Reaper about the creatures from his realm.

When Cordelia and I walked from Pills & Potions to Daggers & Dynamite, gossiping about the latest House scandal, a flash of white-blonde burst out of the shrubs.

Aubrey sprinted to me, eyes fixed on my wrists.

Where my shadows were spreading, thriving. In broad

daylight. Not into beautiful, elegant bangles but into grotesque, ominous shackles.

Shackles, which are growing in visibility by the second. Shackles that would get me discovered. Shackles that lead straight home with nothing but my mother for company—

Breathe, breathe, breathe.

They faded.

Like downing a fire, they extinguished into nothing.

Aubrey glanced around, determined no other students saw, then beckoned me away.

We followed her into a meadow beyond the bushes, ignoring the chatter and laughter around me. I was numb. Emotionless. In control.

We passed deep into the edge of campus, where only truly bored students ever roamed.

She examined my wrists, turning them over in her delicate hands.

"I can explain," I said anxiously.

"No need," she said gently. "I have secrets too."

"Like what?"

Her and Cordelia shared a look. A glance that conveyed this secret was among us three instead of whatever was going on between the two. I'd pry into that relationship later.

"Make sure you keep these under control," Aubrey said. Her voice sounded wary. She assessed me—the clean outfit, the fake confidence, the pleasant smile.

"Sometimes, when you try to hide too much of who you are, it backfires."

WAITING in the thicket of the Whispering Woods, I hoped my attempt at reconciliation would work.

Like a schoolgirl, I'd tossed a note into the very mirror I stumbled out of recently.

It did not toss a note back.

The flap of wings instead caught my attention.

"Samjoko." I bowed, displaying deference to the sun god before me. "I am honored to be in your presence."

When I rose, the three-legged crow only blinked.

I held out an offering. "Do you like red bean cakes? Gaksi does, so I thought I would provide them as a blessing to you."

The crow swept forward, took the cake in one claw, and balanced on the other two to eat it in the branch above.

"Would you be so kind as to contact the Reaper for me? I wish to speak with him."

"Always an ulterior motive with you," Reaper said immediately. Like he'd been waiting all along. He stepped out of the tree to catch the crow on his arm. She nestled into his chest, munching away.

"What caused you to summon me, seraphim?"

"Gaksi says you can teach me how to control my shadows."

"Gaksi told me this, mother told me that." He tilted his head with each phrase. "Have you ever acted on your own wishes? It would be good for you."

I ignored the twinge of embarrassment. This immortal could read me like a book.

"Fine, then. Teach me to control these." The shackles had re-formed, holding my arms stuck together.

He frowned. "That is...unfortunate."

He stepped forward. Samjoko hopped up to his shoulder, where she gazed down at me with contempt. Snack finished. Sun god back.

"Shadows are a manifestation of what we feel inside."

He came closer, and the hold on my wrists tightened. I growled, "So these handcuffs represent your relationship with me?"

He smiled suggestively. "It could progress to that point if you prefer."

I glared at him. Desperate, seductive demon.

"Dissolve them on your own." His voice left no room for argument.

I stared at the shadows swarming around each other in defiance.

Minutes passed.

I tried to think of happy memories. Winning the spelling bee, with Mom and Dad clapping in the audience. Receiving my acceptance letter to Aether University. Getting my House list back with every single House for the next round.

Shadows swirled and swirled but remained exactly the same.

When my vision swirled, too, Reaper spoke.

"Any time now."

"I'm trying my best."

"Tell me about yourself," Reaper asked. "What brings you joy?"

Achievements. Planning. Getting work done. None of those thoughts impacted my ever-growing shadows.

"Arguing with you," I answered sarcastically.

He snorted. "My favorite pastime as well."

The shadows lessened.

"Ah," Reaper said. "You like...chaos."

"Nobody likes chaos."

The swirling ceased.

"Well, then, perhaps you just like...me." His grin was devilish.

"I have never liked you." He had the gall to look wounded.

My traitorous, worthless, otherworldly shadows reformed.

"Too bad you're stuck with me, then." He dipped his finger into the shadow bridge. They circled him, forging a path away from my arms.

"Perhaps we should make another deal, then."

I cursed at him.

"That was not ladylike."

"Forgive me if your deals give me unladylike levels of aggravation."

"Hmm." He circled me, pacing in tune with my aggressive darkness.

I doubted I liked chaos, but a petty part of me craved the conversation that company brought. Would Reaper, being a demon prince, have a crown?

"Where's your crown?" I asked him, eager for a distraction.

"I don't wear one. I wear a gat, a traditional hat of my people, but I rarely wear it lately. It impedes the four essentials of demon survival."

"Which are?"

"Fighting, fleeing, feeding, and... fornicating." He sounded like he held back a laugh at the last word.

"And how often do you do those?" I snapped.

"Not enough of any, unfortunately." Crow cawed in a high-pitched sound that resembled laughter.

"My lovers are few and far between," Reaper admitted.

"Why?"

"Why? Who would want me?" He chuckled darkly. "The transporter of the dead? Why not date an actual corpse at that point?"

"But—"

You're so handsome, I almost tacked on. But his ego was big enough already.

"But what, seraphim? Do you think you're the only one that has hurt me with your rejection? Every generation, the same thing happens."

His voice took on different voices, all higher-pitched as if they were to resemble women. "My mother said no. My dad threatened to kill you. The elders have forbidden it. Fate foretells doom."

His normal voice returned. "I have had no shortage of once-interested options but nobody to actually share the burden of my reign with."

He pivoted toward me. "Tell me about your House system."

"What?"

He loved changing the subject as soon as I learned something new about him, and I could never quite figure out why.

"I imagine you also desire community. Explain to me why you started the process."

"Well…" I shifted on my feet. "Pleasing my mom…it's all I've ever wanted. She sacrificed her free time to be a mom for me, gave up working, stayed in touch with Aether, and ignored her own wants to provide for mine. It feels disrespectful to her hard work to not pursue the best for myself."

He prodded me with another question. "Do you still desire to join a House?"

I took in a suffering breath. I didn't have to be honest,

but Reaper just revealed something about himself, so I felt like I should repay him.

"I should. I fear... that everything I do will be for naught. That I will be stuck in the spinning wheel of life, always making progress, but never being able to catch up to who I could become." I can only be honest about that with him, a fellow shadow wielder, who never quite fit into any predetermined mold.

"Why?"

"Because when I go to those top Houses, it's like, they're all perfect. Perfect grades, perfect use of magic, perfect social circles. They even have perfect skin! How am I supposed to feel like I belong in a place where nobody has problems but me?"

I almost refrained from finishing the sentence. My problems seemed so insignificant, inconsequential, compared to him having to run a kingdom. Why would he care?

"Do you enjoy being the prince?" Now, he looked uncomfortable.

A harrowed, pinched look contorted his features. "It is a responsibility I cannot evade. One I do not take lightly. Fulfilling this responsibility demands sacrifice. Sacrifice of my own wants and needs. I strive to be the opposite of how my father rules: through terror and power. I am rather an embodiment of self-sufficiency and devotion. We all have a duty we fulfill, and this is mine."

Terror and power. The quintessential traits of every great demon. But why break away from that? For duty?

Was that why he pursued the gumiho and rogue demons so diligently? Because he viewed it as his only purpose in life? As his relentless calling?

"Despite being a deranged bargain maker, you sound like a wonderful prince."

He reappeared in front of me. "Wonderful?"

I tripped him before he could materialize. He wobbled over me, laughed, and intertwined our fingers. "If you attempt that again, I shall take you down with me." His voice lightened in promise, though his face was worn.

I saw him then.

The exhaustion. The stress. The lonely, haunted gaze in his eyes. How long had he been laboring alone?

Without thinking, I leaned forward and kissed his cheek, his skin serene and welcoming under my lips. It was brief, just a second, a moment, but he looked back at me like he would cherish it forever.

The stress on his face eased when I drew back, shyly ducking my head to watch the last of my shadows dissolve.

"Until next time," he promised, wrapping wings of darkness around us to take me home.

CHAPTER
TWENTY

THE ORACLE MUSINGS

It's mental breakdown season! It's the midway point of the school year, the crunch time of winter finals before the first big break. The pressure is getting to everyone, it seems. Countess Dracula will face expulsion for ripping out a freshman's neck (but they won't expel her). Fireworks will explode from Fae House. Even Rose House—bless their happy little baking hearts—will have an outbreak of food poisoning. Time to separate the weak from the strong before the next round. Who will thrive? Who will perish? Don't be the one who loses control, reader dearest!

A NOTHER WEEK PASSED FILLED with idle chatter, doing all the work in group projects, and checking the leaderboard hourly.

Mother said that when she was in school in the 90s, they would publish class rankings daily on a sheet of paper outside the main lecture hall. Because there was no internet, that paper was the only way to see how you did.

Now, faculty posted class rankings daily on a continually updating screen on the school clock tower. Any time there was so much as a late assignment, you could see your place in school drop in real-time.

It was 'motivational,' according to our professors.

'Necessary,' to weed out the weak from the strong.

'Sadistic,' was what I would call it.

Initially, when the Oracle published that column about my relationship, I felt like the laughingstock of the school.

Cameras flashed every time I left my room. Hype and chatter died down as soon as I strode by. Fangirls repeatedly stopped me to ask what their favorite man was "really like" to date.

"Isn't he just spectacular?" They'd be gushing.

"Spectacularly annoying." I'd be fuming.

My playlists became increasingly more animated as I used them to drown out any surrounding noise.

But now? With my name continually near the top of the leaderboard? The critics had fallen silent.

Some of them had even sheepishly deleted their stalker photos of me, approaching me after class to ask what my study tips were or if I could share my notes.

Sometimes people would tell kids nonsense like '*grades aren't everything*.' But I'd never had that problem. My grades were perfect. 4.0 since grade school.

Grades weren't everything, but your reputation as a smart person sure was.

That was what they should know me for.

That was who I was. That was what I did best.

Kept my life together. Concealed my external wounds with makeup. Concealed my internal shadows with breathing exercises and sometimes a little help from Gaksi. Successful, put together, competent. I belonged at this University.

～

"You almost hit that spot at least once today," Reaper remarked.

"That sounds like an insult."

"Perhaps it was."

"I think it was, sloppy seraphim," Gaksi said.

"Don't call me that!" I responded. Reaper's eyebrows rose. I resisted the urge to gag. Gaksi using Reaper's nickname for me was so foul my lunch threatened to reappear.

"*I don't even like him,*" I grumbled in my head.

"*Is that why butterflies possess your stomach every time he looks—*"

I blocked him out.

Then missed the target again.

And again.

And again.

～

Classes came and went, along with exams. Hunter's gang left me well alone, swamped with the intensity of their own schoolwork. They must be too busy and scared to torment me, with school and recruitment pressure amping up.

Cracks were showing in every student's carefully constructed facade.

Aubrey broke first.

Crying, she confided in me that being first generation made her feel lost at Aether.

Cordelia's downfall was her homesickness: Aubrey caught her trying to drown herself in the ocean, drifting away more than a mile from shore. Aubrey watched her like a hawk after that.

Brayden broke down publicly, crying in the middle of an exam. He must have still passed, though, because he returned the next day. And the next. And again after that.

Even Hunter peered over my shoulder a little in class sometimes. Of course, I didn't let him, but I noticed the desperation for the right answer was there.

I had what was close to my own escape plan after spending ten hours on a lab report from potions class. I barely passed. Somehow, I created a 200% yield, meaning I created matter out of thin air. Considering I didn't have light magic yet, creation was impossible, which meant my calculations were way off.

My GPA sunk so low, if it wasn't for Flora's deal, I might not have a House come the next round of recruitment.

By the last exam, I was ready to kill everyone at this university, demonic or angelic, finishing with myself. I'd spent so much time in the library that students scampered away in fear when they saw me approach my spot. Lest I stare daggers at them until they left and I could reclaim my tragic, depressing enclosure.

"Think of what shadows are. Then visualize your surroundings. Imagine sending a shadow straight from you to wherever you picture it in the environment."

Reaper's voice was my only distraction from school. My eyes drifted closed, and I imagined I was a thundercloud, shadows swirling around me.

I pictured a bolt of black lightning hitting the Reaper who stood before me, and shadows jutted out of me—

Until they dropped lifelessly to the ground a foot in front of him.

"Ugh!" I screamed. "Why won't it extend?"

"You're too calm. Imagine what riles you up," Reaper proposed.

"Think about your daydream of Reaper earlier," Gaksi suggested aloud.

My cheeks heated. "Gaksi!"

Untamed, my hair lifted with the force of shadows.

"Good," Reaper commented, blissfully ignoring Gaksi's last statement. "Emotions fuel shadows. Harness those and keep going."

I aimed left, and a shadow bolt hit right.

I aimed right, and a shadow bolt struck behind me.

I even stared at the sky, furious, while shadows seeped out of the surrounding earth.

Hail rained down, pattering against the students who didn't suspect it.

Focus on school. Concentrate emotions outside of school. See the shadows in your head, hold them, possess them, own them, and then spread them out. Direct them into streaks of energy, controlled bursts of power, manageable waves of mischief—

Control them.

Pick a start and an endpoint, then connect the dots.

Control the pathway.

Grab hold of your own power. Get it together. Don't feel

terror, don't feel anxiety, just do it correctly. Again, again, again.

CONTROL IT.

I made small talk with actives. Caught any minor demons that came my way. But the most grueling part of my day remained shadow training with Reaper.

Some days I fell asleep without even moisturizing and dealt with the aftereffects later.

My days fell into a routine of studying, training, and impressing at the expense of my health.

I was drained and stressed, and my skin deteriorated to show it.

I sat in a bath of bleach, wondering if I should start drinking it. I remembered the first time my doctor told my parents they should start adding bleach to my bathwater to kill the bacteria that worsened eczema symptoms.

Dad's horrified expression scared me.

My mother's face? Excited. Thrilled to try something new.

The doctor described it like a recipe. 1/4 cup bleach to every 40 gallons water. Dump the kid in, neck down (can't have her drinking any, boohoo), and let her soak for ten minutes. Then rinse, pat dry, and moisturize.

Never mind how I, the patient, felt about being surrounded by bleach and misery three times a week.

It had stung so badly the first time that I thought I might dissolve. However, mom had pushed me down until Gaksi whacked her with the shower curtain.

Now, as an adult, my bleach baths don't really hurt. Only smelled.

I expected this, my skin problems, to disappear as I got older.

For most people, it did.

But I'd never been most people.

Miserable, I texted Reaper out of the blue.

Luna: *Do souls have skin problems?*

Gaksi had added an unknown number to my phone last night. I called it, thinking he had finally caught up to modern technology, only for a baffled Reaper to answer instead. How Gaksi snuck a phone onto an ancient prince, I'd never know. Perhaps he collaborated with Mother somehow, and Reaper answered with the one my mother left in his palace.

I stared at my phone in the tub. Probably not a good idea to text in the bath, but I'd always done it. Maybe I'd drop it and never be stuck in a bath again.

I wasn't even done after this. On skincare day, it was bleach bath first. Moisturize second. Wet wraps third, depending on how bad the flare-ups were.

Fourth, I jabbed a needle filled with monoclonal antibodies in my stomach, which blocked the inflammation that worsened my symptoms the most. But only if I got up the courage to do it and not be labeled non-compliant. I was hopelessly, irrationally scared of needles, so injection day was by far the worst day of the week.

Maybe if I felt especially risky, I'd throw on some sunscreen before leaving the house.

Heaven forbid it was a chemical sunscreen, though, or I'd be back to tomato color for the rest of the week.

Luna: *When you transport souls to the other side, does their skin come with them?*

He was going to think I was insane. I was going to be mortified in the future that this was the first text I'd sent him. But I was in a horrible mood, and it wasn't like I could get this answer from anywhere else.

Luna: *Do souls have skin problems in the afterlife? Or are they free? What do they look like?*

Would I have to deal with this forever? Was there a future that excluded my problems and insecurities but included me? With no skin problems, where I finally look the same as everyone else? Would I finally be beautiful in death?

He responded after a long while.

Reaper: *Souls don't have bodies.*

Reaper: *And they are all beautiful in their own way. Just as they were in life.*

Hope swelled in my chest. One day, eventually, I wouldn't have to worry about this kind of stuff anymore.

Reaper: *Wishing for death is foolish when there are so many beautiful creatures to behold yet in life.*

A small, fragile part of me smiled when I saw that. His Highness was definitely referencing his own vanity, but maybe I'd be somebody's beautiful creature someday.

Provided my eczema was in check. And my shadows. A fearful, ashamed part of me worried they were linked and served as a punishment for some unknown crime.

It shouldn't still affect me. Almost everyone grew out of their eczema with age.

Not me.

Nothing ever went easily for me.

I scratched the back of my neck as I went up to the usual barren wasteland for training. My skin eruption stretched from one shoulder to another, and guessing by how tight and dry my face felt, it was likely all over that, too.

This was the worst I'd looked in weeks, and I had to skirt the edges of campus to avoid being seen.

"You're late."

Reaper's annoying, heartless voice rang out.

"I was trying to find an outfit that hid my entire body," I snapped.

My black turtleneck and jeans covered almost everything but my face, but each blink irritated me.

"Can this wait? I'm uncomfortable and stretched tight right now."

His eyes roamed my body, then settled on my face. Steel lined his gaze. "Demons are more likely to attack you if they sense you're weak prey. You need to learn how not to show how you feel."

"How can I not show it when it's all over my skin?" I burst out, crankier than I'd been in years.

"*Careful*," Gaksi warned. "*He is a prince.*"

"*Anyone with perfect skin can go off themself right about now.*"

"It's not the skin that's the problem," Reaper said. "It's the fidgeting. The scratching. The looking down at your feet and wearing clothes you don't even like. Demons can sense the lack of confidence, as can most of your classmates."

He stepped forward and cut through space. "Stay still," he murmured. His head leaned over me.

I was reminded of our bargain, where we were in this exact position.

But this time, his fingers brushed my hair aside, settling something heavy and cold along my neck. I think my heart stopped beating. He smirked, sensing my reaction to his nearness.

Deft hands clicked something behind me, and he drew back to assess. Hands rested on my shoulders.

"Divine," he breathed.

"Tortured," I responded, shoving him off. "What is this thing?"

I pretended I didn't see how much his face fell. "It's a magic amulet. Large enough for Gaksi to possess, small enough for you to wear every day. Thick enough to cover our bargain."

"Why are you giving me this?" I asked, unimpressed.

"It imbues the owner with confidence. Hold it when you need energy, and it'll remind you of your self-worth."

"How?" I was in no mood for presents, and this one sounded absolutely ridiculous.

"I filled it with my belief in you this morning."

"You believe I am your sworn enemy."

"I believe you could be. Or if not, I believe you could even be my friend."

Oh. Some of my earlier irritation dissolved. A softer feeling blossomed in my chest in its place. Was he being truthful?

"It's powered by emotions from dark magic. Gaksi can also fill it with his magic when mine runs out."

"Thank you," I said, voice quiet. I'd been ornery, and he appeared sincere enough, which meant I'd been rude to someone offering me a present.

He settled his hands on his hips, flexing his biceps. Even underneath his garments, I could see how muscular his frame was. I wondered what it would be like to run my hands down them, to feel what other parts of him were hard—

"Gawking at me is not part of your training."

A shadow of embarrassment burst from my skin, blocking the sky. Foolish emotions.

I clutched the necklace like a lifeline.

"It won't control your shadows for you. But think of it like a grounding point and imagine your shadows centering there before spreading out."

I closed my eyes and imagined all the tingling, hesitant energy lines in my body moving to one place. They traveled from my toes to my ankles, up my chest, and settled eventually at the amulet above my heart. When I opened my eyes, the black center swirled amidst neon blue lights.

"Well done, Luna!" Gaksi cheered.

I glimpsed Reaper for a second before a shadow wrapped around my ankles, knocking me flat on my behind in the frigid snow.

"Fight me," Reaper said, dragging me by my ankles toward him, creating divots from my body in the ice. "Show me the worst you can do with your training."

I held my arm out and envisioned a shadow launching straight from my heart, curling up my arm, and dragging Reaper down by the waist until he landed on top of me. I waited until I'd been dragged close enough to him for it to work and then wrenched my arm down.

A shadow tendril shoved Reaper from behind, and he landed between my thighs on the snow.

Success!

Before I could summon another, he'd sprung forward, pinning my hands over my head.

Hot.

Too hot, this demon at my front, with the biting cold in the back.

The emotional rollercoaster made it even more successful.

From this angle, I could see the hard planes of his face. The way his eyes darkened and his full lips pressed together. His weight settled over his hips, and he restrained my wrists tighter. I willed my face not to heat.

"Tell me, seraphim, what advantage do you think this position can give you? The shadow work was your best yet, but for what end?"

His lips brushed my ear, his breath warm. "I can't say I'm disappointed, but—"

I gripped my legs around his back and flipped him to the side. Shadows twisted around his neck.

I said from on top, our fiery bodies flushed together, "I knew the advantage of you being easily distracted." My shadows dove around his neck like a chain, and I imagined them pinning themselves to the frost, locking him down. More of my shadows rose around his ankles and wrists, too, and he watched with a darkened gaze as they pinned him in place.

"I assumed you'd be too busy looking at my pretty face to notice the shadows I'd grown like vines from the ground. Like how you pinned Lukas all those months ago."

He eyed my amulet, looking amused by its instant effect on my mood.

"Word of advice, seraphim, few men want to speak of other men while their partner has them chained and in position."

A scowl crossed my face. "I wouldn't need that advice, though, would I? Because this is only a training position, and we are only *friends*." I emphasized the last word, which I knew would drive him crazy.

Based on the way my shadows ripped in two, I was right.

He rose, pulling me up along his body. "Friends don't tease friends like this, sultry seraphim."

"I'm too hot to be your friend, anyway," I said.

I stepped back, visualizing him in my head. In my mind, he was falling back into the Beyond, confidence swirling in his shadows, performing a teleportation he'd done a thousand times. Dazzling my heart, gracefully vanishing into the deep.

When my step finished in my dorm room, I knew I'd done it.

Teleportation!

I clutched my blanket to my heart that night, giggling and kicking my feet because I just did all that and flirted with the Reaper the whole time.

CHAPTER
TWENTY-ONE

THE ORACLE MUSINGS

*M*ade any friends yet? Data from years of crunching recruitment numbers revealed that the more friends a freshman has, the more favorably she's looked upon by Houses, who view it as a sign of social status to be charismatic. An unlikely friendship will form today, though if it is the result of charisma is unclear even to this Oracle.

I WAS STUDYING at the library when I heard a horrifying screech. The sound reverberated through the space above me, capturing my attention and sending a jolt of fear through my heart.

"Samjoko!" I gasped, eyes widened with respect and reverence. Hastily, I dropped into a deep bow, surprised by the intrusion. Reaper's three-legged crow perched precariously on a light fixture above my head.

"Caw!" she squealed.

I whipped my phone out for a photo before I forgot. She didn't seem to mind and even ruffled out her feathers, posing them just so. "This is not a photo shoot, your highness," I said disapprovingly, but secretly, I was thrilled. "Did Reaper send you?" I held up my phone, sending photos to The Eternal via Bluetooth without losing sight of her.

Flora: *Cute bird. The hell does it have to do with me?*
Luna: *I saw her with the Reaper! Look at the three legs!*

Three dots popped up. Then disappeared, then reappeared, then disappeared again.

Flora: *How do you know it's a her?*

"It's a her," Gaksi affirmed. I didn't know how I knew that, though. It just felt right.

Luna: *Gaksi said so!*
Flora: *Eyes on the other demon, fish. Unless you want to end up sleeping with the fishes.*

What in the Beyond was it doing here? I glanced back up at where she sat. The crow focused her eyes on me like a smirk. With a tap, its *pastel pink* talons rapped against the light fixture. I choked.

"Thief!"

Forget respect. How did it get access to my limited edition Chanel polish? I'd been missing it since recruitment started!

"How did you get into my room? What do you want?" I demanded. The bird fluffed her wings, unperturbed.

"Where's my nail polish?"

No response.

"You're suspicious." The crow blinked in affirmation.

What do I do about this? I couldn't kill it. And the portal to the Beyond was so far away. And it had been in my room! My safe space! How did it even get in? My hands clenched into fists. Why did I even bother trying to study when I had to deal with nonsense like this?

Having Reaper in and out of my room was enough!

"How did you allow this, Gaksi?"

"She asked so nicely. We demons have little options in the way of accessorizing." His tone was amused, as usual.

"This isn't over." I threatened the sun god with a wag of my finger.

Without a further word, I fled.

In the Barren Fields, Reaper set up an obstacle course. I scaled fake cliffs, landed on my shadows as a cushion, then jumped between moving obstacles.

When I called him nearly as evil as Lukas, he added fire to the mix.

"I didn't injure him badly enough," Reaper said, hurling ebony fire at me. "He was only leaning on you after our first encounter because he enjoyed being touched and cared for by a pretty woman."

"Don't be ridiculous," I responded. "He was bleeding all over that time!" I dodged a blast of flame. "And how did you even see that? I thought you disappeared?"

A ghost of a smile lined Reaper's stern features. "He could have healed himself. Sirens possess mending magic."

"That's something an abuser would say." I retorted. "'Yeah, it doesn't matter that I hit her. She can heal herself.' As I spoke, I made finger quotes with my hands, and he narrowed his eyes.

"Whatever kind of finger magic you're using right now, it's not working."

"It's not magic. It's quotations!" I replied, annoyed.

"And you didn't answer my questions. How did you see what happened after you left, and how could you pretend Lukas wasn't even that injured?"

"You only asked the second question just now."

"And are you going to respond?"

"Sam collects info for me." Reaper shrugged. "She's nosy, like Gaksi. And I knew Lukas wasn't that injured because if I wanted him to be, he would be."

"That's sick," I responded.

Reaper raised a brow. "Didn't realize you were so attached to him."

"At least he started off nice," I said.

Reaper smiled and shook his head. "Nice enough to hit on his own student?"

I shook my head, ducking under a torrent of fire. "He was only a couple of years older than me."

"But dumb enough to ask you if you were a freshman in a freshman-level class," Gaksi interrupted.

"Maybe I'll find a spell to banish you permanently to the other side," I threatened, hopping over the blue fire bursting at my feet.

"Is that why the Samjoko visited me at the library yesterday?" I asked.

"Yes, she's my spymaster," Reaper replied.

I slipped at the admission, skidding to the ground.

Reaper ceased firing, extinguishing any remaining flames on the earth. "You should take this seriously. Don't you have any battle training coming up?"

"They mostly leave that to the Houses since it's magic specific." I sat up, only to meet his disapproving stare.

"So you receive no fight training at all? They just send you out with textbook knowledge?"

"I take an elective in dagger throwing." He circled shadows around my waist, lifting me from the floor.

"You need to take that elective seriously." Cool shadows swirled around my waist, unwilling to let go.

"Why?" I asked.

"There are vicious creatures out there," Reaper said, serious, despite his shadow extensions tickling my midriff. "They might come after you if they detect traces of me on yourself."

"Leave me then," I said, pushing his shadows off with my own.

He threw one of my daggers at me, which I caught midair with a shadow hand. "Can't leave the most vicious creature of all, now, can I?"

That damn bird showed up so often I fought with it in my delirium.

When I walked to class, I saw it hopping between trees.

On my way to the gym, it spied like a creep through the window.

My hands had to hover protectively over my food in the Cornucopia lest she fly down and eat it straight off my plate.

At midnight tonight, it plopped down in my seat in the library, daring me to fight it.

I tipped the chair, throwing it off.

"Sun god, huh? I'm the moon. Come back in the morning. It's my turn now."

Sam had the audacity to look flabbergasted.

"What? Are you going to complain to Reaper? Report back all my activities? Tell him I need to study! And vanish through the portal, with witnesses, while you're at it. I need more points."

The crow blinked, then pecked me with a sharp beak. "Ow!"

I rubbed the peck as it cackled and flew away.

The next time, Sam was actually minding her business and sat above my usual seat. But I hated being stared at, or even monitored, while I worked until the late hours of the night. I directed my hand to the window. "Out."

It squinted at the window, eyeballed me, then flipped a page of its book.

"Don't make me feud with you. Is there no more valuable use of your time right now? Don't you have any powers to wield?"

She straightened out, glowing faintly red-gold, as the temperature escalated several levels. Rays beamed from her like she was the rising sun.

"Good, you're a heater. Begone now."

Her wings snapped in with a crack. The heat abruptly vanished.

"Now you've done it," Gaksi warned. *"She's vicious when she's angry."*

"But not as vicious as me," I retorted. I stood up on my tiptoes so I was level with the crow engrossed in a copy of *Twilight: Breaking Dawn*. "I'm prettier than you," I whispered.

"*Caw?*" She slammed the book closed with her wings. "That's why Reaper sends you to stalk me and not the other way around."

A deep chuckle sounded behind me, igniting my mood in the otherwise somber stacks. "Speak of the devil," I muttered.

"Don't bully my bird," his raspy voice chided. "She once held a favorable opinion of you."

"The girls are fighting!" Gaksi announced from the bookend. The crow knocked it off the table with the viciousness of a cat and a table salt on a countertop.

Reaper approached, and his face in the dark night was... absolutely flawless.

My heart thrummed. Every part of my body heated, warmed with the possibility of getting closer, flushed with anticipation of what we could do alone in the library...

His lips turned up, catching me daydreaming. Reaper's long, thin hands flipped a blade between them, juggling it without effort.

"This is a strange place," Reaper mused.

He was one to talk. "How so?"

"The way administrators here hoard magic and make children compete for it... is rather sadistic."

Sadistic. That was exactly how I'd describe the clock tower to any other student, but I felt defensive right now, with my University under attack by an onlooker.

"It's orderly. Everyone gets an equal chance to be whoever they want to be."

Reaper's voice was laced with condescension. "Do they? Or do they get forced into the same House their parents were in?"

Legacies were preferred in every House's process, but that was beside the point.

"Being... gently pushed into something is a lot better than born something you never wanted to be. Than having rogue fairytale creatures and humans intermingling."

He slid the dagger into a sheath, then presented it to me. It was one of mine. I must have dropped it during practice.

"More like a dangle of hope for something they could never achieve. And given that you, mischievous one, are currently a mortal among immortals, it doesn't seem like these 'fairy-tale' creatures have separated much from humans at all."

"Wouldn't you have wanted the option to choose? "

"I make questionable choices every day," he said, pulling me forward by a lock of hair.

I grabbed a fistful of his hair in return, and, at his overjoyed expression, yanked it toward the other side of the library, where an ancient map of the island hung.

"What are the green spots on the map?"

I'd been staring at it for hours between studying sessions and had nobody else to question. If I didn't figure it out, I might go crazy.

He waved my hands off his head. "That is the garden of prosperity. Magic created fruit so sweet it rivaled candy, trees that reached to heaven, and animals so wild they would delight any zoologist. That's what you study, isn't it?"

"Yeah. I like learning about exotic animals and otherworldly creatures," I said, mind wandering to the zoo I spent most of my time in on campus.

"I must be fascinating to you, then."

Charmer. "Don't flatter yourself. What happened to the garden?"

The maps we covered in our history class only mentioned it as the Barren Fields.

"Take a guess."

"Demons razed it to the earth?"

He snorted. "That's the impression they want to give."

"As opposed to what?"

"I know the past of this place well enough. You mortals

can barely keep a memory alive for more than one generation without someone else rewriting it."

"The memory of what? Some magic paradise? Forgive me if that seems a little far-fetched."

"You can figure it out, shrewd seraphim. Don't let me down."

REAPER BECAME scarce as weeks passed. Sam, the most visible shadow I had, followed me from place to place. I complained to Reaper via text, and he said he couldn't control her whereabouts. No proper conversations passed between us. Day after day, I had peace from him, save for the occasional message. It was actually kind of relaxing. I fell into the familiar patterns of school, studying, resting instead of shadow training, then to bed. I even looked forward to Sam's familiar flap of wings. It was nice to have company that wasn't of the handsome variety.

So when Reaper stopped responding altogether, I felt an uncomfortable pit in my stomach. I checked my phone a couple more times throughout the day. Nothing. Empty.

What's up? I almost texted. I deleted it before I hit send. One didn't just greet the carrier of corpses with *What's Up?* I wasn't a sleazy siren. *What's up?* was what you texted to an ex at witching hour after one too many seltzers.

So... how do I contact him? Should I? My thumb tapped my phone screen as if that would bring him back. It was 4 P.M. He always texted me by 4 P.M. It was right after my last class let out.

Are you alive? I almost sent.

Stars, that was worse. Had he ever been alive? Could he be alive? Or was he like an undead ghost? Maybe I'd ask him that. Take a couple of shots and start getting nosy with my knowledge gaps.

"Maybe you should get a hobby," Gaksi suggested, "other than stalking your boyfriend."

"My whom? He's not a boy. Not even a friend!"

"I heard the panic in your thoughts there," Gaksi countered.

"I'm busy," I told him and busied myself with cleaning my apartment instead.

I'd compiled such a stockpile of information about Reaper that Flora wasn't a concern, but it left me wanting.

Where was he?

Worry churning in my stomach, I decided on one last text.

Luna: *Are you okay?*

Please respond. What if he wasn't? What if he needed me right now? Reaper lived by an organized, dutiful schedule. If something was amiss, it must be horribly serious...

Reaper: *...*

Reaper: *...*

Luna: *Do you need a rescuer?*

If I brought Gaksi, I could probably intervene in whatever situation he became trapped in. Worry somersaulted in my gut, matching the torrent of emotions in my soul.

Reaper's response catapulted my spirit.

Reaper: *No, but you might after I tell your mother you're so devoted to me.*

I almost collapsed laughing. He—I—would be alright.

CHAPTER
TWENTY-TWO

THE ORACLE MUSINGS

Hoarding secrets is no fun. Sharing secrets means you've won. How do you make even the most serious of men sweat? Alcohol, bets, and a delicious game they'll never forget.

Flora: *I need something against Reaper I can actually use.*
  Luna: *What do you mean?*
  Flora: *Hopes? Fears? Dreams?*
  Luna: *Why do you need those?*
  Flora: *Hopes direct his current motivations. Fears show if there's anyone stronger than him he's afraid of. We can interpret dreams as either an indicator he sleeps (a vulnerable position), or how corrupt his ambitions are.*

No wonder Flora led the Fae. She was clever at getting key info out of people. I supposed that when other faeries couldn't lie, you had to subtly ask them the right questions to get them to spill.

I released a sigh. I'd need to catch at least three demons, and it usually took me a week just to chase down one.

"How am I going to get so much out of him at once?" I asked Cordelia.

We studied on adjacent hammocks together on the Diamond. Gaksi had cast a sound barrier around our blanket so that our conversation was private, while we got to enjoy people-watching in public. Bicyclists rode by, students threw frisbees above, and birds sang. Midday, it felt so peaceful and free. So... university. If I never got entangled in this mess, would my life be this serene?

"Maybe you should get him to play strip poker," Cordelia swooned. "Then you can at least learn more about his body."

"Stars, Cordelia! How would I even suggest that?" I sputtered.

"Start stripping?"

"While I'm catching a demon? Should I ask the lost virgin ghost to join too?"

"Yeah, keep it spicy."

We dissolved into giggles.

Cordelia stopped laughing first, which was out of character for her. Usually, she was the silly one I had to reel in. Her face indicated that her next prompt was serious.

"You should ask him out on a date."

My jaw dropped. "What? He's off limits!"

Cordelia frowned, as if she'd forgotten. "Keep it undercover."

"Cordelia, I'm only doing this because I have to! I can't make a dangerous situation any worse than it already is!"

I collapsed onto the blanket, remembering how badly I

was treated when the oracle implied we were dating. If I went through with this, that meant she was right. I couldn't give her the satisfaction.

"Yeah, but if you're already stuck with him, you might as well have some fun," Cordelia prompted.

"I'm not sure a date with him would be fun," I said. Reckless, sure. Interesting, absolutely. Memorable? Undoubtably. But if my recent Beyond adventure was our last date, I shuddered to think what he would follow that one up with.

"Well, there's only one way to find out!" Cordelia pushed.

"Cordelia, I have to be responsible. My standing and reputation at this University are at stake." Just thinking about the hours I spent studying this week made me nauseous.

Sparks flew in Cordelia's eyes. "Just go on one date with him to get information. Bring some alcohol to loosen him up. Get dressed up, and get enough info to placate Flora for a while!"

I forced my eyes shut, haunted. "I've never, in my eighteen years of living, found a human man to go on a date with me. How am I supposed to get the Reaper to do so?"

"Just ask him!"

Heavens above, she sounded just like Gaksi. I bet he gave her the script for this conversation. Maybe I should get better friends.

"What if he says no?" I asked quietly. Cordelia swatted my arm. "Hey!"

She rubbed it reassuringly. "He's already admitted that he finds you attractive. And I feel like you don't give yourself enough credit. You could have a lot more in life if you just went for it."

Her hope in me was unwarranted. "You sound like my mother."

"Maybe she has some brilliant advice you've been putting off."

My face scrunched. "Maybe you give her too much credit, too."

"You're deflecting," Cordelia said. "Just admit that you're scared—"

"I am not scared—"

"Your fear doesn't involve *him*. You're scared of your feelings being hurt!"

I scowled and crossed my arms, sitting up. "I think I'll go study by myself now."

"Yeah, keep running from your problems. It's not like he'll be back for you, regardless."

My lips clamped shut. There was nothing worse than your closest friend knowing your soul far better than she should.

Regarding Reaper, I should be fearful of him. My feet should hit the ground running at his presence. Anxiety should fill my heart whenever I thought of the bond he snared me in.

I shouldn't be thinking of which types of soju he'd like best.

MY SCALP PRICKLED. I resisted the urge to stare.

Reaper appeared in the brewery I'd drawn my latest wraith to. I sat at a white linen-coated table set for two, surrounded by stacks of alcohol. I opened two bottles of soju in front of me, but I hadn't drank any yet. Once I saw Reaper, his presence would intoxicate me enough.

There was nothing more venomous to my future than his smile.

I held out a chalice. "Care for a drink?"

Reaper paused, eyes widened.

Why ask him on a date when I could bring the date to him? I silenced the voice in my head that told me how awkward this was. Setting the candles, the fae lights, and the table in advance made the date guaranteed to happen. This way, he could never reject me. And my fragile little heart could remain intact for a while longer.

His gaze lingered on the alcohol. "Are you drunk?"

I might as well be. The intensity of his gaze made me want to drown in liquor.

"Stone cold sober." I waved the drink at him. "Come sit down and play with me." I gestured to the playing cards I set on the table.

He pulled a chair out slowly. Sat. Took the drink from me and downed it. The muscles in his neck flexed, capturing my attention. Noticing my blatant stare, he dragged the bottle away. "You've had enough."

My cheeks flushed. Well, that was rude. Especially because it was inaccurate.

He flicked his wrist behind him. The ghost disappeared.

This wasn't going well. My mind raced, searching for a way to capture his attention.

"I made a deal with Gaksi."

He raised his eyebrows.

My hands flexed uncomfortably under the table. I swallowed hard and continued. "I made a deal with Gaksi. Just one date, and he would stop hounding me about dating for the rest of the year."

"So..." I released a breath. "Please stay. For Gaksi." Not for me. Never for me. Despite the pit of my stomach screaming, begging for him to stay. He was like a puzzle, and I wanted to put him together, handling every part of him until he was complete.

A smile lit up his face. His eyes twinkled as if my discomfort amused him.

"Very well, sweet seraphim." He returned the soju I set out and poured it into my glass first, then into his own.

"I thought I'd had enough?" I asked.

"You've never had enough of me, have you?" He chuckled. "Why would alcohol be any different?"

With no suitable response to that, I took my first sip. It burned, in a good way. Like a wound that pushed you forward in its agony.

He fingered the cards. "Let's play, then."

Reaper shuffled the cards, used magic to suspend them midair, then whipped them around themselves in a frenzy.

"Show off," I teased. He winked.

His shadows reached out, tenderly, cautiously, dealing me my cards.

"Stakes?" Reaper asked.

"Secrets," I replied. "What else?"

Cordelia would be disappointed it wasn't clothes. She would survive.

"Deal," Reaper responded. "Do you know how to play blackjack?"

That was specific. I'd studied the rules of poker before this, assuming that was what he'd want to play. Poker just seemed like a demonic game to me.

"Yes," I responded. Gaksi taught me all kinds of card games as a kid. For counting practice. Whoever got closer to 21 wins.

It was a game of push and pull. Push too hard, and you

got a high final tally and lost. Pull back too far, and you didn't have nearly enough.

"Good," Reaper said. Then he snapped, and the cards flipped.

I told him to deal and deal again, and my eagerness resulted in a house win.

I grimaced and took another hit of soju. This wasn't going well so far.

Reaper leaned over the table, deep voice steady. "Why does Gaksi want you to go on a date?"

I inhaled. Might as well rip off the band-aid.

I answered evenly, even though my insides were quaking. "Because he knows I'm lonely."

Reaper remained expressionless. Which was good, because I could never handle the shame of him thinking I was defective.

"Elaborate," he pressed. Perhaps it was the alcohol or the comforting shawl of his shadows, but the words burst through me.

"Because I am lonely. I have been for a while. Mom's whole life is her children, so whenever I messed up, it's like she took it personally as a failure of her parenting. So I avoided her out of my fear of failure, and my only real companion became Gaksi, which meant I had to be homeschooled because I refused to go anywhere without him. Despite my excitement to meet new people at Aether, Cordelia and Aubrey are my only friends. Everyone else is just more competition. An adversary waiting to happen. I was always on the defensive growing up, waiting for my mom to find some new flaw in me, for someone at cheer practice to treat me like garbage, or for Gaksi to push me too far, and I think my inherent standoffishness impedes me making real friends."

My spirit howled. I'd never spoken that much in one setting, let alone been that vulnerable with anybody. I finished my glass. The shadows tipped the soju, refilling it for me.

Reaper was silent, brow furrowed. I could tell he was deep in thought, but thankfully, he only re-dealt. I won. Thankfully. I needed a break.

"What's your greatest fear?" There. It was a two-way street; if I opened up, he should too. Karma.

He swirled his chalice absentmindedly. "I won't bring my kingdom back to where it used to be." He took a sip.

"Elaborate," I enccuraged, repeating his own words back to him.

"My job has been relatively static for years. Transport souls, do whatever odd tasks my father requests of me, but all that has been upset recently. The veil weakened, the gumiho jumped out, and I've been here for months without any real leads. My father already thinks of me as a failed prince. An unworthy, dishonorable child. Eventually, my kingdom will share the same belief. They already think I am a rather young and foolhardy prince as it is."

His lip curled in disgust. So he was insecure then, too. I wondered how many dead souls lived in his kingdom. Were there consequences to them disliking him? Or was it like an honor thing? That he took it personally when he was disliked? We had that in common.

Perhaps I should not have called him worthless earlier...

He dealt another hand.

Seven and three for me, which made ten. I've already gotten here. Might as well make the night memorable and *push*.

"Again."

One.

"Again."

Seven.

"Again."

"You're bold." He glanced at me over the cards. "You know, I have a personal question waiting for you next. If you lose, I get to ask." He smiled at me like I was a meager fly, trapped in a mastermind spider's web.

"Again," I repeated. I wasn't afraid. What was he going to do, try to kill me again? He'd never succeeded.

Three.

"Blackjack!" I shouted, slamming my hands down on the table.

He cleared his throat. "Go on then."

I pursed my lips for a moment, thinking.

How should I ask him what his biggest hopes were? I could ask, 'What are your hopes and dreams in life?' but that sounded ridiculous.

What do you want out of life? That might work. Except I didn't know if he was alive or something in between.

"If you had one wish, what would it be?" I asked.

Surprise flickered in his eyes. "Do you have wishes to grant?"

"Yes, in my magic lamp," I answered sarcastically. "Answer the question."

"So demanding," he murmured. He stared off into the distance. "That I could tell the future."

"Why?" I asked.

"So I could know when I'm free of this... date." He said it in jest, with his eyes crinkled.

"I'm not answering seriously if you don't." I took another sip. I knew he was teasing, but I wanted him to be honest. "From now on, can we promise not to lie to each other?"

He regarded me thoughtfully before nodding. "If I knew how this would play out, I could save us a lot of trouble." His twinkling eyes met mine. "I could look down on the rest of humanity, much like how I imagine your oracle does. I'd know that everything I do is meaningful and isn't just being swept away. I'd know that my work has meaning, and I'm not just throwing all my efforts into nothing."

He sounded so... defeated. Was he permanently tired, being an immortal? Forced to work forever with no end in sight?

I reached out my hand, tapping his. He startled, but let me hold it. I ran my thumb in small circles on his palm. "You're too hard on yourself." That was what a good date would say, right? Never mind that my hand felt so small and warm in his.

His thumb brushed the back of my hand in return. He slanted forward, bringing his knees to brush mine. "Is this a strategy of yours?" he said. "Touch and distract me so that it's easier for you to win?"

I drew our conjoined hands together, pressing a chaste kiss to his hand. The alcohol was making me extra adventurous tonight. Beneath the table, he couldn't see my ankles cross and uncross with my nervousness. "Yes."

He laughed. Rubbing comforting circles into my hand, he retreated into his seat, pulling away. "Next round, then."

He dealt. I pushed until I felt ready, then told him to flip.

I won again. He cursed.

A shadow crossed over his face. One that I had begun to recognize. Eyes bright, smile wide. Trouble. Lust. Disaster.

Reaper released my hand, then stood and strode over. Soft thuds of his feet echoed in the glass bottles of the brewery. Chimes sounded with every step.

When he was beside me, he tilted my chin up with two fingers. "Look at me."

I did.

"You wore my gift." He slid his hand down the arch of my neck, hooking beneath my necklace. My pulse thrummed like a drumbeat beneath his fingers. He moved them aside and replaced the elegant necklace with his lips, lingering longest in the center and moving to his mark.

He sucked lightly on my skin. I fought the urge to swallow. Or faint. Or pass out.

"If you get to play dirty, I do too."

His teeth grazed my neck as he withdrew. Shadows emerged into a newer, grander seat beneath him, right beside me instead of across the table. "Ask your question."

Time to push one last time, before I lost all my nerve. I took a deep breath to steady myself. "What do you dream of?"

His arm dropped behind my back, tracing my spine. "I dream of a great many things."

"Answer the question," I said, blood rushing.

"Are your own dreams not variable?" he asked, fingers dancing around my collarbone.

"Yes, but I didn't lose." I stuck my tongue out at him. He fixated on it for too long before I pulled it back in.

His hands slip up to cup my face. "I always dream of what I shouldn't have. Freedom. Peace."

Still vague. I wanted to goad him, but his shadows billowed around him, pulsing and throbbing with anger, like a storm might erupt if I triggered them.

"I dream of what I have always desired." He set his pupils, which darkened, back on me.

He couldn't possibly mean me, did he?

But he was staring at me like he did. Like a man starved of air, and I was his only oxygen.

"Would Gaksi expect a kiss to finish a first date?" His nose brushed mine. Now it was I who needed air.

I should say no. I should pull back, accept the information I have received, and report back to Flora like the docile, virtuous girl I should be.

But you don't win blackjack by pulling back.

"Yes," I dared.

He swept me up in capable arms, stealing my breath away. He pressed his lips to mine, shocking me with the electrifying intensity. His kiss was raw. Exploratory. Passionate. Sparks flew so brightly, I'd kissed no one before, but I never needed to kiss another again.

I wanted... more.

When he pulled back, I pushed forward. When I returned his kiss, one of his hands tightened around my shoulders, moving my lips in a tender rhythm against him, igniting every corner of my soul.

When his tongue parted my lips, I receded.

That's enough, I thought. If this went any further, I didn't know if I'd ever stop. First, his tongue would be in my mouth, then mine in his, then I'd be begging him to put it all over me...

Reaper's face was stricken. Devoted. Devastated.

"Was that—a good date?"

His hesitation broke my heart. "Yes," I said, placing my hands on his cheeks and kissing his nose.

"If you weren't forbidden, I would do it all over again."

CHAPTER
TWENTY-THREE

THE ORACLE MUSINGS

Revealed: Hunter and Co. will be training on the Diamond today, shirtless, for anyone who cares to see. And I would certainly care to see that pretty boy very much, abhorrent personality aside.

Dallying with any man is a form of sickness in itself.

"Was it a good kiss?"

I nearly leaped out of bed. When I returned home last night, a silver twin bed inlaid with jewels rested against my window. A glossy marble desk faced the other side, and an oak bookshelf sat empty on the far wall. I'd thanked the stars for Gaksi's refurnishing, slid between the downy sheets of my new bed, and slept like the dead.

"Mind your business, Gaksi." My stomach flipped, sickness stirring within.

"Oh, it's everyone's business, girl. All the demons in the Beyond are chattering," Gaksi said.

I rubbed my eyes. "What?"

Did he tell people? Bile rose to my throat. I threw back my sheets, hurtled across the clean floor to my bathroom, and retched.

"Many of them are quite loyal to Reaper," Gaksi said, voice trailing in my necklace. "It brings them joy to see him succeed."

Strands of energy pulled my hair back, preventing the worst of the vomit from spreading as I fought my hangover—and regret—over the toilet.

I was glad the demons felt joyful. Someone should be able to see hope in my idiocy, amusement in my audacity. "Why wouldn't they be loyal to their prince? Has he done anything wrong?"

Had *he* ever faced the consequences of his own mistakes the morning after?

Gaksi swiped the light on, illuminating the room. "No. He spends all his time catering to them, then absorbing the wrath of humanity for their mistakes."

Last night Reaper feared his kingdom would think of him as dishonorably as his father did. An unexpected burst of rage slammed into me. How dare his father make him think so little of himself? When he worked so tirelessly for his kingdom?

Another wave of nausea hit, and I vomited.

Could immortals feel sickness?

"Dr. Ansi said that all demons came here to harass and sicken humanity."

Luna Deokhye, exhibit A.

"Harass," Gaksi scorned. "Do you feel harassed by me?"

"Yes."

My hair collapsed back around my face, sticking to my emissions. "Hey!"

I eased away, careful not to pick up any of the vomit on the side of the toilet, and reclined onto the tile floor.

"Now, that's harassment," Gaksi chortled. "Unlike Aether's perceptions, not all demons were formed in the Beyond before coming here. Many were created in this universe and hold no ill will to humans. They're just lost and wandering."

My mind went back to the ghosts. They didn't even seem like they knew how to attack. They just... floated. But why would school teach us that all unhoused demons were inherently evil?

Why kill all of them if some were harmless?

I supposed if they were never alive, it wasn't really killing.

Recognition suddenly hit me. "Is that why you like him? Was someone about to kill you? Or were you lost?"

"No," he answered. "I was very much present."

My necklace flickered out.

The smell of the campus zoo enveloped me like a lover, excrement and syrupy light magic swirling. I loved it here.

I spent at least one day a week feeding, cleaning, or studying the mythical and regular creatures that lived here for school. Just last week, I finished my report on the mechanics of flying versus grounded pigs. Sometimes, I even engaged in unplanned side quests, indulging a pegasus for a ride. For enough carrots, I could coax one to soar high above the tree line, granting me a captivating view of the entire zoo and its inhabitants.

Today, Joseph danced at me, performing just past the guest entrance. Jonah, the sullen brother, only stared at me from beyond the gate. When my brothers said they wanted to visit, I could think of no better place.

Mythical and regular animals roamed their exhibits, eyeing students and visitors as they walked by. I stopped to feed a sheep-growing vegetable plant before I reached my siblings, letting the excited animals nibble gratefully. The true magic of this place was that when visitors, like family members, left the premises, they'd only remember the sheep and vegetables separately. Conversations were edited so that they would make sense from any university, and the truth remained seamlessly hidden.

When I reached them, Joseph locked me in a hug, and Jonah patted me gently on the back.

"Sister!" Joseph yelled, unable to contain his enthusiasm.

"Luna," Jonah greeted, bored.

"Brothers of unnatural height," I teased. Even though they were in high school, they towered over me, which was a horrible trait for little brothers to possess.

"You've been gone a long time," Joseph accused. He was Jonah's slightly younger twin, albeit polar opposite attitude. "Has anything tried to kill you yet?"

"Good to see you too, Joseph."

Jonah stalked away to the griffin exhibit, clearly annoyed by Joseph's antics. Even as kids, they always needed ten feet of space between them, with me serving as the dutiful buffer.

"That's evading the question," Joseph pressed, his curiosity evident.

Wings flapped ahead of us, showing the eagle-headed, lion-bodied griffins landing from flight.

"Yeah, they have tried to kill me," I confessed.

With bird feed in hand, Joseph reached into the exhibit, only for a sharp beak to snap at him.

"They want meat, Joseph," Jonah said, handing him a piece of jerky. "Use your brain."

"No, you use your brain!"

The griffins inched forward, eyeing them both with interest. It was just as Professor Ansi said. Any discordance or bickering drew the ire of demons, who sought to strike at your most vulnerable.

"Well, why are you still here, then?" Jonah asked, dodging Joseph's attempts to snatch his jerky.

"Because they didn't succeed," I said.

I was struck by how true that statement was. Everything I'd gone through so far, and I was not afraid to talk about it. Because I survived.

"Do you even like being in a place where you could die all the time?" Joseph asked.

"It has its benefits." My friends. Learning new things. Shadow training and not hiding.

Watching them whirl around each other, a pang of homesickness almost overwhelmed me. I missed seeing my siblings grow up. It was lonesome, watching them fight from the sides when just a few months ago, I would have joined in.

"You're frowning. Are you lying?" Jonah asked.

He'd always been the most like dad. The smart one, the observant, astute one.

"No... it's just different, realizing you guys are growing up without me."

And I was growing up without them. Forging my path, fine-tuning my identity... I'd done more personal growth in these past months than I had in my entire life.

"Do you want to drop out, then?" Jonah continued.

"No!" At their confused faces, I went on. "I never thought... that I could love college enough to see it as my haven."

My home. My hearth. My haven or my haunt, depending on who I was speaking to.

"I really feel like... I hate to admit it, but Mom was right. Aether is where I'm meant to be."

A griffin plummeted down, aiming for a snack, and I caught it by the neck. Joseph and Jonah stared at me in shock as I redirected the wriggling beast, thankful for my honed reflexes.

After checking to see that nobody besides family was around, I sent my shadows along the enclosure line, feeling for the break, then slammed the griffin back through. It let out a squeak of consternation as it tumbled back into its enclosure.

When I hugged my siblings goodbye at the exit, I had no regrets.

If I wanted to give up, now would be the time. I could go home with my siblings, and it would be like I never came. I'd save myself before round two of recruitment, where cuts would be the most intense. Eliminate myself before the competition did. That way, I would never have to feel the weight of my failure.

My shadows writhed with the thought. Ditching was the safe option. The path of least destruction and most stability.

An explosion of shadows wouldn't end with my expulsion. My skin could bask in its hideous glory. In an online school, Luna Deokhye would be perfectly sequestered from the comfort of home.

But my mother would always know I gave up. And she would be disappointed, and I would never feel the shoddy warmth of her half-baked approval again. Even if I ran from her physical presence, I could never hide from her spying reach, her lingering effects on my psyche.

Yet a smaller part of me thought that maybe... my mom was actually right. That I needed to prove I belonged here. That I wanted to be here. And amidst the chaos, uncertainty, and peril, I would miss this place if I were to leave.

I didn't need to go home. I already was.

CHAPTER
TWENTY-FOUR

THE ORACLE MUSINGS

I foresee a grand showdown tonight!

Evil always comes in threes, regardless of gender. On one side of the ring, we have our testosterone-fueled fae heir, second-year repeat, and school crybaby. On the other, we have mommy issues, orphan issues, and abandonment issues (what abandonment issues, you ask? To be continued in a later column).

Who will get the most points after a heated night? May the best trio win!

Spring Equinox was always "Balance Day."

It was the one day a year when the university opened all portals they knew of and aimed the demons coming through at ourselves.

Affectionately nicknamed "cleanup day," it eliminated a sizable chunk of the humanity-curious demon population on our campus before they could spread.

Balance out the population, as you will, on the day of equal balance between day and night.

Seniors saw it as their last day of glory before heading out into the real world, where they were unlikely to encounter more than one or two more demons in their lifetime.

Freshmen saw it as their last chance to prove themselves to a House.

It was the deadliest day of the year, but not for us.

It was the day predators learned what it was like to be prey.

"You've reviewed all the books, right?" Audrey asked. She was staring up at the sky, ready to rumble. She surpassed me in points last night, and her competitive streak demanded she ended up on top today. There were only five points between her and Hunter, and then she'd be at the top of the class.

"Yeah. I doubt there's anything that could surprise me tonight." I tightened the boots on my laces. "Run away from anything crazy," Aubrey added. "You can always go back for the kill in a couple of years when you have House magic on your side."

"Agreed." She hugged me goodbye. "I'll see you after tonight."

Another set of arms hugged from behind. I turned around once she released me. "Good luck out there. Call me if you need anything," her kind voice said.

"Sure you don't want to follow me around, Cordelia?" I asked.

She shook her head. "Not tonight." She was already in a silk bonnet, cartoon pajamas on.

We parted in three separate directions. How unusual

our odd little trio was, always pushing away from each other with the same end goal of being Housed.

Judging by the position of the moon and the state of the constellations in the sky, it was nearly midnight.

The coppery scent of blood surrounded me, as well as the screams of banshees, wails of students, and triumphant yelling of Houses as the clock tower updated. Today there was a dual screen: House Rankings on top, and individual unhoused on the bottom.

I'd come across some centaurs, a wandering ghost, and even a lost troll—

All of them got swiped by an upperclassman before I could approach.

I kept wandering campus, wary. What if I wasted all night? Every time I'd come close, something else came in my way.

I kept far from the wolves, knowing that they'd work as one. Fae were already deep in the forest, so I avoided the Whispering Woods, too. I stayed far from the beach, Siren territory, and I kept clear of Angels every time I spotted white light.

However, vampires liked to lurk in dark corners, and they kept threatening to rip my neck out when I distracted them from their kill.

Vivienne had already threatened to bite me, lock me in a coffin, and leave me there for a century. Twice.

The second time I saw her, she was neck-deep in an ogre twice her size. I should get away from hiding before she turned her fangs on me next.

"If you get a view from above, you might select one you can

handle," Gaksi said. *"If you're far enough away from others, you can even practice your shadow work."*

"Good idea." I made my way to the clock tower and started climbing the fire escape. The ladder shook and creaked, slowing my progress when I checked to see if anything heard me, but otherwise, it was mercifully quiet.

When I reached the rooftop, I surveyed the campus.

The few demons I saw were engaged in battle with upperclassmen. Fae House was on top on the leaderboard, with Vamp House close behind. On the Diamond, a few freshmen meandered from place to place, looking distraught at how empty it was.

Thank heavens. They were struggling to be productive too. I didn't realize how... useless we were when the upperclassmen showed up.

"There's nothing out here! If I can't kill any demons today, maybe I should just start with you motley crew!"

No. I stopped breathing. I knew that voice.

Hunter.

Hunter and his crew of demon hunters were here.

I flattened against the clock tower on my stomach, hoping I could crush myself enough that they wouldn't spot me. The tower was ten stories tall, so unless they were craning their necks straight up, they shouldn't.

"Where is she?" Zain said in a voice devoid of emotion. "If we don't get that thing she always totes around, we aren't getting any real kills in tonight."

"And where she goes, that psycho prince follows," Brayden added.

Bloodlust dripped from their voices. With Gaksi and Reaper on my side, they'd just identified me as their next target.

"Bring out your shadows," Gaksi advised.

"I'm on the clock tower! In the middle of campus! Everyone will see me if I fight them that way up here!"

I checked my clothes. From my chest down, I only had five daggers on me.

I'd taken them once, with the element of surprise on my side. Could I do it again?

"WHERE IS SHE?" Zain shouted. His screech contorted, and I counted three voices around him. Wait, three?

"Answer, red!" Hunter roared.

Red. *Cordelia.*

I heard sobbing and had the overwhelming premonition that my next choice might be the death of me.

That wouldn't stop me. I knew what I had to do.

"Stay away from Cordelia!"

I jumped up, feet clanging against the metal surface. "And if you want me and Gaksi, come and get us!"

Hoots and hollers vocalized from the boys as they spotted me. To my horror, Zain grabbed Cordelia by the braid and towed her up the stairs with them. Two stories up, I flung my first dagger.

"Witch!" Zain hissed, hand sliced clean open by my blade.

Cordelia shot me a grateful, tear-stricken look, then ran back down the stairs.

Good. I'd be less worried about hitting her when she was gone.

"Forget her!" Hunter commanded. "How many points do you think a goblin is worth, huh?" He cackled maniacally.

Something was off about him. He was usually hateful, but the tenor of his voice made him sound downright diabolical.

The terrible three's steps echoed like a drumbeat as they climbed the stairs, in time to my racing heart.

They were five stories up. *"Go take Cordelia home,"* I told Gaksi.

"You need me more here."

"Cordelia can encounter all kinds of demons on the way home. I can survive here on my own."

And I couldn't lose you, I thought to myself. I might die, but the family line would live on with Jason and Joseph.

"I do not leave my bonded."

"I do not leave my friends behind! Go, Gaksi!"

I felt his disappointment, anger, and concern, but my shadows soothed when he jumped out of my head.

When the men reached the lip of the stairs, Hunter led the charge. The roof curved, propping Hunter up as the tallest leader of his gang, menace radiating from his figure.

"In a way, we're doing you a favor." Hunter held up a fae light, which twinkled enough to illuminate the brutal shadows of his face.

"How?" I asked.

He stepped forward. I moved backward. I had approximately five more steps before I fell ten stories and splattered on the pavement.

"You never would have matched a House here anyway, would you? Mythical beings are supposed to be pretty, and you've always been so...patchy. Like a quilt!"

His gang of degenerates laughed.

Embarrassment tightened my face, urging my shadows to strike. A simple wire, and I could trip them all over the edge.

But I wouldn't. Because I was always in hiding, even when I was in the place I considered home.

In the distance, drones flew by, centering on the tower.

Bored freshmen must be using toys to live stream this encounter.

Hunter charged, screaming bloody murder.

Before he could reach me, an infernal shriek screeched from the side. His steps wavered, and I seized my opportunity and struck. I flipped my blade out at his neck, and he collapsed with a bellow.

He groaned on the floor, clutching what was left of his trachea.

"Hard to make fun of someone when you can't speak, isn't it?" I taunted.

Brayden ran next. I struck right between his legs, and he crumpled. Served him right.

He should have suspected I'd attack the same place twice. Not that he had much going on down there, anyway.

"That's to prevent such a dumb fool from reproducing," I explained.

Air whooshed behind me, and I hit the ground before Zain's blade decapitated me.

"What would it take to kill a bonded goblin? It's not fair!" he huffed, jabbing at me. I jumped over Brayden's writhing body, heading to the stairwell.

"You have every advantage here while the rest of us are fighting for our lives!" Zain roared.

I flew another dagger at him, and he deflected it. Cursed. He had second-year training, and it showed.

He cut again, slicing straight into my arm. I yowled, red-hot blood streaming down my arm.

"Come out, come out, Gaksi goblin! Don't tell me I have to kill your favorite mortal for you to die."

"He's not here," I said before Zain tackled me. He threw me down on my ruined arm before slicing my other one clean, shoulder to elbow.

I screamed, white agony lighting up my chest.

My shadows throbbed. *Out, out, out*, they begged. They wanted to come out, to strangle, to seek revenge—

The macabre sound of bloody coughing came from my right, and Hunter dragged himself off the ground to finish me.

This was it. They were going to kill me.

Zain pressed his sword into my neck, straining as blood seeped out.

"I'll cut her straight open," Zain said. "Don't tempt me, Gaksi. I will kill you, but not after I take out this pompous loser."

The moon reached its peak above me. The kiss of metal cooled my neck and my back. My mind searched for consolation. At least I lasted a long time at this school. Cordelia made it. Gaksi made it. And once Zain eradicated me, I'd be able to tell Reaper I almost made it, too.

A torrent of wind distracted my thoughts, slamming so hard into my side that I cried out as Zain got thrown off.

His hulking body bounced twice off the roof before the cataclysm pushed him off the side.

Taking in a shaky breath, I braced myself.

My heart crashed back into reality as I heard the infernal shriek again.

Standing taller than any man, brighter than any sun, was my past nemesis.

The Bulgae.

And my dagger was still lodged in its back.

He howled, shaking the entire tower with his wrath. It vibrated and pulsed as I crawled away, inch by inch, panicking.

I only had one dagger left, but I was too weak to throw it.

Hunter chuffed, spurting blood ahead of me, and barreled toward it.

The hound stepped forward, hackles raised. The hairs on my neck shot up, dread consuming my soul.

"No!" I whispered, frozen solid in fright.

The hound opened its maw, sparks flying, fire combusting in a tornado of heat.

Warmth blasted.

Hunter screamed.

When I reopened my eyes, Hunter was gone. Instead, the odorous smell of roasted barbeque lingered, wafting from the smoking metal where Hunter once stood.

"Stars," I murmured.

I breathed through my nose, urging myself to think. I was in no condition to fight, but this creature obviously was.

"You ugly beast," Zain hissed. He unsheathed his blade, dragging himself along the floor.

Light blinded me.

"Demons are notoriously vain," a familiar voice advised in my head.

Vain as Zain, now ash.

The demon barked steam, then centered its golden eyes on me.

What did my animal science textbook say?

Don't look a dog in the eyes. It was a sign of aggression. At least, for a normal dog, if you hadn't already stabbed it. How did you de-escalate a fire-breathing demon?

Its large nostrils flared, my fear scented.

The hound approached slowly, growling faintly.

"Just do it," I said. "I'm sure I'll see you again on the other side." I laughed to myself. The clock struck twelve, echoing through campus. I'd lost my mind.

Drone flashes lit up the sky, closing in a circle around me. Great. Everyone could see my death, too. I hoped I went viral.

The Bulgae may have rescued me from my tormentors, but I was still too weak to save myself.

A bang resonated from my right. "Stay away from her!"

Cordelia.

In her cartoon seashell pajamas, unarmed and untrained, Cordelia came back for me, the deadbeat accepting defeat on the floor.

"If you die now, you'll be stuck with that hideous outfit on forever," Aubrey added next to her, arms crossed. She was covered in black and red blood from hair to toe, white hair nearly as scarlet as Cordelia's.

I was so tired of this. Tired of being rescued.

Tired of needing to be saved because I refused to use the weapons at my disposal.

Screw this.

My shadows lashed up and out, knocking drones out of the sky.

I teleported sideways, landing between the Bulgae and Cordelia. If I had to become a demon to protect the innocent, so be it.

Darkness called my ego, and I let it, succumbing to the eclipse of energy in my soul, spirit, and self. I was the absence of light, the night where the moon rose.

My black eyes opened.

Bands of power wrapped around my arms, holding my wounds closed.

Limbs of smoke and shadow extended in arching, hungry claws around the beast.

The Bulgae fell back, but I advanced.

I was the unbreakable, unwavering night, and it was a fool for crossing me.

"Demons feast on negative energy, don't they?"

My shadow claws stabbed into hard muscle. The Bulgae arched in pain and roared, flames lighting the sky. I didn't care. Pain delighted me.

My mother cautioned me that once the shadows were let in, there was no going back.

Good.

How many times had I wondered whether I would ever be enough? How many times had I let myself doubt?

I turned my shadows into invisible shackles, rooting around the Bulgae until he was immobilized. Then I curled smokey, near-invisible strings around the fallen drones, moving them back to witness my glory.

When in sight, I yanked my first dagger out of Bulgae flesh, smiling at its misery.

How much hell could a hellhound take?

"Should I make you my sacrificial lamb?"

He growled, and I thrust the dagger back in. Rough sinew vibrated against my blade.

"This is for every one of you who mocked me for having bad skin."

Out. Gushing blood sprayed my face. In. Warm flesh coated my hand.

How much time had I spent worrying about what was out of my control? I could control *shadows*. I was *more* than my appearance.

"This is for everyone that's mocked my association with demons."

Out. My shadows constricted around its throat, cutting off circulation. I removed my last dagger from my pocket, holding one in each hand.

My family never spoke ill of me the way this two-faced, self-righteous, hypocritical community has.

"This one's for my fans."

I plunged both daggers in, and the Bulgae ignited, dissolving into a haze of red dust.

I turned and bowed to the drones, laughing at their red eyes and blaring white flashes.

"I hope you enjoyed the show!"

CHAPTER
TWENTY-FIVE

THE ORACLE MUSINGS

After a smoke show of footage was released yesterday, it has become clear that campus busybodies lack proper filming techniques. Despite many of you fools attempting to clarify film today, there's too much residual magic in any of the drones for the efforts to be worth your while. Only Luna's audio speech, and the Bulgae's roar of defeat, are salvageable.

As a whole, campus is covered these days with simpering fools. Just this morning in the dormitories, I counted nearly a dozen freshmen attempting to break into their classmates' rooms, looking for the coveted Fae Masquerade invite. It is difficult to discern who, of all the ridiculous freshmen, is most desperate, but I would have to suggest our leaderboard queens: Misses Luna, Aubrey, and Cordelia are not as composed as they appear.

I DUG my hands in the dirt, fulfilling the compulsory volunteering the school required of us each year. Cordelia and Aubrey pulled out weeds beside me.

"Can't Rose House just do this themselves?" Aubrey complained.

"No, they can't," Wisteria shouted from her megaphone. Every House had charity events we could sign up for, but I wanted to guarantee I'd be with friends, so we all picked Rose House together.

There were only a dozen freshmen here.

And only six of them were new freshmen. Hyacinth was here, along with six other sophomores.

"I heard the Sirens are going surfing," Aubrey muttered. "Next time, we might have to go our separate ways."

"It's not that bad—ah!" I pricked my hand on a rose thorn.

A girl who got cut from the first exam ran over. "Here, let me help with that!" She pulled my finger, squeezing out the thorn. I fought a grimace.

She was trying to prove herself, I supposed. Cuts could rush again next year. Hopefully, if they made enough friends the first year, they could easily slide into a House with them.

Everywhere I went, people were being oddly nice to me.

When I so much as glanced at a cafeteria table, people picked up their plates and left.

Students I'd never spoken to were making their way to approach me.

When the three of us walked to Daggers & Dynamite, the grass around us was packed with bodies, but at a glare from Aubrey, they quickly vacated.

"Are you all right?" she asked with a gentleness I'd never heard from her.

"I feel guilty," I admitted. My stomach soured, searching for boys that weren't coming.

"The Bulgae killed them, not you," she said.

"But I didn't save them, either." Wasn't that what we existed for? Slayers of demons, protectors of humanity?

"They kidnapped me, Luna," Cordelia said. "I won't miss them." She flipped her braid over her shoulder like Aubrey usually did. Our trio was rubbing off on each other.

"Forget the deceased, Luna. I'm ready to be Housed," Aubrey grumbled.

Sophomores from each House arrived in rambunctious bundles to their seats. This was one of the few mixed-grade classes where we all learned together.

"Aren't we all?" Cordelia added. The longing was so plain on her face as she watched the Sirens swim up to the shore. Since the weather was so nice, we had class outside today, and Sirens watched from the sea.

"Maybe the Antikythera will add you back to the roster for the last round," I said. "It's done crazier things before."

"I wouldn't count on that old piece of work," Aubrey said. "Unpredictable is never good."

As if to prove her point, a frisbee glided out from the side and smacked her in the face.

"Aubrey! Are you okay?" Cordelia asked.

A gangly werewolf ran up. "Maybe you should have sat out of the path of progress—" His eyes roved to me.

"Ah, sorry. Didn't know you were with the sun slayer."

Sun slayer?

Aubrey whacked him in the face with the frisbee. "Aubrey!" Cordelia scolded, but she covered her mouth to suppress a laugh.

He faced me, dodging Aubrey's attacks. "Apologies. I didn't know you were friends with her."

"You don't have to apologize to me," I said, but he'd already run off, Aubrey still holding his frisbee like a mallet.

"People have been treating me differently lately, don't you think?" I asked my friends.

"They've finally been showing you the respect you deserve," Aubrey spat. "Although, they should show all of us the respect we deserve." She ripped the frisbee into daggers and hurled them at the boy. All missed, and Cordelia shot me a grin. "You're next, fin lover." Cordelia gulped.

"I didn't do anything to deserve their respect."

"You killed a massive sun beast. They're respecting who they think will be a future house leader," Cordelia said.

"Everyone bows to power," Aubrey added. Her gaze lingered on me, and I swore she was watching the shadows swimming beneath the surface. "And you're a cauldron ready to burst."

"Could you ask a boy from back home?"

"A high schooler? Gross!"

"Human boys are worthless. Real men have power," Mom would remind me.

"Is that why you married Dad?" I'd ask her. Then she'd get all offended and huff away. She married for love. But she was insecure about it, so she always pushed me to be different. More.

You've always been smarter than me.

More supported than me.

You'll accomplish more than I ever did.

And anytime I would get distracted—whether it was high school crushes, sneaking out to go to the movies, or slacking at school, she'd remind me of my goals in life.

"You won't find Mr. Right skipping class," she'd say. *"I did. That's how I ended up married to your father."*

"Hey!" Dad would say. Then they'd exchange one of their rare smiles at each other, and it would be like the conversation never happened. But I remembered it. I always did.

"If I made it into Fae house, there's no excuse for you," she'd promoted. "We don't do bottom tier. Not in our family."

Dad usually wasn't around for the second part of the conversation.

"This is your last chance to impress the Houses before the final round of cuts." I heard her stern tone through the phone as Aubrey entered. Gaksi's bird form winked once, then flew out the window.

"I've arrived in your daughter's room, Mrs. Deokhye!" Aubrey chimed.

"Hello, darling!" Mom screamed. I winced, cringing. She was so loud when she wanted to be.

Mom met Aubrey once when she tried to FaceTime me when we were braiding our hair together. Aubrey was a master at it, so it was usually spent with her doing my hair over and over again.

Once she realized Aubrey was just like her, she exploded with joy. "I knew you would end up in the right crowd eventually," she'd said, "and Aubrey is definitely the right crowd for you. Smart, beautiful, well-mannered girl."

To be honest, I thought my mother would be happier if Aubrey was her daughter and not me.

Especially when she learned Aubrey was an orphan. She'd all but cried and told her she was welcome to call her anytime. She'd even invited her to holiday dinners.

Cordelia wasn't, though, which was a little awkward.

My mom liked Cordelia. But, "She won't push you. Not like Aubrey will. Aubrey has ambition." Never mind that Aubrey initially wanted to be an angel. As soon as she realized faeries were on top, she'd changed her tune. And when mom destroyed my room, Aubrey had agreed it was adequate punishment.

That made Mom like her. Overdramatic social climbers thought alike.

"You look like sin!" Aubrey exclaimed when I turned around.

I swirled my lavender dress around. It had a nude lining to give the illusion of wearing nothing underneath, cinching at the waist and flaring into a mermaid style at the knees. It draped across the bust, making my bosom look even larger, and fell in diagonals across, making my curves look especially striking. Gaksi had styled my hair into loose, effortless waves and painted black smoke along my eyes to make them look huge. Bejeweled earrings hung in my ears. Reaper's amulet hung around my neck, rubbing against my brand with every movement, heightening my anxiety.

I curtsied. "And you as well, Aubrey."

Aubrey dressed like a princess. She wore a bedazzled gold tiara, a spun-gold dress that reached the floor, and sparkling gold shoes. With red lipstick and simple eyeshadow, she looked like she just stepped out of a modern-day palace.

"Thank you," Aubrey said. "But you... you look like you're trying to raise the dead tonight."

If only she knew. That I had been dealing with the dead and their master for weeks.

But enough of that. I'd had enough thinking about Reaper to last a lifetime.

"Let's hope it doesn't come to that," I said. "Should we put on our masks?"

Each of us put on our fae house-gifted masks.

Mine shifted again into a luminous white swan, the glow making me shine in the light.

At first, Aubrey's had no effect. It changed to a flesh color, almost resembling her skin.

She tapped it. "Come on, work," she muttered. It morphed into a chameleon mask, changing color depending on what she looked at.

"That's pretty cool, Aubrey."

She readjusted it slightly. "It'll do." She linked arms with me. "Let's go, bestie."

I felt a pang of guilt. Cordelia, my first bestie, loved dressing up for stuff like this. But she was getting ready at Wolf House with some of Xavier's pack members.

We took a carriage to arrive. The butler held up a gloved hand to let me into the cushioned interior, and the horses clop-clop-clopped their way along to Faery Castle, the upgraded version of Fae House.

We arrived fifteen minutes early. Fae, who were both tidy and punctual, frowned upon tardiness. Students stared and whispered at us as we passed. I was glad Gaksi paid off who knew who to get us this ride. We looked positively regal compared to the desperate hopefuls walking.

When the butler helped us out, a crowd had already gathered. Bouncers checked names, unafraid to haul out anyone uninvited.

"How embarrassing for them," Aubrey mentioned to me.

"Yeah, for real."

Fresh ivy lined the white bricks making up Faery Castle. Pastel spires ascended high into the sky, making me crane my neck to look up at them. They decorated the entrance with lightning bugs, darting to and fro high above the bouncers. It was ethereal and enchanting. Perfect for a masquerade ball.

Once we were let in, we were bombarded with waiters

offering food.

"Wine?"

"Cheese?"

"Crackers?"

"They're trying to make us fat," Aubrey insisted, grabbing my hand. "It's a trap. If you take the food, you won't make it into the House." She threw her head around, looking for our escape route.

"What?" I said, cheese in hand. "Why would they do that?"

"Because nobody likes a glutton! Come on, let's go," she insisted, tugging me along. I threw the cheese back on the tray before I left.

"Sorry!" I said.

I would miss that cheese. It looked like gouda, my favorite.

She pulled us past ancient-looking tapestries and hand-painted murals. Cherubs lined the ceiling, smiling through scene after scene of precious art. To the sides, iridescent crystals served as tables, where most of the upperclassmen sat and laughed with each other. Unhoused danced in the center, twirling under the shining chandeliers that swung to the tune of the music.

"Mingling time," Aubrey announced. We started conversations with "important-looking" people that strode by. She introduced us to upperclassman after upperclassman, and I worried I wouldn't be able to remember any of their names. Although with the predatory gaze some fae gave my dress, I was hoping they wouldn't be able to remember me either.

I was shifting uncomfortably on my feet when a hum went through the room.

"See, look! Everyone who took the wine and food is

dancing like an idiot!" Aubrey said.

In the middle of the dance floor, possessed freshmen contorted their bodies in crazy positions. Jerking, slapping, falling over. Twisted, painful movements, like puppets on a string. The lights above strobed in tune with their convulsive movements. Eerie.

Actives laughed hysterically around them. They mimed their movements, then fell over themselves in mockery.

"That could have been us," Aubrey said. "We have to stay responsible so we don't fall into mass hysteria. This entire night is one big test."

Beyond them, a crowd gathered near the entrance. Newly set-out velvet ropes held them off, and their phone lights glimmered like spirits at a wake.

Aubrey elbowed me to pay attention. "Look, that's Flora!"

It was acceptable for the leaders of the Houses to arrive fashionably late. After all, once housed, always housed. No lack of decorum could result in an expulsion. Sometimes I wondered if they came late just for the notoriety. Just to remind us they could do anything, anytime, and we'd still grovel and watch like peasants.

Flora arrived, dressed in diamonds, with the male Fae House leader, Fabian, on her side. I had never seen Fabian before, as he only recruited the males to Fae House, but I was stricken by how attractive he was. He had bronzed skin, earthy brown hair, and pointed ears that looked delicious enough to nibble on.

"Fabian's cuter than I thought," I told Aubrey.

"All fae are pretty," Aubrey said. "Imagine how good we'd look with some light magic inside us."

Light magic. Did it ensure that outcome? Make you even more beautiful? Was that why I'd never arrived on a man's arm before? Because dark magic, in contrast, made me ugly?

"The night sky is more beautiful than any sunrise, little moon." My necklace warmed, insecurity forgotten, as the remaining House leaders entered.

Angel House arrived next, donned in impeccable white feathers for clothes that blended seamlessly into their wings. Vamp House wore vintage, lacy black clothes reminiscent of 18th-century barons and baronesses. Sirens wore as many scales as they could out of the water, with a mermaid skirt for the female leader and a trident accessory for the male who replaced Lukas.

Xavier and the female leader of Wolf House arrived next, dressed in a simple button-down and cocktail dress. They both arrived with dates, and on Xavier's arm was the most well-dressed version of my friend I'd ever seen.

"Cordelia!" I called.

She didn't see me, but that was okay. I'd seen her. Her pink chiffon dress made her look like a happy cupcake, and I was going to tell her that the next time I saw her. I was so glad she came.

She smiled and waved at every person she met like she was having the time of her life. When I got the chance, I'd tell her she was a natural at parties.

"We're going to be like that one day," Aubrey promised.

"Definitely," I affirmed.

I longed to imitate them. To be a leader not only in this school but in life. To be so well known that an entire campus of freshmen would do anything to be just like you.

"Luna."

A shadow tendril coiled around my ear.

A chill bolted through my spine, rooting me to the spot. He was here.

CHAPTER
TWENTY-SIX

THE ORACLE MUSINGS

The annual Fae Masquerade ball is tonight! This oracle, unfortunately, did not receive an invitation. So, I am delighted to inform you that most of the candidates who did will have a rather horrific time.

MY SHADOWS THRUMMED WITH ANTICIPATION. My palms suddenly felt sweaty, breaths coming in too fast.

"Luna?" Aubrey asked. I was immobilized.

Then she saw him, too, appearing out of thin air. He strode toward us, a tempestuous shadow mask covering his upper face. Partiers thrashed behind him, providing a sharp contrast to his calm demeanor.

His suit was black, with a simple moon embroidered on the breast pocket. His dark hair hung, untamed, around his head, like he spontaneously planned to arrive at the ball. He walked with the audacity of a man who had just practiced dark magic publicly, in a room full of witnesses, and knew they couldn't do anything about it. He walked as if he didn't threaten my very life and purpose with his presence.

He walked with a smile.

His eyes drank in my body, moving with an intimacy that left me feeling naked, even in a room filled with people.

He might have spent all night lusting over me if Aubrey hadn't jumped in.

"Dance with me," Aubrey suggested, holding out her hand to the Reaper.

My rage nearly toppled me over with intensity. How dare she—

He stopped in his tracks, staring at the hand in surprise.

"Of course," he said, kissing her exposed hand.

The chandelier lights sputtered and cracked, glass pelting the students below.

Dark energy pulsed within me, demanding more. More violence. More destruction. More vengeance.

I hurried away, following the students that scattered from glass shards, determined to get my emotions under control while Aubrey and my Reaper danced.

Not *my* Reaper, I corrected myself. Not *my* anything.

I should find Cordelia. She could calm me down. Or at least let me rant to her about the absurdity of this situation.

I couldn't react now. Not with the dramatics I just did. Pixies were already working to clean up glass shards off the floor, some pieces bigger than themselves.

Relax. Aubrey didn't know he was the Reaper. She was just socializing like she always did. Calm down.

"If it isn't my favorite fish," a sharp, feminine voice chirped.

"Flora," I said. The fae approached in a cloud of snowy mist and kissed my cheeks. I fought the urge to recoil.

"I couldn't miss the show, now, could I? You left your mission over there." She pointed to Reaper, who was dancing with Aubrey in his arms. Aubrey leaned close to whisper something in his ear. Fortunately, I couldn't see Reaper's expression as he spun away. If he looked happy, I might have to walk over and kill him. For real this time.

He danced in the middle of the dance floor, performing well, all spins and fanfare and dips, drawing attention to himself like a reckless, insufferable fool—

"Does anyone besides us know who he is?" I asked Flora.

"No," Flora said. "I only know because you've been staring at him like a slighted lover since he arrived."

"I am not—" I let out an exasperated breath. "He and I—"

She held her hands up. "Look, fish, I don't actually care. But I need you to keep getting information from him."

My nails ached, pulsing with her magic. I stopped clenching my fists. Any harder, and they might just cut into my skin.

"I need to get his attention," I told Flora.

She eyed me with disbelief. "He's been watching you all night. You already have it."

I pretended I didn't hear that. "Can you get me a dance with Fabian?"

Frostbite burnt my fingers.

"My mate?"

I cringed. Mates were what starborn souls were called among Faeries. Nothing came between them. And if you tried to make a move on one, you were lucky if their partner's jealousy didn't strike you dead.

She would rip me to shreds for that slight later. Blood already dripped from my fingertips, splattering on the floor.

"I need to make Reaper jealous," I insisted.

"By dancing with my mate." She gave me a frigid, deadpan stare. My fingers were starting to lose circulation, numbing to the pain.

"If Reaper has been watching me all night, then he definitely saw me staring at Fabian earlier when he arrived with you. If he sees me dancing with him, too, he'll be convinced I'm interested."

"Ow!" I yelped. I dropped my hands to my sides. Pain was radiating up to my elbows now. Flora was strong, especially when fuming.

"Watch yourself, girl."

She deserted me. Discomfort ebbed away from my elbows, then my wrists, and finally localized to my throbbing hands.

"If you kiss him, I will rip off your hands, then shove them down Cordelia's throat," Flora said when she returned, hand arched like a claw over Fabian's shoulder.

He grinned mischievously. "Both of us get to make our loves jealous today, won't we?" He pressed his hand into the small of my back, then cut us a path into the crowd. Flora watched us apprehensively, icicles dripping down from the ceiling.

"So... you are in love with a demon?" Fabian asked, twirling me.

The way he said it sounded absolutely ridiculous. Demons were the pure embodiment of evil. Wicked, foul, hideous, and fundamentally untrustworthy. Although the more time I spent with Reaper, the more I questioned whether everything rumored was true.

"I have a bargain with Flora," I answered as Fabian led me through more steps. He was a superb dancer. Shame I actually had to pay attention and not talk to him. It would be interesting to see how much Flora told him about my situation.

I spared a glance at Aubrey, who had wrapped herself in Reaper's arms. Reaper noticed me, only briefly, before he slid his hands up her back and around her neck to grip her face. She batted her eyelashes and spoke something I couldn't hear. Reaper winked like a thief, conspiring on some great heist with his new partner in crime.

"Flora sets lots of bargains," Fabian responded. "None as charming as you."

Heat rose to my cheeks. I hoped Flora wasn't listening to this. I was on her hit list already.

"Thank you," I said, a little mortified.

Reaper's hand now combed through Aubrey's hair while the other slid lower on her back. Dangerously low. He smiled endearingly at her, pulling her closer.

I hoped they both died. Then I would never have to watch something so disgusting ever again.

"You know," Fabian said conspiratorially, "the more I compliment you, the better the nightlife will be with Flora later."

He pecked my cheek. Then said, a bit louder, "So, darling, you're really doing both of us a favor."

I whimpered. Ice bit at my hands again. I couldn't move them at all.

A deep, ravaging force buzzed behind me.

"Seraph."

His wrath blazed over my skin, moving all the way down to my soul.

I curtsied politely to Fabian. "Thank you for the dance."

He bowed. "Anytime, sweetheart." Flora appeared instantly, gave me a look that could freeze me into an ice sculpture, and dragged him away. He laughed the entire way, ruffling Flora's perfectly manicured hair. She snapped at him.

"Seraphim."

Shadows curled around my ankles, forcing me to turn.

I hesitated to look up. I was fearful, for a moment, of what jealousy could do to him.

"Please recall your shadows," I murmured. "We're in public."

They dissolved.

Graceful fingers pushed my hair beyond my ear. Traced the bond along my skin, then ghosted over my collarbone.

"Do you go out of your way to torture me?" I breathed.

"This is torture?" He chuckled lightly. "You are very sensitive."

"Did you come to dance with me or to confront and prod me in public?" Although my tone was a tad irritated, I was actually feeling quite shy. I'd never danced with someone I liked before. Not that I was allowed to like him. Those feelings were purely imaginary.

He twisted me up against him and spun me around. He was so much taller and stronger than me that he led me effortlessly, letting me follow his cocky rhythm.

His body remained aligned with mine, rumbling deep in his chest every time we drew closer. He spun and spun me, delighting the chaotic shadows within, distracting me from actually having to converse with him. Perhaps that was a strategy in itself. Work me so hard that I ignored the flaming chemistry between us.

Too bad my shadows thrived on conflict. "Why not keep dancing with Aubrey?"

He threw me into another move as an answer. "What do you have against her? She is your friend?"

"She looked like your lover just a minute ago."

"She insisted we dance. It was out of my control."

"You, the walker of worlds, the transporter of the dead to the Beyond, cannot control a little human girl."

He squeezed our entwined fingers tighter. Possessively. "Are you so bothered?"

"No," I said, ducking beneath his arm. And I was not bothered. I was positively feral, a cobra waiting to strike against an unexpected predator. If he looked into my eyes, he'd see the smoky black awaiting.

He lifted me in an elaborate hold, face as smug as I'd ever seen it. "I knew it. You desire my company."

"I am forced into your company."

The smug bravado disappeared. "You are not my hostage."

I shimmied with the music. "No, but I might as well be."

"Well, as a hostage, why would you care if I've had any lovers?"

"How many have you had? Since I shouldn't care, it wouldn't even affect me to know."

He frowned. So did I. A ball had dropped in my stomach. I feared whatever number it was, it would be too high for me to handle. The lights above me flared with my unease. This was bad. My emotions were too high, and my dark magic was spiraling out of control.

"None, seraphim."

None?

My lovers are few and far between.

I disregarded the excited little skip in my intestines. The entire room glowed brighter as my energy sparked every candle, light fixture, and phone in the room. We basked in the glow as the room illuminated. Several "oohs" and "ahhs" erupted from the crowd.

Flora smiled and waved, expertly taking credit. Good. It

looked like she'd been running the show, and not that I let my powers get the best of me.

I forced myself to abate. Demons were known to lie. What Reaper said might be fabricated. How did I know he wasn't just telling me what I wanted to hear? The lights above dimmed back to a normal level.

"Your shadow control is all over the place," Reaper observed.

"Don't be rude," I snapped back.

"Don't be bratty. It was just a critique."

"A critique." My nose scrunched. "A critique? After you set your sights on me and locked me into a bond? After you've attempted my demise and shown up publicly with no regard for decorum?"

"You're causing more of a scene than me," he said.

Heads turned to witness our argument. I quieted my voice.

"Here's a critique for you: you vex me."

"You've been reading too many romance novels," he said, swatting my nose. "And you vex me too, seraphim."

Past him, the crowd watched us with hushed voices and intense stares. The level of attention made my insides squirm. The overall noise level had dissipated as onlookers listened in. Every House leader was staring, watching us interact. If they figured out who my dance partner was, I was done, and I'd never be able to recover.

I pressed off him. "I don't want you here. I don't care about you," I burst out. "I can't do this. Go away."

Something akin to—hurt?—flashed across his handsome face.

"Do you want to know a critique you can never deny?" his gravelly voice asked.

"Last one, before I find some way to kick you out," I said.

"You may not like me, but you have always been attracted to me," he declared.

Reaper pressed his mouth to mine.

I swayed, surprised, while he folded himself into me. Lips and teeth collided. He kissed me in a frenzied, impassioned way, like he hadn't ever kissed someone before. Like he'd never kiss again. I kissed him back like I was haunted, impassioned, devout. Like the stars themselves had collided, bringing us with them, and I was cursed to desire this man until the end of time, when our stars inevitably burned out.

But I couldn't. Because we were in public, and it was forbidden. My self-preservation won, and I shoved him away.

He stared at me for a moment, enraptured, before vanishing without a goodbye.

CHAPTER
TWENTY-SEVEN

THE ORACLE MUSINGS

Who's the mystery man from the Fae masquerade? Luna Deokhye and Aubrey Hahm were found dancing with a beautiful stranger during the last round of recruitment: is he a notable alumnus, an estranged lover, or what? Will he drive a wedge between friends from week one? Only they can decide. The future is tumultuous and uncertain.

In other news: The second to last round of cuts is in! This one should be brutal: Houses only want their best for preference round. What are you willing to lose to belong?

BLUE FLAME TWINKLED in my necklace as I navigated the library stacks.

"You don't have to follow me in here, Gaksi. It's just the library." A flexible, shimmery ward had appeared around library doors last night, offering protection from wandering demons. The University expressed gratitude for the anonymous House gift via an ad space in The Eternal. Gaksi had cackled like a witch when he read it this morning.

"It's cozy in here," Gaksi answered. "Besides, I enjoy learning what you do. Consider me your personal Cheshire cat."

I rolled my eyes.

Vivienne waved her fingers at me, nodding at the seat across her. Her red sweater dress matched the liquid in her see-through bottle.

"Good morning, Vivienne!" Gaksi said.

Her pleasant demeanor disappeared.

"Gaksi," she answered with a tight-lipped smile. "So nice to see you've joined our study date."

Vivienne's shoulders tensed as I sat. "Have you ever lived without... company?" She sipped from her bottle, sloshing the dark liquid. It stained her lips maroon, the same color as freshly-bitten flesh.

"No, Gaksi is family. We've always had him."

She frowned. "Should we get to studying, then?"

The abrupt subject change unsettled me. "Sure."

We flipped through Vamp House history, University History, and chiropterology (bat science). Almost all Vampires took a bat class, so she was quick with my zoology homework, pointing out the structural features of fangs and wings.

Her lips pursed when Gaksi turned the pages for us. "Does Gaksi ever help you with exams?"

He snickered in my head.

"No, he rarely knows the answer."

"Hey!"

"And if he did, it was because I learned it first."

"I see," Vivienne said. She flipped through a flashcard

set before asking another question. "You know you would have to get rid of him to join Vamp House, right?"

My brows creased in confusion.

"Vampires don't share. We can't have an unidentified demon living in sacred vampire space."

Ouch. Unease spread within me, worry weighing on my spirit like a jinx.

"I see," was all I could get out.

Should I give up on Vamp House, then? Did all Houses have a similar rule?

"You have the potential to be a great vampire if you ditch the imaginary friend," she continued, throwing her stuff into a scarlet portal. Within it, I could see the Vamp House foyer.

"That's house promising," Gaksi mentioned. *"The houses aren't supposed to tell you that you belong there before offering the official bid."*

Could I do it? Could I give up Gaksi to belong? I'd gained exquisite control of my shadows, so I needed him much less than I used to. Would it be so much to give up my childhood best friend, too? Maybe Joseph or Jason would like a companion...

My necklace bounced off my chest.

"I can feel your guilt and indecision from here, moonbeam."

Tears swelled. I almost cried, hearing my childhood nickname. I wasn't losing Gaksi.

"Nice to study with you," I told Vivienne.

"I won't ever be doing so again."

Since the masquerade, I woke up to the smell of freshly brewed tea on my nightstand. Warm and earthy, I sipped it gratefully. I reached out with my mind to Gaksi, but he was never nearby.

Thank you, Gaksi, I wrote on a piece of paper instead. It faded without a trace.

I got into a routine of texting Flora tidbits of info at a time. Not all at once, because I realized that when I did that, she would pester me for more. So I fed her bits and pieces, and when the next round of cuts dropped, I knew she was upholding her end of the deal.

The final round comprised us visiting only three houses, even if more wanted us. So, Flora had asked me which were my top three.

It was a painstaking decision. Wolf and Rose, I wanted to avoid because of their bottom-tier nature. Siren House traumatized me at their most recent rager. Fae House reminded me too much of my mother, Vamp House wanted me to get rid of Gaksi, and Angel House felt so quintessentially antithetical to my shadows that I didn't see myself there at all.

Fae, Angel, and Siren, I ultimately told her. Two top and one mid-tier. If I was going to stay here, I was going big.

Fae, Angel, and Rose House appeared on my invite card today.

"What the hell, Flora?" I asked over the phone.

"Rose House has you at the top of their bid list, Luna," Flora said. "And no, you're not supposed to know that. It would look incredibly suspicious on my end for them not to have you this round, given how highly they ranked you."

After that, I was a little flattered. Rose House was my favorite House to learn about before I got caught up in the fanfare of it all. It was sweet to know they thought well of me.

Cordelia's melancholy on her selections preoccupied my thoughts after I finished my conversation with Flora.

"Wolf House has very strong pack bonds," I encouraged. "You would have such a strong relationship with everyone in that House."

"What if they decide they don't like me anymore?" Cordelia despaired. "Then I might end up in Rose! With nothing but a gardening shovel to bury and kill myself with."

"Hey, don't talk like that," I insisted. "Reaper would have to be the one to bail you out."

"Well, in that case…" Her tears dried up a little. Sometimes, it was nice to know her boy crazy thoughts won out over much else.

"I don't even know if this process is worth it anymore," Cordelia admitted. "It seems like I'm just putting on a show, not being the real me."

I bristled with the accuracy of the statement. I felt it, too, especially when strategizing how to keep myself interesting. We both moved like disco balls, constantly spinning, doing everything to keep the party going despite the crowd being empty.

"Whatever you do, I'll support you," I said. "Do what feels most right for you."

She took a breath, like she wanted to speak, but faltered. "I'll see you tomorrow," Cordelia said. "I'm going to nap and watch reality television until I feel better."

"Take Gaksi with you," I offered. "He loves that stuff."

Gaksi's pigeon darted out with Cordelia. She couldn't hear him talk to her, but hopefully, he would provide some company.

The next day, before class, Aubrey dialed, presumably to discuss our House rankings.

I slid on a face mask from my desk that morning. Gaksi had really outdone himself. It smelled like rose and cotton candy.

"Fae and Angel for me. You?" Damn, Aubrey got straight to business.

I shared my list. She squealed and explained that it's incredible to get 3/3, when most have 2/3, 1/3, or got dropped entirely. They removed over 100 students from recruitment this round, which meant they wouldn't get a chance again until next year.

"Nothing is guaranteed in this process," Aubrey said. "We need to chase our destiny."

"Agreed."

"Speaking of..." her voice trailed off. "We should consider our reputation."

"What do you mean?" I asked, flopping down on my bed. "We erased our social media presence a few days ago."

We had a wine night to "polish up" our image, but it mostly just comprised of Aubrey deleting questionable nonsense from my digital footprint. Fanfiction, mostly. It wasn't under my name, but she was paranoid. And it was pretty cringe. But it was fun to reread as an adult.

"Who we associate with is pretty important." There was a long pause on the other end of the line. "Do you think it's time you distanced yourself from Cordelia?"

My body stiffened. The mask displaced, and I scrambled to right it.

"I mean, she's completely nice and all," Aubrey rushed to clarify, "But like, you won't spend as much time with her in the future, so it's better to wean her off now. It's hard to be around clingy people!" Her voice filled the void of my silence. "She's got what, just Wolf and Rose, right?"

"How did you know?"

"I mean, we're besties, right? So can I be honest with you?"

"Yes?" I asked cautiously.

"Well, first off, there's nothing wrong with either of those houses," she began, words careful. "I thought Wolf House was so welcoming, and Rose House was so nice during recruitment. They definitely care about attracting kind girls."

"But they're... also a little more homely, you know? They don't party as hard. They don't finish off their appearance before school every day. They don't attract the youngest, the fiercest, the best and brightest. This is the last round. We've got to shape into the best versions of ourselves. Everything we've ever worked for has come to this moment." Aubrey pressed on. "We have to belong. We have to rise to the occasion."

Guilt gnawed at my stomach, but... a begrudging part of me knew she was right. I could still maintain a casual relationship with Cordelia. But when I saw the top-tier girls, all their friends were Fae or Angel associated, with the occasional Vamp/Siren. Keeping the right friends was an integral part of cultivating the right image.

I despised myself for even noticing. But, I told myself, this was temporary. Just until recruitment was over. Extreme measures had to be taken sometimes.

"Agreed," I said quietly.

"Are you going to suicide bid Fae House?" Aubrey's voice pierced through my emotional turmoil, and, for the first time in the night, I heard a hint of worry in her voice.

Suicide bidding was a common, though frowned upon, practice. In it, you only selected one of the three Houses left for the final round. Considered a form of "social suicide" because if that House rejected you, there were no backups.

You had to wait a whole year to try again, but by that time, you were old news. Rejected candidates were unlikely to be desirable as older, traumatized students.

"I don't think anyone should suicide bid," I said. "Melody specifically told us that actually hurts our odds with the Antikythera."

Aether revived the Antikythera after sirens found it in Atlantis decades ago. The machine was perfected for matching potential new members to the right House. It was marketed as a mutual selection process, but gossip insisted the Antikythera had a mind of its own and did not take kindly to being questioned.

"I'm scared of that thing," Aubrey confessed, "It almost sounds like dark magic."

"Don't say that!" I said, voice dropping to a hushed tone. "You never know who could be listening."

"I know, I know," Aubrey said. "We have to stay fighting, Luna."

"Fighting," I agreed, because I would fight, even if it meant sacrificing something I cared about.

CHAPTER
TWENTY-EIGHT

THE ORACLE MUSINGS

Everyone has their biggest college regret.

Xavier's was stepping up as Alpha. Sorry, cinnamon roll, but you're more like an Omega than an Alpha! President Ansi's was coming back to this university in the first place (yeah, I foretold you complaining!). Mine is that I didn't start monetizing this column sooner. I should have had y'all put bets on which future was most likely. Sometimes the in-betweens are muddier, but absolutes always come through. One absolute of today: a little entropy would do you good.

I SET a trap for my favorite demon today.

My shadows craved disorder, and studying nonstop was agony, so I distracted myself by satisfying them.

With the fruits of trees finally growing, I made a massive, heaping pile of them. I then practiced levitating the fruits, one by one, until I had them suspended in the tree that shed them. And once Gaksi flew through them, I was going to collapse them on him.

He used to prank me all the time. He'd set out candies made of vegetables, toys that were really treats, and love letters from 'secret admirers' that were really just from him.

I'd been waiting years for revenge.

Every dawn, he flew in with his favorite form, pigeon, through the tree by my window after going on a fly.

Today, I set my alarm uncharacteristically early. Rested innocently in bed.

Then, when I heard a noise, I pounced.

I unfolded hundreds of pomegranates down.

Where Reaper stood, unfazed, holding up a layer of fruit like a shield.

"Well," he merely said, "now I know why Gaksi sent me to retrieve you. He said you looked 'devoutly pleased' all week and must have been up to something."

He shook the fruit away, genuinely amused, then rerouted them. "Revenge time," he threatened, an impish grin crossing his face.

I shrieked and ducked while he chased me with them, hastily throwing up smoke to shield us from prying eyes. For a moment, it was like we were training again and not avoiding each other post-masquerade. I hadn't contacted him, and he hadn't contacted me either.

"You have such a pretty dance when you cower," he said, eyes watching me with rapt fascination. "Have you considered fighting back?"

Cower? I was not cowering from anything, least of all him. I stood straight up, hands outstretched. The fruits stopped, gripped by my shadows, until I yearned for them to drop. They did.

"Good," Reaper said, stepping through the wall of my dorm inside.

I hesitated, unsure of what to say to him. What were we now? He didn't have to come here. Gaksi sent him, but he didn't have to listen.

Reaper rubbed his neck. Perhaps he sensed the awkwardness, too. "Gaksi would like to reward you for obeying his request this year."

"From our date?" I asked. I was surprised he remembered.

"Yes," Reaper answered. "He would like you to see his true form in his home."

"He has a true form?" That was news to me. "I thought he was only a spirit?"

"Goblins have a true form on the other side, yes," Reaper confirmed. "They can access it here, but rarely do so."

He had a proper body? All the years we'd spent together, and he'd never once mentioned it. What else didn't I know about my lifelong companion?

"Can I return from his home once I visit?" I asked.

Demons were known to offer appealing deals before kidnapping naïve girls. I wasn't falling for that trap. He'd already threatened to leave me in the Beyond once.

"Yes," Reaper said, "Gaksi promised to return you."

And without the promise, would he have left me there? As if sensing my hesitation, Reaper continued, "We promised not to lie to each other, remember?"

He extended an arm. I took it timidly, and he drew me into him, back flushed against his chest.

"But it might not be what you expect, so brace yourself." His voice rang with finality.

I felt hot all over, even though he'd only touched me for a minute.

"Are you ready?" he breathed against my ear.

"Yes," I mustered back.

We fell backward, air whipping past as we made our descent.

We arrived seconds later in a wasteland I'd never seen before, similar to the Barren Fields. Sam perched on a tree, whistling at our arrival. "Where are we?" I asked.

"Gaksi's favorite haunt," he said, stepping away from me and calling out, "Gaksi goblin! Your progeny is here."

I was awed when a creature emerged from the mist.

A winged beast with blazing blue eyes flew down, landing on a single leg. Arched grey wings, large enough to take out a horse, rose above us. Sharp teeth protruded from his mouth, pointed enough to rip out any throat. A decorated belt hugged his bulbous body, and bird-like talons gripped the floor.

I loved him immediately.

"My lord," he bowed to Reaper. "My dear Luna," he saluted me.

Reaper stared at me, frown deepening. Why? "Luna, Gaksi wanted to spend time with you in this form. Would you like to be chaperoned by him for a while?"

"Yes!" I said enthusiastically. Gaksi laughed.

"Just as I told you, Reaper," Gaksi mocked, "I knew she'd like me in this form, as I am her favorite demon."

"Watch yourself," Reaper warned. He bent down to kiss my hair, the softest press against me. "Enjoy."

My cheeks blossomed pink. He'd never done anything

like that in front of company before. Gaksi's eyes warmed in amusement, like a proud father. I wasn't sure if Reaper even liked me after I shoved him away at the masquerade.

Reaper dissipated, leaving me in the privacy of Gaksi and Sam. I rotated to the former.

"Gaksi! Why didn't you tell me you looked like this?"

His blood-red lips curled into a smile. "My other offspring would have been afraid."

My jaw dropped. "You have kids?"

"Yes, Luna." He chortled to himself. "I have more descendants than you know. Than even Reaper can keep track of."

How peculiar. I'd never thought of Gaksi as a… dad. I supposed he raised me like one, but that begged a better question: where were his kids?

I searched the sky, looking for smaller Gaksis to begin flying down, but Gaksi skipped away, hopping on one foot, and I had to hustle to keep up. Sam trailed above us.

If he had kids, did that mean he…reproduced? Ah! What a horrible thought.

He bounced, carefree, as he spoke.

"I am excited to have you here with me today. After all the time I spend in your universe, it seems only right for you to do me the favor of hanging out here."

I grinned. "Perhaps I should come here more often." Moving beside him, all kinds of mystical creatures pranced away when they saw us. I saw ghosts, humanoid figures, beasts, and all kinds of animals. It was very exciting. Would I find undiscovered animals here? I should have brought my notebook for documenting.

"Why haven't I come here before?" I asked.

"You weren't ready," he said, "but after you took down

the Bulgae, there's not much that can threaten you." He spoke with the unmistakable sound of pride.

His mirth was comforting. It made me feel so relaxed, so comfortable, so at home. Like this was where I was meant to be. That must be a component of dark energy from surrounding demons—to make the receiver feel more at ease. Gaksi used it more in this form to keep me calm as unknown creatures passed beside us.

Tricky demon, even though I trusted him.

"Do you miss Reaper now that he has departed?" Gaksi questioned.

Yes. Although I would never admit that out loud. Lately, I'd been reaching for my neck, searching for the pulse point of the mark, only to remind myself I had bigger problems.

"He misses you," Gaksi said. "He spends too much time with the dying when they're frightened and alone. Your spark and company keep him rejuvenated."

His admission shocked me. He saw me as a spark? Compared to the mortals dying alone, I was at least fighting to stay alive.

"Do not worry about him, though. He would never miss it for anything. Some souls are even ready to greet him and the comfort and certainty of the end." Gaksi's favorable opinion of him was showing. "Shall we tour my home?"

"Yes!" I wanted to capture everything.

Gaksi threw me a camera and I snapped photos of everything as we traveled.

Poison trees. Scaly animals. A dodo! Weren't those extinct? How did Reaper get one here?

I put my camera down when we reached a village. Gaksi slowed his pace.

Music played from a harp, stationed alone with no

musician. Little houses were built from the grey earth, with translucent people drifting between them.

"What is this place?" I asked cautiously. I thought we were in an unknown piece of the earth, where demons roamed alone, not in the company of people. A sinking feeling compressed my chest. Something wasn't right. Dodos? Translucency?

"You'll learn soon enough," Gaksi said, remaining cryptic as ever. I debated, brushing my hands against the dagger, but decided against it. Why would Gaksi put me in a position of danger? Maybe my eyes were playing tricks on me.

"Why are so many holding hands?" Some apparitions floated alone, but others were locked onto others. Some held only one hand out, fingers splayed like they were waiting for something. It felt like I was intruding on something private, something sacred.

"They're starborn souls," Gaksi explained. "They were made for each other, so they spend an eternity together, too."

"An eternity?"

We'd drawn close enough that I could determine the apparitions were not human. They were luminous, floating above the ground, wandering without purpose. Souls.

Souls lived here, not humans.

Gaksi loved it here. Sam was here.

Extinct animals existed here.

Nausea crawled up my throat. I knew where we were. Why Gaksi's true form came out here. I forced myself to ask another question instead of collapsing. "And the ones with only one hand out?"

"Their true love is in the realm of the living," Gaksi continued. "They hold their hand out so that the moment their loved one passes, they'll be welcomed by their lover's waiting grip."

That was...so precious. My heart hurt as I looked at all the lonely souls. Then the ones that were bonded together forever. So sadly romantic. When would it be my turn to be happy? Would I ever be like one of them, content and loved by my chosen one forever?

Perhaps never, if I only got here because Reaper killed me, and I fell into the Beyond willingly.

Unbothered. Confident. I couldn't be dead, was I? Gaksi wouldn't have sent Reaper to kill me without me noticing. He knew I was too young to die.

"A certain prince of ours walks much like the waiting ones." Gaksi wiggled his eyes at me.

My stomach sank to the floor. Reaper had a lover?

He was waiting for someone?

Then I couldn't have him.

The revelation hit me like a hurricane. Of course, this was a waste of time. Of course, I would fall for someone I could never have.

Thunder boomed above. I reeled in my emotions, focusing only on Gaksi beside me and not the rising panic that I'd been kidnapped or killed.

Did I even know this demon? Why did he bring me here?

"Interesting," was all I could say.

Gaksi continued hopping, and I scurried behind him, terrified of being left behind in unfamiliar land. We passed a massive statue of Reaper, traditional gat on his head, completing the lovely rendition.

"He commissioned this of himself?" I asked.

"No," Gaksi replied. "The souls built it for him."

"Why?"

"They admire him," Gaksi said simply. "For many, he was their last memory of earth, and for some, he was their best."

How horrible was a life that Reaper was their best memory? With his red cloth of names, did he often comfort people before they officially died? Without meaning to, a vision of him came to my head, holding a soul's hand gently before they passed on. It softened my heart a bit, making me unusually fond of him.

Ghosts and phantoms roamed every few paces, several of them now bowing their heads as they passed. I bowed back. One of them, a gwisin, I recognized. She bowed lower than the rest, holding her glasses on to do so before departing.

"Reaper holds the escaped demons hostage here?"

Gaksi gave me a skeptical look. "No, child. They always live here. But they get pulled, like a vortex, out to the other side when there's an imbalance of energy."

"What do you mean? I thought they enjoyed tormenting mortals."

That was what all the texts said. That they drew energy from draining ours. Dark magic was built on stolen energy, and when humans weren't being drained, lights flickered, and the earth rumbled from energy being stolen from the environment.

"We've been over this. They were mortal once, too. They have no reason to harm you."

A younger soul, dressed in jeans and a t-shirt, waved at me. His chubby little fingers reminded me of Joseph.

I waved back. He giggled and ran away.

Joy. I was playing with the dead. I wondered if his parents were here too or if he was alone.

"Reaper enjoys tormenting me," I insisted. "He only made that bargain to do so."

"You know him much less than you think you do," Gaksi replied. "Reaper made that bargain with you because he was desperate. He had to find a way to determine whether you were the gumiho, lest the rest of his kingdom fall into disarray between this universe and yours. He has never desired to harm a mortal. He feels enough of their pain during their demise."

I fell silent. I never considered many ulterior motives for Reaper's deal-making. I had always assumed he was inherently evil, like all demons, which was sufficient for his motivations. Sure, he'd told me he needed to ascertain my identity, but I'd never dwelled on *why*.

I hadn't dug into his identity at all.

But that didn't justify everything he put me through. Sending a hound at me, mocking me, pushing my boundaries at school—he was inherently devious.

"Why do you defend him?" I accused.

Why did he do all this for others and go out of his way to torment me? Why did he tell me so little about his life while spying on all whereabouts of mine? Did he want me to despise him?

Gaksi snickered. "He does not feel the need to convince you his actions have merit."

My earlier words rang in my head. *"You are a worthless immortal,"* I had snapped at him, and he had dumped me into my bed like I'd offended him.

Guilt quickened my breaths. Cruelty wasn't my habit, not even to demons. But at the moment, I meant it. He had hurt me, and I felt conflicted about that.

"Reaper never speaks of this place," I said.

Gaksi waited before answering. "He keeps those things

he finds precious close to his heart," he said. "He rarely speaks of you to others, either."

There went Gaksi, implying that men were obsessed with me. So I was important to Reaper, really? What an insane comment. I shamefully craved his affection, yet he despised what I could represent. The gumiho, who only brought him more trouble and torment.

"It is best if he never speaks of me. Rather, it would be best if we never spoke again," I confirmed. "You know as well as I do that I cannot be with him."

"Would not is different than cannot," Gaksi said. "And, my dear Luna, I do not believe there is anything that you cannot do."

"Could I escape the Beyond if Reaper just killed me to bring me here?" I demanded.

Gaksi's saucer-sized eyes crinkled with amusement. "I knew you'd figure it out. You've always been a smart girl."

"You didn't think the village of dead people would give it away?" Souls turned their heads toward me. They could stare all they'd like. They'd get an eternity to deal with me if I were dead.

He laughed, the sound echoing off the brisk wind. "Living creatures pass through the Beyond all the time, just as the dead return to the land of the living to haunt them. I wanted you to see this place before making a decision."

"Before making what decision?" I asked. "To kill myself and join them?"

"To accept your destiny," he said, clouds swirling around me.

When they disappeared, I was back in my dorm room, heart pounding hard enough to know I was fully alive.

CHAPTER
TWENTY-NINE

THE ORACLE MUSINGS

Time for a history lesson!

Once upon a time, a young goddess was lonely and desperate for companionship. She tested boundaries, day by day, until she found a young man she was ready to become one with.

However, there was a problem: he was to die, and she could not. So, she snuck around. Made some deals she was not qualified to make. Found a magic-infused herb that could bring her to mortality.

And as soon as she took it, her humanity kicked in, and after thousands of years of living, the goddess Circe died.

All good things must come to an end.

WEEKS PASSED with nothing significant happening, save a few demon sightings. I tried to send some away, but others usually beat me to it. I didn't have any motivation to work harder, given that my Bulgae move had secured me so high above the competition it was hardly a fair fight.

It made me wonder whether Reaper or Gaksi had sent the Bulgae deliberately to help me climb the leaderboard. But they knew it was risky—I almost died the first time. So, who sent him?

We lost three more of our freshmen that night. One died the night of, charred to a crisp by a phoenix. The second followed a kelpie into the ocean and drowned. The third died in the infirmary last night after failing to recover from a cyclops beating.

So...why was I still here? Did I even deserve to be here?

"Yes." My necklace warmed over my heart.

"You almost let me become a statistic last night. A zombie nearly ate my brains!"

"How was I supposed to know a recently deceased student could turn that fast?"

That entire area of campus got torched, leaving an ugly black shadow of death in the middle of the Diamond.

"You didn't need me. You held your own without me."

My necklace flickered out, as it usually did, with Gaksi spending less and less time with me as I grew stronger.

"Luna, I have been holding my tongue. I have been trying very hard to be a good friend to you, but this must cease."

I glanced at Aubrey. She came to our wine night with a bottle of pink vodka and a platter of crackers, but she tossed them onto my desk so hard it rattled.

She wore pajamas, but her expression promised death.

Her hands settled on her hips, and she shot me the most intimidating glare I had ever seen from her.

"What's your problem?" I asked. I popped a cracker in my mouth. Knowing Aubrey, this could be serious or just a 'fashion intervention, because my eyes bleed around you.'

"First, I demand you hear me out till the end." Aubrey began.

"Okay?" I grabbed another cracker.

Aubrey inhaled deeply. "Your relationship with the Reaper threatens everything."

I swallowed. "I know."

I wouldn't ask how she knew I still saw him. I trusted she had a reason for bringing it up now.

"I'm not finished," Aubrey continued.

I stared her down. If she wanted to go there, she could. "Talk, then."

"You seem to think this relationship can continue forever," Aubrey stated.

I flinched. "I never said that."

"No, but you act like it," Aubrey said. "You continually disappear for hours—and I know you're with him that whole time—"

"You don't own my company," I said simply.

"It's not about me!" Aubrey yelled. "It's about how obvious it is that you're with him! I know your patterns and behaviors because I know you well. But it won't take long for others to connect the dots and realize you're still seeing him. That you go out of your way to spend time with him because you *care for him*!" She screeched the last few words.

I reared back in shock. "I do not—"

"You don't have to admit something to me for it to be true," she declared. "Anyone with any bit of sense can tell you're too smart not to spend your time strategically. I mean, you're a straight-A student! You're at the top of the freshmen class after weeks of nonsense assignments! You wouldn't spend your time away from all that unless it was for a damned good reason."

She looked like she was about to pull her hair out in frustration. "You have no idea how dangerous he is. He's immortal! He has centuries on you of practicing his magic! Of becoming lethal! Of molding himself into this perfectly charming weapon of mass destruction!"

He had committed no acts of mass destruction so far, I reminded myself. And the only magic he regularly practiced was teleportation for his job.

I gritted my teeth. "You don't know him at all."

I didn't know what drove me to defend him. But with such blatant lies, it just felt right.

"You don't know how well he can manipulate and control!" Aubrey shouted at me.

"I'm more of a control freak than he is," I said. "And he cannot manipulate me easily with a goblin of my own at my side."

Aubrey stomped her foot, indignant. Her eyes flashed. "Why would he want you?"

"What?" I inhaled.

"Why would he want you?" The seriousness of her tone hit me like a hurricane. "A human girl with no throne? A stranger to him, even better yet, a child? You don't think it's a little predatory for someone that experienced in life to let a kid who just left her home—"

"I am not a kid." My dorm room trembled. I desperately willed my shadows to extinguish, despite my righteous anger.

"You don't think it's questionable how he just picked you at random?" Aubrey scowled at my shaking room. "How the only tie he has to you is that your own goblin doesn't see a problem with this? Have you slept with him yet?"

"What?" I repeated, voice shaky. "No! That is none of your business, anyway."

"You will regret this." Aubrey crossed the room. "Once he gets what he wants from you, I doubt he will ever reappear in your life again. If you continue to see him, I will take matters into my own hands."

"By doing what?" I retorted.

"I will find the principal myself and tell him I've seen you two together over and over again," Aubrey said. "I'll kidnap Cordelia if I have to. Make her my witness."

"Leave Cordelia out of it! Isn't she a little too *homely* for us anyways? And if I had any choice, I would not want to be with him again." My breaths panted out, in tune with my racing heart.

"Actions speak louder than words," Aubrey said, face-to-face now. "You've checked out every book about demons, monsters, and immortals in the library, but not one on bargains."

I was struck silent, hating how she pointed out the obvious. That if I wanted to escape this bargain, I could have put more effort into it.

"Tell me, Luna, do you really know him?" Her white teeth flashed.

"I know him better than you!" I shoved her out of my personal space.

"You don't know anything about anyone, Luna! I doubt you even know your friends at this point. You're too busy chasing a monster," Aubrey said, backing up only inches.

"I know you're crossing a line right now! What's there to know about my friends?" I couldn't believe she really came here just to fight with me—

Aubrey ripped the cracker from my hands and crushed it. "Focus, you self-absorbed freak!" She huffed out a breath. "How old is Cordelia?"

"What?"

"How old is Cordelia?" Aubrey repeated.

My mind went blank. "18. She's a freshman like us."

"She's *sixteen*, Luna. Sixteen. And when I rescued her from her suicide attempt, you couldn't even be bothered to talk to her after because you were so busy focusing on Reaper and school and yourself! Because if you took more than half a second to look up at the world around you, you'd realize one of our friends is a child who needs to *go home*! And she can't do that if she's surrounded by friends here!"

Cordelia was a kid? She never drank. Or partied. Or fought.

The room spun, guilt washing over me so intently I could drown in it. I never knew she was so young.

"You don't even know the people around you, and you think you know the Reaper?"

I watched the storm forming in Aubrey's eyes, processing. Boldly, I decided to ask what I was really thinking. "Are you jealous that I'm dating him?"

Her smile became sadistic. "No, because me and him have history."

My shadows sank deep, retreating into the pit of my stomach. How long? When? How?

"You aren't special. You aren't the only one he's pursued. He's not dumb enough to flaunt his past in front of you, but I've known him longer than you have."

My shadows burst from my skin, whipping around me.

"I'm going to pretend I don't see those." Aubrey scrutinized my shadows with distaste.

"Prove it," I gutted out. "Prove you and him have history."

"He acts the way he does because he has a father that detests him," Aubrey held up a finger with each truth she revealed about him. "He has a kingdom and citizens that adore him because he showed them kindness in death. Preventing the gumiho from taking lives is his life's mission."

My knees met the floor. There was no way she would know that unless...

"And between every toxic love story between the immortal and the object of his fascination, the mortal always has the most to lose."

I HAD the most to lose. In that, Aubrey was right. I blocked her number the moment she stalked out of my room, downing the vodka she left behind in the meantime. It stung, and I wondered if it was intentional. Vodka instead of wine as some kind of subtle, irritating punishment. Her words plagued me the most, in the deepest part of my mind, because I knew she was right.

So, I threw myself back into my first goal in this university: school.

I didn't like to think or ponder about my problems. The secret to my 4.0 at school? When I felt overwhelmed, I worked through my emotions by being productive, not by facing my feelings. If I kept myself busy and booked enough, I never had to feel anything at all.

My mind was a horrible place to be, and I did everything in my power to stay out of it.

Besides school, House recruitment was winding up.

Rose House invited pledges for a simple dinner at their home for the final round. Eager for the distraction, I RSVP'd.

"This is an optional, low-stakes invitation. Please come as you are :)" read the invitation.

Low-stakes, easy, relaxing. That was what I wanted right now.

They had decked their entire House in roses. Glowing pink roses lined the doors to the entryway. A carpet of red roses coated the entrance. An active member with bleached white hair, who introduced herself as Daisy, led me to a velvet chair on a long dinner table loaded with plates. Among the feast set out, little white roses served as magic, self-cleaning napkins.

"Please, eat," the house chef insisted, a thicker woman with a colorful apron. She came out solely to address us. "No traps here."

The food was divine. Savory, sweet, and heavenly—it made me feel genuinely full for the first time on campus.

President Wisteria came personally to talk to me. She surprised me by pulling me in for a hug. "I'm so glad you're here, Luna." Her face was genuine. "You are welcome to socialize with the actives here. They're glad you're here, too."

I spent most of my time, however, chatting with the other girls my age. I was unfamiliar with many names since I hadn't seen any of them in other Houses. It seemed a pretty even mix of those faking happiness because this House was their consolation prize and those that were genuinely happy to be here. An interesting dichotomy.

Cordelia was also here but seated away from me at the table's edge. When I beckoned her over, she waved me off mid-conversation. Another time then. I wanted to know why she was here when she was so young. Now that I'd ruined my relationship with Aubrey, she was all I had left.

I eavesdropped on some of the active's conversations as I ate. Unlike past rounds, where potential new members were paired off one new member to one active, I was now surrounded by a semicircle of older girls.

"Why did you decide to buy The Oracle Musing's merch?" a brunette with a McKenna name tag asked across the table.

"It's cute!" Daisy spun herself off her seat. "It's got the insignia of every House on it! All House love!"

"She only did that so more House girls would buy it!" McKenna snorted.

"Why would she aim her personal merchandise at House girls?" A blonde named Cassie asked.

"Because she knows we're all gossipy, two-faced bitches who love to know the tea!" McKenna near-shouted. The actives collapsed into laughter beside me.

I was taken aback by how at ease they were. They weren't even trying to impress me. Just having a conversation. Every so often, they would ask my opinion of something. It bewildered me every time. They spoke to me as if we were already old friends.

I felt a pang of sadness upon leaving.

I had to leave early to get to Fae House. They didn't bother to check the double booking because it was unusual for a new member to be invited to both top and bottom Houses.

The house mom snuck a pastry, wrapped in a to-go box, in my purse when I left. I munched on it while I went over to Fae house. No eating could happen there.

I walked alone to that House, adding jewelry as I went.

Their house was exactly as I remembered. Enchanted, magic-spun, whimsical.

Many of them flexed their ears to tea-sipping potential new members, while berating those that had been dropped. Eating macarons with them, I saw what my future could be.

Dainty and delicate as their pointed ears, yet sharp enough to cut a threat to shreds.

Their garden party passed in a blur, and the next day, I redressed myself in finery for Angel House.

Angel House prepared their entire house in shades of white and black. The theme was film noir, and we chatted over silent movies while classical instruments played. It was a safe and regal affair. I felt bored the whole time, which disappointed me. Although lovely and classic, I ached for more.

When I glanced at the perfectly made-up faces around me, darkness roamed and twisted my soul. It should be easy to live in a place like this. Where everybody was pretty and polite and universally well-liked.

But, after hearing enough classical songs to kill me, I decided I didn't need to be well-liked.

I worked like a maniac. I chased demons because I could. When darkness called, I ran toward it.

I was restless for an identity of my own, not a comfortable box to fit into. I spent so much time crafting an ideal image of myself that I no longer recognized who I wanted to become.

I didn't like Angel House at all. I may have been insecure, but I'd always be filled with lust for more.

Better to be thought of as vicious and beautiful than soft and pretty.

Melody messaged our group at the end of all the parties.

Melody: *Just remember, freshman: it's not just four years. It's for life. Is this the person you want to be? The values you want to share? You have time to think it over before you make your final choices. Choose carefully.*

CHAPTER
THIRTY

THE ORACLE MUSINGS

We've got spirits, yes we do! We've got spirits, how about you? One of our cheerleaders (past or present) will have a dramatic encounter led by a spirit today.

THERE WAS a dragon in the lagoon.

I knew there was a dragon in the lagoon, because Cordelia texted me for the first time in weeks with a picture of a scaly red beast. It sprouted a long beard, whiskers, and arched red ears sprouting above its head. Instead of wings, it carried a swirling blue orb.

It appeared good-natured, given that Cordelia was taking a selfie with it.

"That's a demon, Cordelia?" I questioned into the phone.

"He's a friendly one!" she enthused. "He's been smiling for photos all day. Look!"

She turned the camera around. The dragon posed for every student waving at him, making sure he aligned his eyes with the camera. A friendly beast.

"Come visit!" Her final words before the phone died.

HYDRA ALERT! HYDRA ALERT!

An unidentified demon has been spotted on campus! Take shelter! Any paranormal activity has the potential for danger!

Raucous laughter echoed from outside my room.

"Do you think Siren House will take us if we kill that thing?"

"Faeries would be impressed by those that can slay a dragon, right?"

"I bet that orb has magic powers! Let's get it!"

"This one's rumored to be weak! If we wanted to practice, now's the perfect time!"

Students shouted and planned outside. A sickening feeling crept into my stomach. The dragon looked like the harmless Yong Dragon I read about from Reaper's kingdom. They were harmless spirits that appeared in water and rerouted irrigation to promote good harvests.

They didn't even breathe fire. There was no reason to hunt them.

Unless you wanted points, of course.

I put aside my feelings for the lord of that kingdom. I had to lead this creature back home on my own.

I sprinted out of my room. My feet pounded the sidewalk as I outran the other student hopefuls. I willed shadow energy to pump my legs faster, making me almost as fast as a vampire.

Rain poured from the sky, first a light drizzle, then a torrential downpour. I heard students slipping and tripping around me, but my shadows cleared a path. Clouds of my making covered the sun. Reaper's shadow training had its merits.

A black shadow flew above me as I ran. Sam was keeping tabs on me, as usual. I flipped a vulgar gesture at her, only to stumble as it tried to poop on me a moment later.

Maybe I'd direct the students to take out that demon instead.

When I split through the Whispering Woods to reach the dragon in the lagoon, students crowded like paparazzi around it.

"Look here, dragon!"

"Smile!"

"Do you think I could ride this thing and go viral?"

"Enough!" I boomed. Heads turned toward me. "Leave that thing alone! It needs to go back home!"

"What are you going to do? Find its house?" a boy mocked.

"Didn't realize she was a demon whisperer," another whispered to her friend.

"Maybe if you rode that thing, it would go viral," a foul vampire male suggested.

CRACK!

A beam of light blasted into the ground, cracking the earth into a massive fissure. Students scrambled and wobbled for footing until a thunderclap rumbled so loud, I thought I might go deaf.

I shrunk on my knees, covering my ears with my hands, shadows cradled around me. The thunder cracked five more times before I cautiously released my hands. The other students collapsed.

"Cordelia!" I called, running to her.

"There's my little beastling," a dark voice rumbled, "always making friends with the beasts instead of humans."

Cordelia lay on her side in the dirt.

I whirled around. "What. Did. You. Do?" I shook with the force of my rage.

"I sent a sound wave infused with enough dark energy to make them pass out," Reaper said, hands resting in his pockets.

"They look dead!"

"I would have a lot more work to do if I killed them," Reaper said, the picture of cocky arrogance. He had the audacity to smile at me as if I could actually stand him right now.

Aubrey's earlier words came back to me. *We have history.*

I turned my back to him, staring at the dragon.

"You know dragons can fly, right?" Reaper questioned. Listening, the dragon shook out its powerful body, spraying rain everywhere. It winked at me, then launched into the sky. "You had nothing to run for. It can handle itself."

"My books didn't say that." I crossed my arms. The magnificent beauty flew away, slithering like a serpent into the clouds. "Where is he going now?" My brow creased with worry, not that he could see it. "Some students have bows and arrows."

His voice shifted in confusion. "You have too much compassion for creatures that are not yours."

"I don't think any being should suffer more than it needs to." Like my sputtering heart right now, thinking of where he could have been before this. "Do you disagree?"

Reaper sent shadows around me. Slithering, teasing.

They gently pressed my hips, encouraging me to rotate. I let them, begrudgingly.

He leaned against a tree, looking as leisurely as a student skipping class. The top of his usual shirt was unbuttoned, exposing the muscular lines of his chest. The desire to taste it rivaled my desire to rip its heart out.

"Does it bother you how much the opinions of others weigh on you?" Reaper implored.

"What does that mean?" I wanted to ask him about what Aubrey said. But I was so angry, so frightened, so scared that he'd say exactly what I didn't want to hear. That I meant nothing to him, and this whole affair was pointless. That Aubrey was right, and he had no reason to really choose me. I was just one of many.

"We go on these cycles." Reaper whirled circles of shadow around me with each sentence. "You act like you hate me, then you kiss me, then we go back to hating, then we continue like lovers. I've been thinking, and I determined there was a common denominator. The opinions of others."

"The guidance of others is valuable to me," I said, affronted.

"You haven't noticed that your mother in particular likes to keep you hostage in her hold?" His shadows tightened, confining me. "I can't tell if it's because she's jealous of you or is afraid of who you can become."

My brows raised. "You spend your free time thinking of my mother?"

"I think of all the mortals that possess a fraction of power," he answered. "And having a soul as wrathful and experienced as your mother pawning you around is a perilous position to navigate."

Pawning. I was not a pawn. "My mother is hardly

ancient. Though you're proving her case. That demons will do anything to try to separate you from family."

Reaper prowled toward me, shadows gleaming, scent and power all-encompassing. The shadows pressed against my back, forming a solid wall, as his hands caged around my head.

I stood my ground, unamused by his antics. This was the attitude of a man who had played me like a fool. Who made my lonely heart hurt a little too hard for a broken man.

"I can't tell you what to believe about your family," he said, warm breath coasting my face. "About your life, about anything you are. But I know that you are capable of being more. And I think you are afraid of that. Your mother knows you're special. Why don't you?"

I gritted my teeth. I hated that—condemnation—that marked his tone. I wasn't oblivious to who I was. And here was he, so determined that he knew everything about me when he'd been fooling around with mortals for years.

"I am special." I rose on my tiptoes to meet his eyes. He smirked. "Special enough to get any man I want. Should I prove it to you?"

His gaze darkened.

"If I took up that boy's offer and rode something that wasn't you, what would do?"

His gaze jumped to my mouth, irises dark. The shadows pressed in closer, near suffocating. "Those are some vile words from such a pretty mouth."

My heart fluttered as he surveyed me. I couldn't tell whether he wanted to hate me or love me.

He brushed his nose to mine. "I am not a jailor. Your life cannot be controlled by myself. I can only hope you will not resort to such...uncivilized options."

"Will do," I said.

"As you wish," he responded, warm breath brushing my forehead as he fell away.

"As *you* wish," I spat.

A small voice in my head told me I was being immature. Irrational. I should just bring up what Aubrey said. How long until he figured out what I was really angry about?

But not yet. I had to play first.

He wasn't in charge now. I was. And he would not pressure me—not until I pressured him first.

I was in control.

Knowing my determination, my shadows manifested themselves as daggers in my waiting hands.

"I would advise," Reaper breathed, eyeing them, "to not show your mother how much you've progressed."

I propelled them at him. Too unexpected, too nimble for him to predict. He only looked at me in amusement as they bounced harmlessly off his body.

"You cannot hurt me with my magic," he quipped. "But you've come a long way from the girl who ran away from me at House recruitment."

"Why do you think my mother is jealous of me?" I asked, recalling my shadows.

The fascination and pride misted off his face, replaced with quiet contemplation.

"She had everything when she was in college," I said. "She got her top House. She married the love of her life. She could have even had Gaksi had she not shoved him away."

Gaksi nodded in quiet approval in my mind.

"Your mother knows you have more control over your powers than she does," Reaper said. "She envies you—it's visible all over her face every time she overreacts to your presence. She knows that kind of power is not granted lightly by the fates. That it is worth more than all the stars in the sky. You're her greatest accomplishment, and that's why she wants you to stay safe within her realm of control."

I staggered back. They were the loveliest words anyone had ever said to me, though they were at the insult of my mother. "She loves me, Reaper. Every mother wants her daughter to be safe."

"It's not whether she loves you. It's whether her love becomes too much. Restricts you from who you could be and instead confines you into her safest version of you. Family love is often the most toxic of all."

CHAPTER
THIRTY-ONE

THE ORACLE MUSINGS

*D**emons are very protective of what they decide is theirs. Especially their homes. Did you know that once a demon brings his lover to his home, he can never love another? It is as binding as the cut strings of the Fates themselves.*

Speaking of demons: A new prediction has emerged! There is nothing more fickle than fate, and I saw a darling new prediction recently: would Aubrey get her true love's kiss after all?

My hand flew to my mouth to cover my choked cry. Shame, so strong I thought it might swallow me, heated my cheeks. Why? Because my friend might be happy? Because the male who spent so much time with me—bickering, flirting, cavorting—had a future life that did not include me?

He didn't owe me anything. Our bargain meant nothing.

And I could attest that Reaper might deserve his own

true love story, too. Didn't I say earlier that no being should suffer needlessly? Who was I to deny him his happiness? We all deserved our happy ending.

Although...for one foolish, fleeting second, I thought I could share mine with him.

I wanted to know that he was mine.

And...I wanted to be his in return.

I had been unchosen, and I had been unchosen for too, too long.

I remembered how engrossed he had been in Aubrey at the masquerade. Had he recognized his fate there and then? Was that the beginning of the end for us?

And it wasn't shame, embarrassment, or wounded pride that took over then. It was longing.

Such pure, unadulterated longing that I collapsed back into bed.

It was a quiet morning after that. No stray demon activity to report. Even Gaksi, sensing my mental anguish, removed himself for my privacy. Nobody to comfort me or judge me —especially when I woke up screaming because a dream monster had carved out my heart to eat, and I was too tired to fight.

Sunlight streamed through my blinds, and it was going to be a beautiful day, but I was lonely. So lonely.

A bargain. I was just a bargain to him, someone to help him toward an end goal. The sooner I accepted that, the better.

I missed home. I wanted my dad to come in my room and tell me that nightmares could never win. I wanted mom to make kimchi pancakes and tell me family is all you need, even if she insulted my character in the same breath. I wanted to go back to the way it was before I showed up at this monstrous university, and I never had to feel much pain or misery at all.

Maybe the bargain, the teasing, all the times we got closer—

Maybe they were just a way of passing the time. A method of making sure he didn't truly turn insane in his quest.

That was okay. It would have to be. I did not want this bargain anyway, I told myself. This was never meant to be. It was for the best.

Forget Audrey. She could rot in hell for all I cared. Traitor.

Reaper could still be my... ally. I didn't want his subjects to be stuck here any more than he did. His loving my former best friend didn't change our end goals.

It was just a fruitless hope to think that someone would choose me as badly as I wanted to choose him.

I DIDN'T BOTHER to keep up with demon news. The last thing I wanted was to help him when he could figure it out all alone.

Presents kept appearing on my windowsill. I assumed that was Gaksi's way of comforting my post—whatever this was.

A mother-of-pearl jewelry box lay there today. It had deep navy hues underneath pearl birds and flowers. It must have cost a fortune. Gaksi surely stole it.

A note rested inside.

We should talk.

"Gaksi?" I reached out tentatively with my mind.

"Yeah, I'll fetch him," Gaksi said. Fetch *him*?

Him? Reaper?

My morning gifts hadn't been from Gaksi?

I was going to throw up.

A moment later, Reaper leaned against the doorframe, looking elated. Joyful, even. Like I'd made his whole day by calling him.

Two-faced bastard.

I observed the relaxed stance, the handsome grin from ear to ear, and cursed. "Why are you here?" I put enough venom into my voice that he seemed shocked.

"Avoiding me is making you moody, is it?"

I shoved the box out at him. "Explain yourself."

His shoulders sagged slightly as he glanced between the box and me. "You dislike it."

"No, it's beautiful," I said. "But why?"

"Why not? You used or ate all my other trinkets."

That confirmed it. He'd sourced them all himself.

"Do you buy your other lovers gifts?"

Reaper dropped his arm from the door. "What nonsense is that?"

"Did you buy me gifts concurrently or in spite of bedding Aubrey?"

Reaper moved forward in practiced, elegant waves. "Is that why I haven't seen or heard from you in weeks? Because you think I'm interested in your friend?"

"I don't think. I know. I have it on good authority. Even the oracle knows, Reaper!"

He arrived at my side, just a hair's breadth away from me, and took me in with a piercing gaze. "Threatened, seraphim?"

"What's there to be threatened of?" I asked icily.

"You've been just as I expected. Toying with your food until something exciting and new comes along."

Reaper bared his teeth like an animal. "Do you think I enjoyed Aubrey's company? That I wasn't repulsed by her ministrations? That I wasn't just biding my time with her to see if I could get a reaction out of you?"

"The oracle seems to think so."

His hiss was low—dangerous. "I do not care for her. And I did not bed her either. She might have thought we were something—I regretfully admit I should not have led her on—but I assumed you knew of my commitment to you first."

His gaze softened. "I expected you to reach out by now." He released a long sigh. "I have shown up at every rogue demon sighting, sometimes even letting them linger long enough to draw human attention, but you are remarkably stubborn."

He reached out to cup my face, and I swatted him away. I felt a primitive, forceful rumble of shadows against my soul. A warning. Though I took it like a flame to a candle—an invitation to alight. "Is that what bothered you? That I'm not at your beck and call? That I'm not a slave for you to control?"

"What bothered me," Reaper continued, taking in deep, shuddering breaths, "is that you were absent, and I had no idea where you were or even whether you were alright."

His shadows pushed into my back, begging me to get closer to him. To embrace him. To collapse into him and never let go. Possessive, desperate, and wanting, they much resembled their master right now.

"Even Gaksi disappeared to do god knows what." He threw his arms back, grabbed his shadows, and hounded them forward. He braced his arms against me, locking me in, powerful wings throbbing into place behind him. Like an angel of death, deranged enough to hold me captive.

"Why are you so desperate to see the worst in me?" he asked. "I cannot function when I am not with you."

My shadow magic misted at that confession, falling like droplets of spilled blood on the bed.

"Tell me what to do to atone."

With each word, his powerful wings beat, sending gusts of wind into my room and spraying my belongings everywhere.

"What?" I asked, confused.

"I am not blind, seraphim. I know how difficult it is for me to be with you. Those with little magic have it easy. They say some cheap phrases, buy even cheaper gifts, and win over their loves without trying. They will never know the duties of serving a great nation. Of having responsibilities beyond your own desires. Of having your honor and dignity at stake every time you pursue the one you keep breathing for. Tell me how to atone for being who I am so that I may pursue you."

My breathing stopped.

Was it possible... that the oracle was talking about someone else?

She never lied, but she never said Aubrey's kiss was with Reaper.

His confession brought me to my feet. He stayed where he was, brooding. Maybe it was the glistening in my eyes or the hollowed-out look in his, but I reached around to hold him.

How could he think I wanted him to change when he had never tried to change me?

I wanted the Reaper who built cities for deeply damaged and wandering souls. The Reaper who lived to fulfill impossible demands. I wanted the demon trapped in the most beautiful, angelic body. The demon who left me presents and taught me to embrace my shadows, not hide from them.

Yet I was just a lonely student, falling in love with an even lonelier demon.

His wings caressed my back as they folded over. I hugged him as hard as I could, knowing our time together was forbidden, and I would always be too afraid to tell him how I really felt because of it.

"This is for the one who keeps breathing for me," I whispered.

His strong arms coiled back in a vice-like grip. His hold was so secure I wondered how I could ever want to be in another. "This is for the one who makes the undead feel alive."

And at that moment, I think I did.

CHAPTER
THIRTY-TWO

THE ORACLE MUSINGS

Did you know that Aether has one of the highest suicide rates of any university in the country? Unlike the usual depression and anxiety, we have good-old-fashioned hazing. Hell week has begun—and desperate freshmen will do anything to knock out the competition. Sometimes permanently.

SAM FOLLOWED me home from the library today, as usual. But unlike usual, she perched on my shoulder.

Her proprietary grasp felt foreboding. Her three talons dug in, even when I hurried.

Students snickered and whispered as I went past.

Yeah, I got it. Tender-hearted animal lover. That was me. The only show of weakness I'd make. My only concession of gentleness: to hopeless little creatures. Like the one spying on me right now.

Phones covered faces as I got closer to home. That was... odd. Why was everyone recording today?

The stench hit me first.

Iron from blood and the cloying, sweet smell of decay.

"Turn around," Gaksi advised. *"Go back to the library."*

"Why?"

"You don't want to see this."

Had the gumiho struck again? My shadows gathered and pulsed. I wasn't running this time.

This was my campus. My school. My territory to defend.

I dashed forward.

Groans, whimpers, and croaky howls echoed ahead. The crow darted in front of me, flapping hard, shielding me from view, and I swiped beside it—

A pile of carnage lay neatly in front of my dormitory. The creatures were stacked like dominos, laid out by the hand of god, dying and writhing in gruesome agony.

On top, standing tall on the bodies of animals, demons, and creatures I couldn't identify...

His skin was charred, layered and colored, like he'd been cooked alive.

His appearance had lost its boyish charm, instead replaced by scars and a reformed face set in a grotesque sneer.

He had thrown his head back to laugh at my shock, covered in blue, black, and red blood that splattered with his amusement.

Sam turned her face away, unable to look any longer.

But I stared at my spirit saboteur as the idiot, as the fool who thought Hunter Consta might be dead when I had never seen his corpse.

As the fool who never realized he'd return, ready to massacre everything I loved dear.

Carrion, of all types and animals, squirmed under his feet. I spotted the horn of a unicorn. The wing of a griffin. The cloak of a ghost. By their movement, some remained alive, going through the throes of death itself.

Beyond his pile, mutilated blood and body bits shaped the macabre words:

DEMON'S WHORE.

Vultures circled above. Students from all Houses and classes cheered. My world spun.

All my favorite animals were here. Desiccated.

I clutched my stomach and vomited.

"Miss me?" He traipsed down the writhing pile, stomping any still-moving creature beneath him. "I have to say, I sure did miss you. What would my life be without a cheater, a seductress, and a demon lover destroying the fabric of this institution?"

"It doesn't have to be like this, Hunter."

I wiped the vomit off my mouth but couldn't stand.

"Yeah, burning me alive was only for fun, huh? Just a brief side excursion besides sleeping with the devil? Killing off my friends was just a little side plot to you, yeah?"

Before he could reach me, the earth exploded.

Students screamed and cowered. When the dust settled, Reaper detonated, throwing Hunter deep into the pile of death he'd created.

Cameras shattered, dropping to the ground. Broken.

A horrible smile graced Reaper's face. "Next one to speak of this incident," he intoned with graceful wrath, "will suffer a fate much worse than that."

Screeching sounded. A horrible crack split the air.

"I'm not afraid to take any of you to the other side early," he threatened. "And I'll have fun on the way down."

Feet hit the earth as students ran away.

Reaper strode toward me. Daring students to say something. Publicly.

They didn't.

I awaited him from the ground, keeled over. Here came the hands that had lifted me up. The mouth that had set me alight. The smile that had forced me to bite back, to stop being so passive, and to resist complacency.

The Prince of Demons. Whose darkness had never been aimed at me. Whose power never frightened me.

And now that he had claimed me so publicly, put me in the worst position of them all.

Exposed.

He kneeled before me.

"What have you done, Reaper?" I whispered, terror filling my voice.

"It's okay, seraphim," he said, the picture of lethal calm. "I'm going to take you home."

He swung me up in his arms, cradling me to his chest.

The darkness rippled, unsettled, as we teleported.

Shadows slit roughly as he stepped between space. But my dorm room didn't greet us.

Instead, we were in a grey bedchamber, large enough to house an army. He placed me down with two emotions rare for him—softness and tenderness.

Then he turned me to him.

Reaper's shoulders were tense, his posture hunched, and his entire demeanor... still.

He was embarrassed, I realized.

His voice was strained. "Forgive me."

I gazed around the room, cagey. "Where did you bring

me?" A silver desk sat across the bed, inlaid with the same jewels as mine at home. My feet sank into a rich chocolate rug. Rows and rows of books covered the wall across from us, where a four-poster bed rested.

His face remained tight, distant. As if he couldn't face me. As if he didn't want to admit what happened. "I should never have engaged with you. Let you see the...destruction of my wrath. Let you be treated like that by your own people." I'd never heard his voice so coarse, so unsure.

I didn't know how to deal with the aftermath of his public altercation. He might as well have declared that I was his lover to the whole world.

But I had not fought his presence there. I had welcomed it. Felt... relieved when I saw him coming to my rescue.

Yet, I tried not to think of the sight that led me here. I would become ill again.

"I'm not used to hearing apologies from you," I said honestly. I took a steadying breath before I continued. "You don't have to feel regret for... taking care of me. Had the situation been reversed, I would have done the same for you." The confession made my lungs burn. It was too true, too raw for what I expected to talk to him about today.

"I cannot believe what I saw today," Reaper snarled. "Those vile, worthless creatures should have been destroyed like the animals they mutilated. You should never have seen your animals like that. You never should have been rescued from that situation in the first place."

He huffed out a tired breath. "I should not have tormented them either. But when it came to you... I could not resist my baser nature."

Should not have tormented them? The same tormentors of animals?

"Yes, you should have. And you didn't answer my earlier question. Where are we?"

He laughed darkly. "I am rubbing off on you. You weren't always this vicious."

I resisted the urge to wander the room. I was feeling antsy, uncertain. In the corner of my eye, a window had nothing but darkness and silver trees outside.

"Where are we?"

"We are in my palace," he growled. "I was going to destroy them. I was going to flay their skin from their bones and boil them alive in their own blood. And I was going to lose my entire reputation as the Reaper, and all the privileges of my power, just to avenge you."

He heaved a ragged breath. "I had to get myself out of there. I had to take you somewhere safe. So I brought you here—to my home. Your worst nightmare. Go on. Fight me. Tell me how resentful you are of our relationship. That everything I do, I do because I am a worthless immortal."

"You are not worthless," I whispered. Tears slid down my face as I recognized the decorations in this room matched the ones in my dorm. I was in his home. He brought me to his palace.

He chose me.

Did you know that once a demon brings his lover to his home, he can never love another?

"You are my... best friend. And you are the Prince of Demons. I know you have the instincts to defend. And to punish. And to seek justice, always. But don't push me away because you think I despise you! Because of how others are treating me! Let it be my choice whether or not I want you in my life!"

Night swelled around him, billowing like ribbons of storm.

"But is it really your choice?"

"Yes—"

"I know that," he rasped. "But do you know how the rest of our worlds would see it?" Reaper's hands trembled like they contained barely leashed agony. "I am the Prince of Demons, here to steal an innocent bride. I am the irresponsible, reckless fool who brought a soul with an expiration date to live with an immortal. I am the monster, the succubus, the beast that corrupted the gentle and good to take home to himself based on his own selfishness."

My people think I am a rather young and foolhardy prince. He'd admit that to me over cards.

But his anguish sparked a chord in me, forcing me to respond. "And what about how I see you?" I asked plainly. "What should it matter what other people—even other demons think? Is my own opinion of you not enough?"

"And what is your opinion of me?"

I held my tongue, gazing out into the Beyond. I hadn't decided yet how I felt about the immortal being so devoted to me. Although with the frequency of tears slipping down my cheek, my body already had.

His response was sour, sharp. "You are in denial still. And if you can't admit you like me, who would even believe it?"

"What about your denial?" I fumed. "I might not be able to admit anything, but neither have you. Where's the 'I love you?' Where's the dating? The romancing? You have been fighting me just as much as I have you. You haven't admitted yet that I am not your enemy! Because what would happen if you did? Then we would have to face the consequences together... and you aren't man enough."

He recoiled.

The demon strong enough to break bones recoiled. And I knew that I had messed up.

I was too honest. Too spot-on with his flaws.

Or his perceived perception of his flaws.

"Reaper—"

In a split second, I saw the decision cross his face.

"Let your presence here be by your choice alone," he said.

His strong, capable hands—a prince's hands—held my neck, and I felt the wrath and warmth from my neck bond dissolve into fragments of nothing.

It left me like water rushing out of a dam, fast and dangerous and wild.

He disappeared with it, leaving me empty and wanting.

Desperate for a new type of bond to form.

CHAPTER
THIRTY-THREE

THE ORACLE MUSINGS

H*ow's the self-sabotage going, overdramatic prima donnas?*

I KEPT REACHING UP, feeling for the familiar warmth of the bond. But it was gone now, as was my lover. I was free.

Maybe it had been because that was what I was afraid of, myself. Of being really and truly free to choose and not being brave enough to actually commit to it.

Yet I kept pretending otherwise.

Pretending like I knew what I was doing. Like I made friends effortlessly, and school came easily. Like I was in control of my life.

And I was so tired of pretending.

Determination swept through me. I knew what I wanted. And I would tell him myself.

I wandered out of the ornate room—the one that he

must have matched my dorm room furniture to. His palace would respect a guest of his, right?

Hall after hall, I strode, admiring the rich tapestries and silver trim. Startled servants, made of spirit and shadow, bowed to me as I passed. I bowed back, which I think bewildered them even more.

I asked them if they knew Reaper's whereabouts, but they only shook their heads. I thanked them before continuing.

I kept roaming, hoping to organize my thoughts before running into him.

Although I hoped I would run into him soon.

I passed what must have been a dining room. A long obsidian table sat empty, lined with high-back chairs on each side.

I thought of what he would look like leading that table. Regal. Magnificent. Confident. Was that where he ate when he wasn't with me? It was larger than the Cornucopia and big enough to feed an army before battle. Was the food here better, too? Did shadow servants need to eat?

I lingered for too long in that room, hoping he would come.

I knew he would return to me, eventually. He always did.

Although, I wondered if this time I had pushed him too far.

I had been hurting, scared, and battered him with my fear. Which was unacceptable. I owed him an apology.

I'd acted like he was a burden, a stressor when really he was a... welcome distraction. And now, without his prodding flirtation, I had no outlet to deal with my emotions.

Did he feel the same? Did he miss what we had?

I had no way to ask, not with him gone.

And I wanted to ask him. I wanted us to be... something. I wasn't sure what yet. But I didn't want to lose him. And I certainly wasn't afraid of him. Nor was I afraid of this spacious castle as I drifted along.

So it was time. To tell him I was ready to admit it. That I was the scared one, but I wasn't anymore. Wherever he went, I was ready to face it.

I was brave and independent, and I chose this.

Not the Reaper, the demon from nighttime legends.

The Reaper who sent me gifts. Who came to my rescue over and over again. The demon who dropped the bond willingly, which I had grown to crave. Who pushed me to embrace myself for who I was, regardless of what others might say.

As long as he was still willing to love someone as broken and indecisive as me.

He wasn't in the garden of spiderwebs and ash trees. Nor was he in the library (which was spectacular). He wasn't in the servant's quarters I accidentally entered (although they were quite surprised to see me there!)

I'd even sent him a note via servant.

Find me.

The spirit had disappeared and never returned. After waiting for what felt like an eternity, I kept moving down the halls.

How much time had passed in the mortal world? How long until people noticed I was absent? If mother realized I was gone, she might summon a portal to the other side herself.

Let her try. I could take her.

I wandered into another wing, sending a different message.

I tire of exercise. You could at least send me a map so that I know where I'm going. This palace is too big.

Like the first, the servant vanished without a trace.

I bluffed to the next one.

Gaksi says you miss me. Come out and prove it.

Nothing. For all I knew, he was frolicking in a meadow with Gaksi right now.

Infuriating demon.

Sam had appeared a moment later, flying and tilting her head for me to follow. Excited, I sprinted after her, only to pause at the entrance to a massive throne room.

Heavy obsidian doors creaked open, revealing a vast, dimly lit space with stone floors and otherworldly stillness. A throne taller than a mountain centered the room. It radiated power, made of solid gold and adorned with intricate patterns and motifs. Atop it sat an older man with Reaper's exact resemblance. I knew who it was immediately.

"Yeomra, King of the Dead, father of my absent friend," I said with equal parts fear and reverence, dropping into a deep bow.

His grey skin and deep black hair resembled an immortal corpse. His eyes, dark as an abyss, flashed with curiosity, anger, or fascination. Perhaps all three.

He lounged back in his chair, exuding an aura of death. In a voice that was both ancient and primal, rasped, "There is the source of my son's frustration."

The power in his voice nearly threw me back to the wall. I instinctively braced my shadows around myself as a shield.

"Your Highness," I said. "Were you expecting me, or may you inform me where your son is?"

Dangerous, dangerous game I was playing. But I was angry, and I was impatient.

He crooked a finger. Wide, arching shadows pushed me from behind, forcing me to stumble forward until I landed on my knees in front of the throne. From this vantage point, he was so much taller, intimidating, godly. "Let me get a good look at you, girl."

He rose and brought his hand to my neck. He—softly, frighteningly—raised my chin so that he could grasp my face. His fingers were stiff. Dead.

"You look like your namesake," he uttered.

"The moon?"

"No, the last Princess Deokhye." He chuckled darkly. He had a classically handsome face, even for his age. Reaper's strong features resembled his.

I never knew Deokhye was a princess. Did that mean I was royalty, too? Then maybe it wouldn't be so unusual for me to be pursued by a prince. Hope surged, so intense I nearly smiled at the vengeful force before me.

"Gaksi did well in choosing your bloodline." He drew back, and the mounting pressure of his shadows released.

"Gaksi is a great asset to my family," I said, pushing the shadows off me so that I could sit back on my knees and look up at him. I refused to be hunched over.

His cruel laughter then could have split mountains.

"Oh, innocent girl, Gaksi is your family." His words hung in the air.

I didn't say anything, confused. I'd always described him as family.

"How ironic, keeping a creature of the dark in the dark." He slid a hand under mine, grasping hard enough for my shadows to burst forth.

"Do you know how Reaper knew to address your shadows?"

I blinked, trying to process the king before me.

"They're Gaksi's shadows, foolish girl. He was the original sin. The demon that leaped through the portal, possessed a human body, and passed his cursed shadows down the line. He is an ancient ancestor of yours."

The... original sin? Demons passed down their shadows when they engaged with a human? Gaksi was... like a grandfather? "Those rumors you hear? Of how dangerous it is to engage with a demon? He was the original source of them all." He brought my hand to his lips, pressing a light, cold kiss there. I shivered. "Your face spills all your emotions, little princess."

Little princess. The only way I could become one would be if I were married to a—

"So many of them, and not one of them is fear," he mused, awaiting a response.

Summoning my courage, I answered, "I'm more scared of my mother."

His black lips twisted into a melancholy smile. "That's what she said, too."

"My mother—"

"Paid me a visit, yes." His head nodded slightly. "Only assassination attempt that surprised me. You can ask your Gaksi all about it. I order him to introduce me to all his descendants."

"Why?"

He cocked his head, studying me in the way Reaper often did. "To see if they are worthy of my son."

"Is your son worthy of me?" I gambled, hoping my audacity wouldn't be punished.

His shadows dropped at once. An arctic chill bit my bones.

"Leave the servants be. My son will find you shortly."

He misted into nothing, leaving me and Sam alone in the devoid throne room.

Was I worthy?

Sam pecked me on the forehead, and I all but smacked her back into my dimension.

"Test me again, bird, and I will ensure the end of you," I seethed.

She pecked again, dropping a note into my hand.

Meet me at moonlight.

I jumped. "Have you been holding this the whole time?" Sam shook her head.

I debated all day whether I should. This was the pivot point. I could feel it. Once I met him at moonlight, there was no going back.

But despite my hesitation and fear of the unknown, when I held onto those words, onto that hope, I had never felt so confident in myself.

Ever since I accepted my place at Aether, my body no longer hummed with anxiety. I slept through every night without nightmares about being late for class or showing up unclothed. I went to class unafraid of a rogue shadow or a scathing text from my mother.

A level of self-assured maturity had hit me, one I never thought I could achieve. I was ready to make my own choices, consequences be damned.

I picked my outfit like I was crafting a new identity.

Magic alone crafted the dress I pulled from the dresser. Glitter lined every curve and crevice, sparkling like stars on a desolate black night. It hugged my curves before trailing like shadows behind me, capped with opalescent gemstones. It dipped low in the front, covered only by a sheer mesh, showing off assets that would have gotten me sent back to my room in childhood. I brushed my hair down, evenly parted into two smooth, straight sections, with diamonds pinned in.

Looking at the vanity mirror, I was wearing the night sky, and my face was its shining moon.

I gathered my shadows and formed a door with them.

I did not mind addressing my shadows, stepping out with them in the light, now that he had taught me. When he had taught me to be strong, and in control, and fearless, and I could be the same with him on my side.

My hand lingered on my shadow knob. Was I ready for this? For my first real date, with Reaper, that I chose for myself?

When I stepped through the door, I knew I made the right decision.

I met him in our first location: The Whispering Woods. Fireflies drifted along the sky. Lone instruments played themselves in a semicircle around a flattened meadow.

And my chest lifted when a shadowed, muscled demon turned around to face me.

"You look like a princess, Luna."

I avoided gawking at Reaper, who wore black slacks fitted low on his hips and a grey sweater that looked casual enough to have come from the school library. He was the picture of relaxation, of normalcy—and his mismatched outfit pieces made me suppress a laugh.

"What's the smile for?"

"Nothing in particular." I hid my grin. "But I think you

should let me be your stylist. Your outfit is fascinating but peculiar."

He frowned. "This is what your computer told me 'fancy wear' for males consists of."

He was trying to dress like a mortal? That was adorable.

"The internet is not as wise as I am," I said.

"Indeed," he murmured, drinking me in.

"So that's what you were doing this whole time? Looking up mortal fashion choices while you avoided me?"

"I was not avoiding you." He scrubbed his face. "But there's only so much 'man' I can muster in one sitting."

Oh. He misinterpreted what I said. That was why he dressed like an adolescent boy.

Reaper said gruffly, "I didn't mean to worry you. I just ... felt guilty. That you were correct, and I have never really been a man to you."

His gaze was lonely. Wistful.

"I didn't mean it that way," I said, "and it was more of a reflection of my cowardice than a reflection on yours. I'm sorry."

He let out a long breath before he replied. "I knew your meaning. And you were right on both implications. I cannot be a human man for you. I do not know how. You were cursed with my love from the moment you met me."

Silence descended. One filled with all the words we should have said but didn't.

"Why did you say I was cursed when you first met me?"

He jolted when I spoke, then came forward to run a piece of my hair through his fingers.

"Do you remember when I told you family love can be the most toxic?"

I nodded.

"I'm not my father's favorite. Never have been, never

will be. Although I describe him as my father, all the demons of the Beyond call him such, and he views them all as his children. But I am the prince, so I have the most responsibilities. When the gumiho—my father's pride and joy—ran away, he blamed me. He banished me from home, following an ancient prophecy's advice, and I cannot permanently return until I retrieve her, his favored child."

The rest of the world faded away. "So you wanted to kill the gumiho—because it would send her back home?"

"Unfortunately," he confessed, "but I have been unable to do so."

"I have no other family to rely on," he went on, "and the closest I have to companions are the fools you know as Gaksi and Sam."

"As soon as I saw your shadows, I knew they were linked to the Beyond. Which meant you were either the gumiho or something worse. Someone I would fall in love with. Someone I would have to kill to keep on my side forever. Someone who I could not have but could not resist."

I looked at Reaper, at my mirror image. At the person who saw into my dark, twisted soul and did not run from it.

I sent my shadows out tentatively. He smiled, letting them wrap around his until we were enveloped in a swirling cocoon.

"You've been practicing," he said.

"The master taught me himself," I teased.

I closed my eyes and let the shadows flow from every pore. They flew from my skin, hair, and heart until I felt like I was glowing with their blue-black energy.

When I reopened my eyes, Reaper's had glazed over.

"You're perfect," he whispered.

"I am not perfect," I said, a tear slipping down my cheek.

"You are perfect for me," he said, drawing me in close. His lips brushed mine, once, twice. On the third, he lingered, heating me from my toes to my rose-tinted cheeks.

"Do you owe me a favor?" I asked him. My breath caressed his skin.

His nose grazed my jaw. "Perhaps," he breathed.

"What are you thinking right now?"

"That I should have led our first encounter like this. That if I weren't so arrogant and desperate, I would have seen what a prize I have in front of me."

Honest, vulnerable. I never thought I could be around a man like this.

He studied my face. When he saw my emotions—the longing, the desire, the overwhelming trust—he slid his tongue in for the next kiss.

Chocolate and salt. That was what he tasted like.

I swallowed his tongue, sucking enough to make him groan. He moved his hand to the small of my back, pressing him into me. He was ready, ready to go, when he pulled back.

"I need to tell you something." Emotion swelled across his face. "I... greatly dislike how every male would die to make you blush."

That admission had my head snapping up. His eyes gleamed like starlight.

"I detest how easily you engage in their pitiful crush."

He pulled me into a dance, spinning me with soft joy.

Invisible bells tolled in the background.

"Everybody wants you," he continued plainly.

My eyes burned. I knew where he was going with this.

"But I don't like a mad hunt." He dragged me close.

"You're mine, moonlit seraphim." He spun me once.

"And if I don't beg this of you, someone else will." He pressed his lips to mine. They tasted like love and power. My heart sang. "I can't wait anymore. From life to death, light to dark, share your soul with me, Luna Deokhye."

CHAPTER
THIRTY-FOUR

THE ORACLE MUSINGS

What would you do to be mortal? There has to be an equivalent exchange in magic.

On one side of the world, a teenage mermaid, desperate to dance with the humans and chase a boy, made a foolish deal with a sea sorceress to gain her legs and lose her tail. The cost? Her voice and identity. Nobody, not even the man she came to chase, recognized her. And she tried to swim home, but her own family threw her back to the earth, convinced she was just another suicidal teenage drama queen and not the youngest heir to the sea king's throne.

On the other, a lonesome demon met a conjurer, who promised an avenue to live the humanity she watched so often from afar. She wanted to fall in love, she said. She wanted to experience a girlhood, and growing up, and not be stuck forever in the same age of nothing.

So the witch made the nine-tailed fox appear as a beautiful woman, enchanting enough to make any man fall to their knees.

Which is convenient, because she was filled with a ravenous hunger at the cost of her magic: she must rip out hearts and eat them to stay alive. However, there is a twist to her curse: should she last more than 1000 hours without killing a single man, the curse will be lifted, and she will become a normal human girl, ready for true love.

Unfortunately, she only made it to hour 999 today.

HYDRA ALERT! HYDRA ALERT!

My dastardly phone beeped a loud, screeching message, ruining the moment. I desperately prodded the screen to turn it off, but it wouldn't shut up.

HYDRA ALERT: RUN, HIDE, FIGHT. THE MYSTERY KILLER IS ON A RAMPAGE AGAIN. OVER 5 DEAD BODIES IN THE PAST 5 HOURS.

Reaper cursed so foully I almost drew away from him.

"She chooses now to do this?" he snarled.

His eyes softened at the emotional wreck that was on my face.

"I'm so sorry, seraphim." He kissed my forehead. "I wanted this to be so special for you."

I said nothing, in shock. Did my proposal just get ruined by... a different demon?

"I have to handle this."

"Take me with you," I blurted. "Please—just don't leave me alone here."

He gripped my hand. "It's too dangerous, remember? I'll take you to your home, but I have to handle this alone. This is my battle to fight."

He dropped me at my dorm without a word.

My shadows writhed with impatience under my skin. They pulsated and throbbed, unsatisfied with just sitting around waiting.

I was ready to go.

I was going to go find the damn creature myself.

I'd spent enough time letting Reaper rescue me. It was my turn to rescue him.

I couldn't just sit here thinking about how my ancestor never told me he was my ancestor. Of how obvious that was in retrospect. He must truly think me the densest of all his descendants for not realizing. I couldn't sit here and simmer about how a demon from the Beyond nearly proposed to me, only to get interrupted by a different demon. Of how I would have definitely accepted had he not run off to chase.

I willed my shadows into a gate and stepped into the Whispering Woods.

I searched far and wide, starting at the portal and expanding until I covered every inch of the earth. I ignored some smaller creatures that hopped through—including the dragon, which waved at me—and begged the woods to whisper a clue at me. Only hisses and growls greeted me, no different from the regular beasts of the woods.

Reaper must be doing the same. Did he always do this? Engage in a frantic search, hunting for a creature more elusive than he was.

These woods were so vast, and the gumiho might be so small—

And when I realized that, I swore at my incompetence.

Hadn't he once said she was beautiful? Was that all I had to go off of?

But if that was all he had, too, then we were on this witch hunt together.

Frustration held me.

Who did the gumiho think she was?

Murdering left and right? Being an eternal source of torture for my companion? Impeding my proposal?

The screams and body parts should have deterred me.

Tracks of flesh and fighting hung in the branches, scattered across bushes, and littered the soil when I got close.

I feared this kind of destruction once. Not anymore.

The gumiho may be deadly, but I was the princess of death.

I crept to the portal. Stepped over what she left of my classmates.

And when a scream lit up the sky, and darkness clouded over the moon, I ran into the darkness toward the gumiho.

Past trees, boulders, and any lingering apprehension, I ran until I localized the source of the sound.

It was as ghastly as I expected.

Blood-streaked hair. Tattered dress. The slurping and drinking sounds characteristic of eating.

I grasped my shadows in my hands.

"Reveal yourself, gumiho," I called out to the thicket of woods.

"Moon princess," a horrifically familiar voice called out. "I missed you."

She turned.

Sweat beaded on her brow. Her skin was clammy and cold as if she was ill. She panted for air.

Blood dribbled down her delicate chin as Aubrey smiled at me.

Shock—shock so cold and gripping, I nearly fainted—hit me like a brick.

"How long," I stuttered. "How long have you—"

"I was born a nine-tailed fox, the gumiho cursed to live

endless lives and never be happy in any of them," she tutted in her valley girl voice, wiping the blood off her chin.

"You were my friend," I spat.

"I still am," she said plainly.

"Aubrey—gumiho—you're the murderer!"

She wrung her hair out like a mop, twisting out droplets of blood. "I never hurt you."

"What's that supposed to mean? You spared one person while slaughtering the rest!"

"And how am I different from any of the vampires here? They survive off human flesh, too."

"They source it from donations!"

"Details." She clicked her tongue, unfazed.

Monster. I was looking at a monster.

I hurled a blade of pure darkness at her. She shimmered into an elegant, nine-tailed fox and jumped out of the way. Her fox form was larger than any werewolf, extending nearly as tall as the tree lines.

Aubrey's voice echoed out of the fox's mouth. "I have one tail for every one of my lives, Luna. I'm a master of escape by now."

Nine tails. So she'd been sent back nine times and kept returning.

"Do you have no remorse? For the lives you've destroyed?"

Her tails extended behind her, flaring like a peacock. "I only killed the worst of this university," she growled. "Rapists and abusers of women only. You should be grateful! I'm a feminist."

All murders were of men, according to the oracle.

"How do you know they were the worst?"

"Because I only went after men I knew for sure hurt people! What do you think triggered my most recent rampage? I was hungry and angry, and there were all these body parts of my friends, some I've known for centuries, strewn about, so I returned the favor."

The fox's eyes narrowed while I processed that.

"You can't prove their guilt, though," I stated, trying to think of a plan.

Should I go on the offensive? Would Aubrey hurt me?

"The vibes were good enough," she said, licking her paw nonchalantly. "Sorry, bestie."

"Bestie? Bestie?"

My blood pumped with rage. "You destroyed Reaper's life off vibes? What about mine?" Bitterness contorted my face, and clouds blanketed the sun. "You don't get to call me bestie."

I should have been scared, staring down a lethal, otherworldly demon, but I only felt fury and betrayal from my friend. "Do you have any idea how much fear and panic you've caused on this campus?"

"Fear strengthens you. Without fear of failure, you never learn to grow." She reared back on her hind legs, stretching. "I always used fear of being Houseless to push you to be better."

"No, you pushed me to be artificial. Fake. An image of myself that made you look good."

I scowled while she looked at me with disdain. This deceitful, traitorous hellion—

"Aubrey, you were friends with my mother! How could you get closer to her than I ever did?"

"Your mother's a viper. I respect that about her."

Bolts of dark lighting struck. Aubrey watched them hit with disinterest. So my shadows didn't affect her, either.

"It was you, wasn't it?" I accused. "You sent the Bulgae."

She blinked. "I always knew you were smart."

"Not as smart as you are deceitful."

"You say all that, and you have just as deceitful of a partner at your side."

"Reaper has never been as vile as you!"

"Now you defend him? After all the times you broke his little heart?"

Flames of shadows arched around me, taller than myself. I had to rein them in to see the fox again. "I was going to not break his heart for once, but you got in the way!"

"Why did you ask him to dance at the masquerade?" I thundered.

She laughed darkly. "I had to throw him off my tails. After I convinced him I was just your vain friend, I'm sure he never thought much of me at all."

Genius. Even I could admit that, as furious as I was. But something didn't click.

"Could he not sense your demon energy?"

"I coated myself with so much of your hair that day, I imagine he couldn't think of anything but you."

Braiding. She was always coming over and braiding my hair.

She flared her canines, watching me process. "Did you know?" She crept closer, tails trailing like a train behind a bride. "He asked me why we wanted to join the House system. He was quite worried about your mental state. Reaper was dancing with me, the most powerful seductress in all demon kind, and the only one he had eyes for was you."

I sent every weapon I had at her at once. My shadows thrust them forward, but she jumped so high up, not a single one landed. When she fell, it was feet from me.

"Why were you always so desperate to join a House?" I

demanded. "Was it because you wanted to look good? Outside your hobby of human sacrifice?"

She prowled forward. I moved my shadows into a circle of black flame. She sat just outside it.

"Because I wanted the same things I imagine your Reaper does."

She punctuated each word with a step, circling me. "Adventure. Friendship. Family. Belonging. Humanity."

Her lips curled up, exposing her teeth. "A chance to evade my curse."

Curse.

Curse.

You're cursed.

"Reaper has a curse?"

"A curse to meet his starborn." She tilted her head again. Looking through Aubrey's puppy tilt and catty personality shattered what was left of my restraint.

"His curse involves his starborn?" Tired of betrayals, I threw my flames at her. She jumped high over my head, fur shimmering, landing gracefully back where she started. I was spent now, panting.

"What's the curse?" I slurred out. Trees dissolved in ash around me. I reignited the flames, sending smoke flying.

"He approaches," she said. "Until we meet again, Princess of the Dark."

"Luna!" Reaper's voice yelled.

The world went white.

CHAPTER
THIRTY-FIVE

THE ORACLE MUSINGS

Demons, mortals, and gossips who read this column: my sources have updated! The visions have aligned! I see clearly now! An absolutely delicious prophecy has been translated from ancient times. Should I share? Of course I will! That's what I live for!

Prince of the Undead, Messenger of the Beyond,
Demon who never had a heart with which to raze,
Either find a way to send the nine-tailed fox back home,
Or find someone who hounds of death could not set ablaze,
A princess captured in an unwanted bond,
A shadow stealer who takes lone demons in stride,
A demon lover, your future bride,
A gossip in which you could always confide,
A seraphim who can free you from the depths of hell,
Only your starborn can grant the peace you seek all too well.

When I awoke, Reaper held me, and the nine-tailed fox was gone.

I shoved away from him.

"What's your prophecy?"

"Luna—?"

"What. Is. Your. Prophecy?"

He blinked, wary. His hands fell to his sides. "Luna."

"You promised not to lie to me. Who am I supposed to trust if not you?"

He swallowed. "Ninetails told you."

"Yes, I found the gumiho."

Reaper stilled. "Luna, the goal of that creature is to drive us apart. Worry not about her statements."

"I think I've figured it out. You're just an old, bored immortal who thinks playing games with our lives is fun." I paced, stalking away from the demon.

"Do you know what would happen to me if I got caught with you? I would be expelled! Disinherited! Alone! And what's the worst that can happen to you? Nothing. Absolutely nothing. You can't die. If you hop back into the Beyond, you won't be found. I have everything to lose and nothing to gain from being with you."

I faced him. "How long have you been stringing me along, knowing that you have a starborn?" My voice cracked on the last word.

The panic on his face dissipated. "On social intelligence, girl, you truly have close to zero."

"I am not a girl!"

I hated the way he was looking at me. Like I was a fool, a fragile object needing close care and handling.

I hated that he was right. I was on the brink of collapse. My heart beat too fast, my sense of betrayal too intense.

"No, you are not a girl," he said quietly. "But you are ruled by your insecurities like one."

Too deep. He hit too deep every time we fought. "My insecurities? My insecurities?" I didn't want him to use that gentle tone with me. I wanted to fight. I needed to rage. Because if I didn't, what fragile pieces of my heart remained would surely fissure and break completely.

"You're the one who can't even take one day to rest because you're worried about what your father thinks of you! You who hid that you have a starborn—"

"My starborn will survive this, I'm sure." I screamed loud enough that the stars shook. My shadows were storming, forming a whirlwind around me.

"I would never do this to someone—" I started.

"You never told me about your bargain with the Fae Queen," Reaper said.

I let out a vicious snarl. "What about her? You and I also had a bargain."

"Had I known none of our relationship would be private, perhaps I would not have entered it," Reaper huffed. "So much for no secrets."

"Perhaps you never should have entered it when you thought I was a murderous monster!"

He scowled. "I knew you weren't the moment you escaped the fire dog."

"What?"

"If you were the gumiho, you would have just transformed to fight it."

"And you still kept me in the bargain, knowing that?"

He chuckled darkly. "The bargain was perfunctory, seraphim. It didn't even do anything. Would your Gaksi allow me to hold you in danger? It was just an excuse to keep visiting you."

"You are... a manipulative devil," I said, pulling a vortex of power out of him and combining it with my enraged cyclone.

"I am a manipulative devil who is devoted to you!" Reaper roared. "I am heartless. I am diligent. I am stubborn. But don't you dare claim that I am disloyal when I would tear apart heaven and hell to get to you!"

"Your own duty imprisons you, Reaper," I countered. "You're heartless. Powerful. Beneath someone like me. Why trust you? Spend time with you? Do you even know me?" Tears streamed down my face. "I can be more free when I'm away from you than when I'm with you!"

"Do I even know you?" His voice had gone hollow, dark.

"You claim that you came here to be yourself, to be free, to be your own person, yet you are ruled by what others think of you! Is that free?

"And you're desperately chasing after Fae house, not even because you like the fae, but because you want to please your mother so badly! Is that free?"

"Making bargains with fae to be popular? Pushing away your friend to fit in? You're worse than heartless! Ninetails may eat out men's hearts, but you carve them out with a rusty knife."

"You think you have no power? You made a bargain with the Ice Queen! You killed the Bulgae! Your shadows control the weather and move trees! Top of the class, and you're still trying to prove you're above everyone by becoming fae, when you exist far below—you're an underworld demon descendant!"

"Keep tearing me down," I spat. "You do not know what it means to be... trapped. To live every day, knowing you can never be yourself and be enough. To be at war with you are to be and who you live to become."

"I know you better than you know yourself," Reaper countered. "And I have never pulled you down. I have only ever dragged you, kicking and screaming, up into your own self. I offered you that bargain because I saw a version of you that you could never actualize alone."

I whirled my shadows closer. "Why would you withhold information?"

"Because I was afraid of your wrath when you found out." He waved at the incoming storm clouds, at the torrent forming from my emotions. "You are your own worst enemy."

My heart shattered. Slammed against the walls of my chest in such a painful and agonizing collapse that my blood went aflame. A cyclone erupted, and his head snapped up when I stole the last darkness from him and wrapped it around me.

A breath passed, both of us silent, shaken.

Two large, black wings of smoke and shadow beat behind my back.

I was a seraph, fallen from heaven after all.

I could see my wings in the reflection of his eyes. They were smooth and feathered, like a black swan's, and they arched up above my head to elegant points.

I panted, muscles in my back flexing, dark magic pounding. My soul felt wicked. Free. Empowered.

My body tensed as I lifted off the ground, wings flapping.

Reaper looked at my flight, at my determination, my magic molding with the last of his to lift me off the ground.

Color had returned to his cheeks. Magic had faded from his eyes, resembling a warm chocolate brown. His arm was creamy pale, no tattoos to be seen.

My dark magic had stolen his power, his energy, and his immortality.

When he smiled, it was without mirth.

"Well, seraphim, it appears you have freed us both."

When my cabbage patch doll started talking, Jason and Joseph ran out of the room. The door slammed and rattled the frame before the room descended in silence. But I had stayed from when the doll first moved location, winked, moved around, and finally, spoke. I'd been afraid, sure—I never thought my toys could be alive! Yet, as I moved forward—tentatively—I realized my curiosity would always overpower my fear.

"Hello?" I whispered, quietly, like I held a new secret.

"Luna!" Gaksi called.

That was the moment that I had really chosen Gaksi—and conversely, when he had chosen me.

I beat my wings fast enough to fly away, as far and as fast as I could.

Gaksi found me in the sky.

"Looking good, Luna!" He flapped by in pigeon form.

"You traitorous liar!" I screamed into the wind. "How dare you not tell me he has a starborn?"

I spiraled higher, hoping to lose him. "How dare you keep me in the dark, *grandfather*?"

I spun through the clouds, impressed by how cold and wet they were. If I wasn't so furious, I might be fascinated. Marveled. Instead, I was shaking off my wings like a wet dog when Gaksi's demon form flew above the cloud cover with me.

"Gaksi! Someone could see you!"

"Above the clouds?" His large, red-rimmed demon eye winked. "Not likely, granddaughter dearest."

"I am not your dearest," I raged, wings sending furious gusts behind me. "How many of your kids have you tried to pimp off to the Reaper?"

"None." He chuckled, large teeth cracking. "Trouble found you all on its own, moon pie. Fly any higher, and we might actually meet your namesake."

"Don't call me that! I'm the way I am because of you!" I shook off the condensation from the clouds.

"Aren't all humans?" he questioned.

"What's that supposed to mean?"

"Every human carries the scars of their past family members," he said as if it were obvious.

My hands shook at my sides. I had to hold myself back from fist-fighting. I couldn't believe that my family member —literally, my family member—was trying to calm me down from thousands of feet in the air. Any higher and us demons might be barred from the gates of heaven.

"Do you know how my species of goblin is created?" Gaksi prompted.

I fumed quietly but did not respond.

"Blood has to be spilled."

At my silence, he continued. "A very long time ago, back when tigers used to smoke, a young soldier boy was dying on a battlefield. His lover, desperate, used dark magic—she was one of the first users of dark magic ever—to create a dokkeabi goblin. Me!" He threw his clawed arms up in the air.

"Soldier boy was dying, of course, so I had to jump into

his head permanently to sustain him. Instead of blood, I filled his veins. With magic." He bared his teeth. "And, of course, when they had children, it passed a piece of me onward every time. With every generation. The trauma might be different, but they always had me to cope."

To cope. That was all I'd ever been doing. Coping. Coping with not knowing what I was doing. Coping with the expectations of my mother. Coping with the trauma that got passed down.

"Mother tried to get rid of you."

"Your mother thinks ignoring her problems will make them go away."

My wings slowed their frantic pace. We were so high up, the oxygen was getting low, and I was tired.

But I didn't want to return to earth. Even angry, scared, and frustrated, I was so... free. Alive. My shadows had been formed into wings, and I was reluctant to ever contain them again.

"But, my little wildebeest, you've always run toward your demons, not away from them. You were always chasing non-humans. Bugs, plants, animals, even demons. That camera of yours was just an excuse. The weird, the occult, has always drawn you to it."

His wings slowed to beat in sync with mine. "Why didn't I tell you Reaper has a starborn? Because I always knew it was you."

I froze. My wings stopped beating, and I free-fell at least a hundred feet.

Gaksi caught me mid-cloud. I was soaked with water, and he was laughing.

"You know who also always knew it was you?"

I swallowed a lump in my throat. Yes.

"Demons chose soulmates based on cunning, loyalty,

and valor," he said, wings flapping hard enough to keep both of us elevated.

"You are the most brilliant Deokhye in generations. The wisest." Praise shined out of his red eyes.

"You are the most loyal to your family, even when it puts you in danger. Your sincerity of devotion knows no bounds." He released me, and I regathered my wings to stay adrift.

"You give no heed to what others think of you, flying above campus with your shadow wings out. The most dauntless."

The clouds cleared beneath, but I kept my wings out high above.

I pondered what he said when I flew to my first home that night. In my heart, I knew he was right, but there were some old demons of mine I had to control first.

It was time to face the most fearsome of them all.

My childhood home no longer felt like the colorful escape it used to be. Dad said that was common when you went to college. That you felt in-between places, with people making you feel at home, not buildings. Perched atop a hill, the glass-domed roof of my family's house served as a testament to my Dad's love of stargazing. That was where my name came from: Dad's love of astronomy and the night sky. I inherited my fondness for darkness from him.

Mother had a conniption when he took out the roof for glass, but it was more beautiful this way, so she let it stay.

The entire house resembled Mother, save the ceiling. The rooms were perfectly tidy. My siblings were obediently behaved. Even my dad mostly kept to himself unless he needed something.

A part of me would always miss the orderly place of my childhood.

But I was grown now.

I peered through the telescope of the main living room. It was night now, and twinkling stars and planets beamed at me. I remembered looking up at the night sky and wanting to fly up there someday. To fly among the shadows and live to tell the tale.

That dream of mine came true.

"Daughter."

I flinched. Not even a first-name basis, then. Mother sat on the couch like a stone, adding a heavy tension to the already thick air.

"It took you long enough." Mother rose and smoothed my hair over my shoulder, exposing my neck. "You've learned that mother knows best, after all. You have removed that hideous mark."

"Actually, Mother, Reaper is a permanent fixture of my life now."

She hardened her gaze. "I have no time for games, girl."

"And I know you knew he was my starborn, and deliberately kept me away from him."

Mother set her hands on my shoulders, gripping them tight enough to crush bone. "You are nobody's starborn. You are my daughter, and you will come to your senses."

"What senses?" I retorted. "My sense that I was going to die alone, unlovable? That I would have to hide my powers until the end of my short, miserable life? You preach of my senses, but where were yours, getting me into this mess?"

"I got you into this mess? You were normal before you got ensnared in that demon's trap! You've changed into a version of yourself I don't know anymore." Mother said it with such disgust it was like she couldn't bear to look at me. Perhaps, deep down, she truly felt that way.

"I have never been normal." I tried to shrug her hands on my shoulders. She gripped tighter, face changing. Like she knew that once I pushed her off, she would never be able to grasp back on.

"I have always been extraordinary, and you kept me trapped in your own ideals of who I should be."

Mother scoffed. "I kept you motivated. I kept you strong. I kept you capable of reaching your limits."

I met her stare. "You know, I always wanted a mother who loved me for who I am and not who she thought I could become."

Her expression soured. "You know not of what love is, child."

"Control isn't love, mother."

"And what is? Surrendering everything you have for a boy? I raised you better than that. What about your House?"

"I refuse to cower to my university anymore. I will date Reaper, express my shadows, join my House, finish my education, and fulfill every goal I originally set out to do. You should be proud."

Her claws dug deeper into my shoulders, overhead lights sputtering out as she stole their electricity. "What will happen when you wrinkle? When you grow gray hairs, and he doesn't love you anymore?"

"I suppose he'll be growing them with me since I took enough of his demon energy to make him mortal." I unfurled my wings, stretching them fully, spanning the room with their shadowy presence. Mother gasped and nearly fell over.

"We share the power now. Both of us will age at exactly the same rate."

"So this is the end of our relationship, then? You came to tell me you're ready to be disowned." Her voice cracked like a whip on the last word. *Disowned.*

"No, I came to tell you I forgive you."

I slipped shadows over my shoulders, displacing her hands.

I had fought enough. My very bones were exhausted. I wanted to go back to the people who made me feel at home, without having to put on a show.

"Because I know exactly who I am, and you never bothered to find out."

I launched into the air, using the full force of my shadows to slide between dimensions and teleport into the sky. The night breeze caressed my face as I soared into the darkness, finally free.

CHAPTER
THIRTY-SIX

THE ORACLE MUSINGS

Alumni only will read my column tonight. I can't spoil the surprise! Freshmen are busy watching their dreams come true, and upperclassmen are preparing their Houses for the celebration of the year. They won't be sent my latest edition until after the festivities tonight.

So! For all the elderly at home, enjoy my final notes on my favorite contestants:

Hyacinth, the sophomore underdog, is running to Rose House, as is to be expected. Sophomores are lucky to get any place at all, and those whose egos couldn't handle Rose House were cut (which was all of them besides her). Will she make the most of her last two years on campus?

Hunter Consta, former dream boy of campus, will straggle his way over to Vamp House. How ironic that the vainest boy, our Faery crown prince, got cut from all the Houses known for having beautiful, ethereal people, and will spend the rest of his life in the dreary Vamp House dungeons instead. Karma mayhaps?

Aubrey Hahm, points champion of her year, has withdrawn from the recruitment process. Was she dissatisfied with her options? Felt that she deserved better? Nobody knows, but her absence has been noted—nobody's seen her for weeks.

Cordelia Port, the youngest hopeful of them all, who wished so dearly on a star to be in Siren House, has surprised us all and earned her spot along the waves.

And Luna Deokhye has surprised us all with her choice. Good thing she, too, will be in for a delightful surprise at initiation: I suspect her House matches her quite well, indeed.

As if to haunt me, my phone dinged. Flora had texted.

Flora: *You're Late.*

I hadn't fed her information in days. Not only had I not done so, but I would never do so again. I was tired of being her pawn.

And I had enough information to be ready to step into my role as queen.

I waited in the bustling cornucopia. I wanted this to be public. I was ready for this to be explosive. She probably wouldn't attack me with students milling about and eating lunch, but I would have loved it if she tried.

I'd spent my morning plotting and filing my nails into sharp, jagged points. If I was a Gaksi descendant, I should present like one too. Coffin nails only—a tribute to the darkness pulsing beneath my flesh. I flexed them in the sunlight now. Maybe the oracle would see them and write an article about me. She and I could be friends, I thought, if we ever managed to meet.

Flora wore a business dress and blazer as she slid into the seat across from me.

"Pretending you're busy, Flora?"

"Watch your tone."

"Watch your House. I know dark energy powers it," I shot back. Flora paled.

"I kept wondering—why do the Barren Fields exist? Why, next to a thriving university, is there a place that steals energy from anyone who visits? Who is stealing that power?"

I let her sit in silence for a moment. "It's the Houses. They all steal energy from the land to keep their magic going."

Nobody had noticed our encounter yet, but I wasn't lowering my voice.

"I know the faeries created the House system. I know they did so because they wanted to ensure they would always end up on top. You gave yourselves away when you resorted to dark, illegal magic to slip a love potion into all the food from your House—and I didn't eat any."

Flora bared her teeth, face frigid. "How do you know we did that?"

"You told me. Just now." I winked. "I am the number one student in 600, don't you know? I'm not dumb."

It just didn't add up. Not a single negative comment about that House came out of the students who attended, not even when they hazed their hopeful new candidates. That must have been the real test. How much abuse can you endure and still adore your abuser?

Flora huffed. "So what? You're going to tell our smitten followers that their love is unrequited?"

"No. You're going to release me from this bargain," I demanded. And you're going to give every single one of the students who rushed this year their top choice."

She snorted in disbelief. "That would destroy the fabric

of this institution. What about the students who were dropped entirely?"

"Send them a phone call. Blame it on the whims of the machine."

"I cannot control the machine."

She moved to leave, and I ensnared her wrists with a tendril of darkness. She hissed in annoyance, startled by my quickness.

"I think you could if you were so motivated," I said with a sly smile.

"You ask a lot for one mere piece of information," she growled.

"I'm not done." My eyes went dark, blackness clouding the whites. Flora's gasp only fueled the confidence of my shadows. I smirked. "You will, as the most prominent House leader, tell our University president that dating demons is no longer forbidden. Neither is becoming one, or having demonic companions."

"You've lost your mind."

"No, I've gained it," I said, the weight of my words jolting the tense air around us.

I pushed up from the table. My fingers stung, but weakly. Flora was scared.

"And what if I don't do any of this, Luna?"

Her doubt amused me. Good thing a wise man once taught me that everyone had a weakness.

"Then I will tell the oracle that you have never been in control of your own darkness, and that's why your ice powers are ruled by your emotions. That you sent me on a chase for Reaper because you were hoping to learn how to control them indirectly from him."

I blew her a kiss. "First rule of the Fae: strongest always wins, right?"

"Are you sure you want to do this?"

Melody peered at me over her glasses. Dark circles rimmed her eyes. She was tired. She should be. It was three in the morning. Final results were due to houses at 3:30. Bid cards would be opened at midnight sharp the next day. Plenty of time for the Houses to make their final selections and prepare their House for the celebration.

Her question asked to every freshman that came to her tonight carried the doubt and uncertainty that had plagued me for months. I saw Cordelia come in before me, trembling and scared. I didn't have to worry about Hunter because, according to Gaksi, he was in the infirmary, too damaged to move. Any other men involved in the slaughter had been taken out by the gumiho, Ninetails. Reaper had broken so many bones he wouldn't be able to walk again for at least another year. I decided it would be best not to visit or send flowers. The last thing I'd want is to set him off again. His recruitment guide had made him write down his answer on a piece of paper that was thrown into the machine earlier.

The clock ticked behind her in the dimly lit room, reminding me that the time had run out.

"Once I submit your final selection to the machine, it cannot be reversed."

I clasped my fingers together. For the first time in months, they were free of any extra emotion, tingling, or threatening. My hands that only I could control.

"I'm sure." And I was. For the first time since coming here. I was sure.

I handed her the slip of paper with my final selection.

My year's worth of work.

My suicide bid.

All or nothing, for my one and only choice.

The machine behind her clicked and whirred, and I knew the Anitkythera had accepted my bid without complaint.

CHAPTER
THIRTY-SEVEN

THE ORACLE MUSINGS

Enjoy bid day, everyone! No bloodthirsty demons will be returning to slaughter for several months: my starborn lovers (as predicted in the first column of this year, let me remind my doubters) will frighten away any future carnage.

Another successful reading delivered. Oracle love and all of mine!

I SAT on my lawn chair, unbothered, while girls around me wiggled and fidgeted. Our bid cards sat underneath our chairs, and Melody threatened to kill us if we dared open them prematurely.

Dad's white gifted dress swayed gently with the wind. I was happy that I wore Dad's dress today as a reminder of home, even though every other girl wore a similar one. Each of us went through our own journey to get here, despite any appearance of conformity.

I swatted my hair out of my face. I skipped concealer today to focus on eyeliner and lip gloss—accentuating rather than covering up—and the wind blew my hair into my face, catching strands in my lip gloss.

Energy buzzed through the open space. There were fewer of us than I thought. Our numbers must have dwindled substantially because there were barely enough freshman spots to fill up half the Diamond. Even classes had plenty of leftover seats.

I made it, even when others didn't.

The Diamond's center was reserved for freshmen, with each house claiming the closest corner. They waved massive signs made of magic, screaming chants for their Houses.

"3...2...1...open!"

Screams lit up the air.

When I opened my card, it transformed into a rose.

"Start running!" Melody yelled.

I scrambled past the stampede. The most time-honored tradition of all: run your way home, or die trying.

I pounded my feet across the lawn to home. Flowers grew with each footstep, bouncing up to give me a boost.

The actives ran ahead, and I chased them as fast as possible. Wisteria's lavender head led the way.

I kept pace with the strangers beside me. I wished I had gotten to know other people better during this process. They were throwing petals like confetti and collapsing into hugs, but I didn't know anyone yet.

I had never been filled with so much excitement yet felt so... incomplete. My eyes kept roaming the alumni, watching, looking for someone who wasn't there. They invited parents to watch, of course, and to make a donation, especially, but mother dearest was conspicuously absent. I hadn't spoken to Cordelia in weeks, either.

My only company so far had been my shadows.

I'd stayed up night after night, reaching dark vines into the sky, wielding weapons made of power, and dancing in their dark. A week had passed since my final fight with Reaper, and I'd spent it alone, thinking. But without my guide, without passion, without my demons—my shadows were as frail as I was.

I missed my demons.

I wanted my demons.

I was ready to embrace them back into my life.

I considered walking back into the Whispering Woods to contact them directly. I knew they would answer. But I also knew that there was no going back once I did.

They would want an apology, and I was too afraid to initiate one.

"WELCOME HOME!" Floral arrangements spelled out the welcoming message in the bushes in front of Rose House.

Leaf confetti fell from the sky in bright and vibrant colors.

When I paused running, the tree nearest me wrapped its branches around me in a rough hug.

"Don't look so panicked!" Wisteria called out while I assessed whether a drop from this height would kill me. The tree had suspended me midair and was dangerously close to cutting off my circulation.

Wisteria gestured her hands downward, and the tree released me with a plop.

"Luna?" a familiar voice rang out.

"Cordelia!"

When I turned around, Cordelia had already attacked

me with one of her vigorous, bone-crushing hugs. Blue and green paint smeared all over me, but I didn't mind.

"I missed you, demon queen," she laughed. "Glad you finally got away from the company you were keeping."

My lips twisted into a grimace. "Don't talk about Reaper that way."

Her eyes widened. "Oh, not Reaper, silly! Aubrey!" She set me down. "She was a toxic influence on you, through and through."

"You didn't like her?"

"Nobody did," Melody cut in. "But we knew you'd grow out of it." She ushered all the new members inside.

"See? I told you I'd bring the best home," Melody told Wisteria as we entered.

"Food is on us, of course," Wisteria chimed from the end of the long table. "Initiation is in two hours. Do what you want until then."

"Cordelia, shouldn't you be with the Sirens?"

"Initiation for Sirens isn't for another few hours, either," Cordelia answered. "I wanted to bid you farewell before I dive under for a few months."

Cordelia and I dug in and caught up.

To adjust to swimming with a tail, Cordelia explained, new Sirens spent the first month of their life completely underwater. She wasn't worried, but we'd have a hard time seeing each other for a while.

Cordelia and Xavier were still in the midst of their "situationship." When I brought up her age, Cordelia paled but insisted Xavier had skipped multiple grades—so he was only 18, a teenager like her. Cordelia had also saved all her notes from when I was gone with Reaper—so I'd be ready to study and catch up when the time came.

I felt myself relaxing in the company I was with. No

straight posture. No fancy talk. Just eating with friends. I didn't witness any expected pompous arrogance from Faeries. No pleasant niceties from Angels. Just boisterous, friendly conversation.

This year drained me. I had learned to fight demons, courted one, and landed myself a permanent place at this University. Through all that, I'd rebuilt myself.

And now, my darkness was included in that picture.

I was not the same girl. I'd started new relationships. Severed others. Made just as many friends as enemies.

Most shockingly, I longed for my relationship with my mother again. I kept waiting for her to text, call, shout, or do something—but she was dead to me.

As dead as the girl I used to be.

I had just finished my dessert—birthday cake to celebrate our "birth in society"—when I heard a familiar rap on the window.

"Gaksi!"

I threw my shadows into the window, aiming to open it, but it shattered instead.

"Sorry!" I yelled apologetically as I hopped over the jagged glass.

"I'll fix it, Luna, don't worry!" Wisteria called behind me.

I smiled to myself. While furniture damage was punishable for the Fae, it was amusing here; laughter filled the room.

Even as I turned to Gaksi, little sprouts had grown and twisted off the floor to pick up broken shards.

My shoulders slumped when I saw the sun god instead.

"I missed you, vain little thing," I said, placating my disappointment. I held out my forearm, where she landed, fixating her gaze on me with those all-knowing eyes.

"We missed you too, princess," a high-pitched, sugary voice spoke into my head.

"Sam?" I jerked my arm away, but she clawed in tighter.

She huffed. *"Don't be rude."* She preened out her feathers. *"I have plenty to say, too."*

"Then why haven't you?"

"We weren't bonded yet."

"Huh?"

"You have to bond with Reaper to get access to the rest of his demons." She peered beady little eyes at me. *"He longs for you."*

Remorse caught me, and tears welled up in my eyes. "I'm busy right now, Sam."

"My master is also busy these days, fearing you don't want him anymore."

She hopped up my arm to my shoulder, then leaned against me. *"Call to him."*

I glanced behind me to where the entire new member class of Rose House, plus Cordelia, were watching me converse telepathically with a bird. Cordelia gave me a thumbs-up.

Sam raised her wings, and a shield of opaque sunlight covered us.

"You can do that?" I asked.

"I am as powerful as I am pretty," she boasted, *"just like all of Reaper's women."*

"If I were his, he would have contacted me by now."

"Is that what this is? You're waiting for him to make the first move?"

"Yes."

I could feel Sam's disapproval in my head.

"Does he not feel deceived by my second bargain?"

"No more than you were by his first."

I sighed, head in hands.

"He exhausts me."

"He loves you. And you love him too, which is how we can communicate now." She nuzzled my ear. *"Call to him."*

My eyes stung. I wiped away my tears, refusing to look like this when I called him back to me. I wished for him to be here so badly that I could imagine him materializing—

"You can be sad around me."

Reaper appeared, making me the happiest woman alive. Donning jeans and a t-shirt, face glowing with youth, he had never looked more human. Or more handsome. He drank me in, longing and sincere, and I decided to be the most vulnerable I'd ever been.

"I'm sorry I never told you how much I love you before." I met his shining, happy brown eyes. "And I'm sorry I pushed you away when I could never predict the future."

A tug pulled at my heart, and the handsome god I knew reappeared, dark eyes smoldering.

"I'm sorry I hid so much from you," Reaper admitted. "That I hid so many of my burdens from you, knowing that we could have shared them together."

We stared at each other for a moment before crashing together.

He picked me up with hands and shadows, keeping me close to his chest. He kissed me with a vengeance, anger, and desire only starborn souls could share. "The sun may stop rising, and the moon might get tired of orbit and spirit away, and the stars may fall down to earth and destroy everything in their path. And darkness may be replaced by light, and smoke consumed with air, and curses extinguished with love, but until the night stops falling, I will always be yours, Luna."

Our lips met, and the light around us faded away.

Cheers erupted from the audience. That was when I knew I had chosen the right House.

"One last favor, seraphim." The tease I knew was back in his voice.

"Be mine."

EPILOGUE

Candles flared, casting human-shaped shadows that shimmied and performed along the dark oak walls of the Rose House basement. The air thrummed with anticipation and unease as the room filled with mysterious actives and wary initiates.

"It's initiation day, pledges!" came Wisteria's voice, laced with command and mischief.

A goblet filled with dark, swirling liquid circulated among the new members. I took a sip and passed it to Hyacinth, who was wavering. "It tastes like grape juice, Hyacinth," I whispered to her. Grape juice and a rich hint of something potent, deeper.

"It mostly is," Wisteria chanted, "but better."

Candlelight danced in front of her head, casting eerie shadows of her flying hair around the dimly lit room.

Before I could take it all in, a hood went over my head, plunging me into darkness. Gentle hands dragged me past gnarled wood and snaking vines, preventing me from stumbling.

My shadows whispered along the walls as we walked as if they had an innate knowledge of the labyrinth.

When the hood was abruptly yanked off, we were positioned around a cauldron in a dungeon. Books lined the stone shelves along the walls, bouncing with energy. Sconces lit the room, but they offered little heat. If the actives noticed my shadows playing and self-soothing along the walls, they said nothing.

Wisteria laughed manically, her voice echoing and growing louder in the crowded space.

"You all have been through hell," she proclaimed. "You've been tortured. Demeaned. Thought less of, for choosing this House. For going to a place that welcomes all women, no matter their background. Demonized for liking the feminine things, for choosing flowers with your fighting."

The cauldron bubbled, spewing pink, glittery liquid into the air. I reached in to touch it, mystified. It felt as soft as sand, as magical as girlhood, and as sturdy as the almighty hands of fate.

"I see our first initiate is ready," Wisteria said, drawing the attention of all the actives.

"Do you, Luna Deokhye, choose Rose House and all it represents?" Her voice rang through the room, her words conveying the ultimate promise.

My words were confident. "I do."

Actives seized me, throwing me in.

Energy buzzed in my soul as the liquid embraced me. Shadows sang, vibrating with euphoria. My wings lifted me, hailing the heavens themselves. Power, stronger than anything my shadows could have mastered alone, coursed through me.

"Everyone here has secrets," the actives chanted in unison.

"We, too, kept a very important secret from you in the name of protecting our values and ensuring only the most noble-hearted join our sisterhood."

The voices grew louder. "We represent the forgotten. The downtrodden. The rejects from society."

A black rose, as pure as rebirth, bloomed in the air in front of me. I took it, and it multiplied and wove itself in my head as a crown.

"To you, this is a rose, but to us, this is our heart!" Their voices merged as one.

"WELCOME TO HOUSE WITCH!"

If you enjoyed reading *The Prince of Demons*, please help others discover it by leaving a review. Thank you!

Acknowledgments

Firstly, thank you to all my readers for taking a chance on Luna and Reaper's story! I hope you enjoyed it. I love hearing from readers, and every email, review, and social media interaction lives in the most cherished piece of my heart. An even bigger thanks to anyone who shares Luna and Reaper's story with their friends.

Secondly, they say it takes three generations to learn how to play an instrument. The first people I would like to thank are my Halmoni and Haraboji (Grandma and Grandpa) for sailing across the world for a better life in the United States. I am grateful every day that my grandparents sacrificed their own comfort to bring their family to the U.S., which let me pursue my own dreams here three generations later. One generation to seek a better life. One generation to get comfortable in a new country. And I was the generation that grew up speaking the language, with enough free time and social support to publish a book and chase my dreams. Although it's a novel and not a classical instrument, the arts are a privilege only afforded to the most fortunate. I am grateful every day that I was able to pursue an endeavor no generation before me was able to. Haraboji, I never got to meet you, because you passed away before I was old enough to remember. But I hope I kept the legends you grew up with alive, and represented them well.

Finally, thank you to my parents, for raising with the principle of Luke 12:48: to whom much is given, much will be required. I wouldn't have the work ethic to finish anything if it weren't for you two ruling our household with an iron fist, and reminding me that privilege comes with expectations. I am grateful for God for my path leading this way, and for the plan he has for me.

About the Author

Hana Hahm writes enemies-to-lovers romances inspired by fairy tales and folklore. When she's not busy writing, she's probably on TikTok, looking for her next book to devour.

- facebook.com/authorhanahahm
- instagram.com/authorhanahahm
- tiktok.com/authorhanahahm

Made in United States
Troutdale, OR
02/25/2024